Tangles of Infinity

The Dimensional Alliance, Volume 8

Bonnie K.T. Dillabough

Published by The Infinite Publishing Alliance, 2024.

This is a work of fiction. Similarities to real people, places, or events are entirely coincidental.

TANGLES OF INFINITY

First edition. April 30, 2024.

Copyright © 2024 Bonnie K.T. Dillabough.

Written by Bonnie K.T. Dillabough.

Dedicated to my readers who are constantly asking, "When is the next book coming out?" I'm writing as fast as I can. I love my readers and cheerleaders. Thank you for your encouragement and support

Tangles of Infinity

By Bonnie K.T. Dillabough
Book Cover Design: Richard McKenzie

Prologue

"Stop that!" Jenny snapped at Burt. Exasperated, she said, "I've got this. Please... you don't have to wait on me hand and foot. I can do most things for myself, you know. I'm not an invalid anymore."

Burt drew his hand back in surprise, looking somewhat hurt at her explosion. "I'm sorry," he said, looking genuinely contrite. "I didn't mean to offend you. Just opening the door for a lady, something I would do for you even if I didn't know how amazing you are."

Now Jenny felt more than a little sheepish. "I'm sorry, Burt. It's just that lately I feel like everyone is still treating me like I'm some kind of porcelain doll or something."

"Ah, so that's simply your point of view, my darling wife. No one who knows you at all would ever think such a thing. If they do, it's because they've never been whacked on the head by your quarterstaff. You know," he said, rubbing the back of his head tenderly, "that still hurts."

She shook her head, realizing that he was sincere, but also knowing how she was feeling at the moment. Even with all the "ride-alongs" she was able to do to stay up to date with the important goings-on within the Alliance, she still felt like they were coddling her, and she found it irritating and condescending.

"You can't possibly think any of us don't realize how much work you put into your job and how epic your breakthroughs have been. We just want to be sure you stick around for as long as we can keep you. Especially me." He put his arm around his wife's shoulders, and she didn't pull away.

Moments later, "the girls" trooped in, ready to start the day in the usual way. Each of them took a different area to examine and evaluate if there were any potential security issues. In a few minutes, they would come back in, ready for breakfast and a briefing on Jenny's schedule so they could allocate their various shifts of "Jenny watch."

Burt was only there for a day or so, as Elizabeth would be by to take him off to Sanglarka, or wherever they were scheduled to go in their duties as liaisons between the various Alliance teams on Earth and the various Alliance work teams throughout the dimensions connected to the Alliance gate network, as well as a few that weren't.

Recently they had begun some covert operations in some of the beleaguered planets now inhabited by tyrannical Inseni overlords. The two had typically chosen planets that had humanoid inhabitants, simply because this allowed them to blend in with the general populace.

The reports they had submitted to the Alliance Council and the various teams working on freeing these dimensions from the Inseni had been both concerning and encouraging—concerning for the atrocities being perpetrated upon their victims, and encouraging as they began to build an underground movement to help these people to undermine the Inseni's efforts to expand their dominion.

In the meantime, Jenny was extremely occupied with her duties as the official Gatekeeper of the Dimensional Alliance gate network. In addition to her regular duties to oversee the gate guardians across the dimensions, she was currently also responsible for the mental communications network, established as a result of her own mental talent to communicate across dimensions.

She now had three assistants that she and Amenia had trained in the technique, and there was a class of three more who were preparing to go to Tarafau's planet to be instructed by her and Amenia in the coming week.

These recruits had been carefully vetted using the linklings' ability to read minds, as this was a high-security position. They would be entrusted with a serious responsibility to keep the mental communications they received completely on a need-to-know basis, conveyed only to specific targets to whom they were allowed to send the information.

Jenny had less and less time to do anything beyond what her current assignments required. Consequently, she felt she was somewhat stagnating in her attempts to improve her own mental abilities. Still, she hoped she would yet have plenty of time to continue to work on them.

As Burt, the girls, Jenny, and Chidwi sat around the dining room table, Lizziebot served them with their preferred favorite breakfasts. It was easy for Jenny to feel more than a little spoiled by all this attention. Between her loving husband, her bodyguards, her close companionship with Chidwi, and the constant care of Lizziebot, she never really lacked for anything.

In fact, it often made her feel a little guilty, considering how many people in the world didn't even have regular meals, much less a cozy little house in a quiet neighborhood and a group of people devoted to seeing to her every need.

However, when she thought about it, she realized that her entire support network came with a heavy price. Her responsibilities had led her into mortal peril more than once; and even with all the protections the Alliance had put into place for her, it seemed that she still might not be safe from the threats of the Inseni, especially if their efforts to dominate the entire multiverse extended to Earth.

By every sign they could determine, there was a definite interest in Earth, even though they weren't even a member of the Alliance. Of course, Jenny's role as the Gatekeeper and the fact that the main gate for the entire Alliance gate network was now in her cozy little house, made it obvious that Earth could no longer hide in the vast complex of interdimensional portals that spanned the multiverse.

The really strange thing about it all was that the Inseni had shown an interest in Earth long before Jenny had been officially named the Gatekeeper for the Alliance. This made her wonder what could possibly be attracting attention from the Inseni and what it would finally take to keep them from going through with whatever plans they had for her home planet.

Of course, Jenny had the entire Alliance gate network, connecting thousands of different dimensions to one another, to take into consideration, and she knew that their fates were all interconnected regardless of anything that happened in the future. This meant that their current efforts to eliminate the Inseni threat were first priority.

Sighing, she spooned another bite of oatmeal into her mouth. Completely wrapped up in her own thoughts, she didn't even notice the faces around her.

"What's that about?" Mynn asked, breaking her apple muffin in half to add some butter to it. "That sound usually means your wheels are turning. Let us in on the secret, will you?"

Jenny looked up from her bowl and realized that every eye was on her, expectantly.

She swallowed and cleared her throat. Why was it people always seemed to ask a question right after you had just put food in your mouth, she wondered.

"Actually, I was just thinking about how much we have to do and how big it all is and how small we all are..." she said distractedly.

"Wow! That's an awful lot for this early in the morning, don't you think?" Mynn replied with a mischievous grin. "Do you think we can solve it all before lunch? I think maybe we need to take this all one step at a time. How about what we're doing today? Let's let the near future sit for a bit, shall we?"

A chuckle went around the table, and Jenny felt more than a little foolish at how clumsily she had answered Mynn's inquiry.

Burt held up his hand for quiet.

"So, along with your usual communications stuff and the other duties of your station, you also have a training to do in about a week. I've talked it over with Liliath, and she agrees that you could use a break before it all gets too much for you. A week to settle your mind and move forward before everything gets really intense."

Jenny started to protest, but once again Burt held up his hand. "So... as I was saying, Liliath and the council agreed to my plan to take you away from all this for a few days. You will still be able to do your usual duties and you will be fully protected, but it will be just you and me together in a secret adventure. I never got that honeymoon, after all." And he winked with a wicked grin.

Her bodyguards didn't seem at all surprised by this announcement, so it was clear he had briefed them before breakfast.

"Um... what do you mean by adventure?" Jenny asked. "You know how I feel about surprises.... And what do you mean by 'just you and me'; what about my bodyguards and all the security stuff?"

"Ah, that is the brilliance of my clever plan. Elizabeth will be by in an hour or so to transport us to a secret location and will be available at once if we need her. She will be staying here with 'the girls,' and if we need them for any reason they will be instantly at our side. I don't expect there to be any issues, as I promise you, no one we don't want to know will have any idea where we are or what we are doing."

Jenny looked into his eyes, which were sparkling with mischief and expectation.

"What should I pack?" was all she replied.

Chapter 1: Before the Storm

Jenny's eyes were closed. Burt had told her to close them before Elizabeth placed her hand on each of their shoulders. As she felt the ground change beneath her feet, she inhaled the scent of foliage and wet stone warmed by the sun. She heard the sound of rushing water and felt sun, warm on her skin.

"Can I open them now?"

"Yes, by all means!" Burt replied, excitement exuding from him like the scents around her.

She opened her eyes to sunlight filtered onto a small sparkling pool surrounded by large stones. The huge slab of stone on which they stood jutted out just slightly into the pool. It was flat and large enough for several people to stand on or just a couple of people to lie on.

"Our pool!" she exclaimed, throwing her arms around Burt in a grateful hug. "For real!"

Elizabeth grinned at the couple entwined happily together. "I'll be off now. Jenny, I'm just a thought away. Burt, if Jenny is disabled somehow, get Lizziebot to contact me. Either way, I'll be here with reinforcements. When you're ready to come home, just let me know. I'll be at with the girls."

Burt nodded and Jenny untangled herself long enough to give Elizabeth a parting hug, with a whispered "Thank you." And Elizabeth faded from their view.

Burt turned to Jenny, lifting her chin to look deep into her eyes. "I've wanted to bring you here ever since that very first time you found me here in my dreams. This has always been my 'happy place.' Having you here takes it beyond that. This is now heaven for me. We get three amazing days to ourselves here, and I want to make the most of it. I came prepared."

And he produced from his MDP a picnic basket, a large blanket, and a cooler. He spread the blanket out on the rock and gestured gallantly for her to have a seat. He then seated himself next to her and began to remove plates, napkins, utensils, and several covered dishes from the picnic basket.

The scent rising from one of them indicated roast chicken, and she could see fluffy white rolls through the transparent lid of another one. There was also potato salad; and for dessert, it looked like Arvid's spicy sugar cookies.

He then pulled two frosty bottles of her favorite root beer from the cooler and waved his hand over the food like a magician revealing his magic trick.

"Wow!" Jenny exclaimed, her eyes wide and her mouth forming an excited '*O*'. "You've been preparing for this for a while, I can tell. Did you have to coerce Arvid to do this, or did you pay him for it?"

"He asked me to get a photo." And he pulled out his cell phone and snapped a picture of Jenny in front of the delicious spread of goodies. She cooperated with an exaggerated look of surprise and delight. "He'll love this," Burt said with satisfaction. "Now, let's dig in!"

Jenny held up one hand and bowed her head in a prayer of gratitude.

Burt waited patiently, and when she was finished, he began to dissect the roast chicken. "You like the thigh, right?" he asked as he picked up a juicy thigh and settled it onto her plate.

He served up potato salad and then offered her rolls. "They're pre-buttered," he added. "Saved us some time, as I know you can't wait to bite into that fluffy amazingness."

And so they sat and ate, the rock partially shaded by the overhanging branches of an enormous redwood tree. The water of the little pool sparkled; and just out of sight, the Merced River tumbled, gushed, and burbled, perfect background music for their romantic picnic.

For a while, they didn't speak, just soaking in the environment and enjoying the delicious meal. When Jenny finally put the last crumb of the delicious cookie into her mouth, washing it down with the final swig of root beer, she sighed happily, looking gratefully at her sweet husband. She had needed this.

"So what do you have in mind? Will we be staying on this rock for the next three days? It might not be all that comfortable come bedtime...."

"Ah, my dear, that is the next layer of the surprise. It may amaze you to know that your hubby owns some property not far from this spot. My parents passed our cabin in the woods down to me, as their only son. We will sleep snug and sound in an antique environment as our forebears before us. I even put new sheets on the bed," he added, his chest puffed out proudly.

"Wow! How thoughtful of you! So, what else is on our agenda?"

"Well, for now, let's just play it by ear. I brought some hiking gear for both of us. I kind of raided your closet for all the necessities, including your well-worn hiking boots," he added sheepishly. "At some point over the next few days I want to explore the many wonders of Yosemite and maybe even do some rock climbing, if you feel up to it."

"That sounds amazing!" Jenny had missed going out with her hiking club since her initial engagement as a gate guardian, but hadn't had the heart for it, since Sam's betrayal. "Just you and me? How did you manage to convince Liliath to allow us to do this? We both know how she is about my security in these perilous times."

"I had to show her how isolated this area is and take some special precautions, such as having your bodyguards on instant call, but also I have a dozen Alliance troopers hanging out for the next three days in my MDP, courtesy of our friends the Nanoites. They have been provided with excellent food and good sleeping accommodations, and they are having a three-day Cubes tournament."

"Cubes? The game Lizzie talked about in the agent training section of her journals?"

"The same. As a matter of fact, it just so happens that I brought my set with me. I always have it in my MDP, and you've told me in the past that you'd like to learn the game. If you'd still like to do that, I can clean up our lunch things and set up the board, so we can play. What do you think?"

Jenny was a bit overwhelmed at the preparations he had made for their special getaway. She nodded happily and watched as Burt invoked his new little robot friend out of his MDP. "He's small, but he has some special features, including the ability to extend his arms and legs just like a Mookookie. I changed his name from Rebus to DAT. Watch him go!"

The little bot immediately started gathering the remains of the meal, holding each item out to Burt to allow him to store them in his MDP. In practically no time they had everything stowed. Then DAT wandered to the edge of the stone outcrop they were sitting on, with his back to them, scanning the forest behind them.

"DAT?" Jenny asked. "What language is that?"

"It stands for 'dastardly alien tech,'" he said smugly. "Appropriate under the circumstances. An extra layer of security," Burt acknowledged, nodding towards the little bot.

"But you didn't give him any instructions, and he just did what you needed...."

"Ah, yes, well, it appears that Cornelium thought it a good idea to give him mindspeech like Fidget. It makes things very simple if you never even have to voice your commands. I noticed that you seldom use mental commands with Lizziebot. Do you just forget that she has that ability, or hasn't it occurred to you to talk to her that way for everyday tasks?"

Jenny blushed. "You're right. It never occurred to me to do it mentally unless I'm communicating with Liliath or Bob. I guess, though, with all the time I spend communicating mentally, it's kind of nice to hear my own voice, if that makes any sense."

Burt laughed. "I guess it actually does. I never think much about how much time you spend inside your own head talking to people across the dimensions and even across our own planet. And you do have a lovely voice. I enjoy hearing your dulcet tones." And he nudged her in the ribs. "So, before we get into a game of Cubes, let me introduce you to my lovely little pool in person...."

He helped her stand and led her to the edge of the rock slab and gestured downward into the pool. As Jenny looked past their reflection, she was amazed at the almost gaudy show of rocks clearly visible at the bottom of the pool. They were of many colors and shapes, all of them smoothed and gently rounded by their watery environment. There were no fish to be seen, but some water plants she didn't recognize swayed gently, peeking between rocks.

The surface of the little pond was as smooth as glass, reflecting their faces back to them as clearly as the mirror in her bathroom at home.

"This is amazing!" Jenny breathed. "Way cooler than what we experience in the mental version. Can we come back here a lot? I mean maybe we do it on our anniversary or other things?"

Burt chuckled, putting his arm around her waist with a satisfied sigh. "Any time we aren't out fighting Inseni bad guys and saving the multiverse from evil, you mean?"

"Right! After all, we need to keep our priorities straight. Do you think we can even do it? I mean, it isn't exactly what I had expected when I took this job. The multiverse is a big place, when all is said and done."

"Yep, but I think we will do what we can and just do our best. That's pretty much all anyone can do, even the Dimensional Alliance, as big as it is."

Jenny stared down into the little pool, nodding in assent. This place was so beautiful, so peaceful. How lovely it would be to just stay here and forget the world and all the burdens she felt so heavily on her shoulders and in her heart. But she would gladly take what she could get, even just a few days of peace and beauty with her sweet husband.

He was probably the one thing that kept her hoping and moving forward. Even though they didn't get to spend much time together just as a couple, her nightly visits to him at the little dream pond had been the one thing she looked forward to every day. She hoped for a time when they could act almost like a regular couple, but she knew that it would never be quite like that. Between her duties as the Gatekeeper and his as an Alliance agent, she knew they would be frequently in different places.

She was so glad she had finally had the chance to come to this very special place and for the next few days, pretend that they were just a newlywed couple finally taking their honeymoon trip, with nothing to worry about or focus on but each other.

Of course, she still had duties to perform, but most of that would happen while she slept, so it needn't interfere with their daytime adventures in such a beautiful place.

"Do we want to play Cubes here? Or would you prefer the cabin?" Jenny asked Burt after a few minutes of quiet contemplation.

"Cubes can be played pretty much anywhere, but it might be nicer in the cabin, so we don't have to interrupt the game much with supper or snacks. I've spent the week stocking the place with everything we need, turned the power on, as it's usually off when no one is there, and checked to make sure all the lightbulbs work and the fridge has had a chance to cool down properly."

Jenny was amazed at how much thought Burt had put into this little get-away, and once again she was grateful for the events that had brought them together.

"Okay, so let's go then. We can come back first thing in the morning. I have my list of visits memorized for tonight. Do we have a cell tower in the area?"

"We have wireless communications installed in the cabin that is connected to the Alliance network, so you shouldn't have any problems connecting via Lizziebot or your tablet."

"Well, it sounds like you've thought of everything." Jenny remarked hooking her arm into his offered elbow. "Let's go see this little archaic cabin of yours."

Burt led them into the woods behind the pool. The Merced River thundered along beside the trail that led up to the two-lane highway. Across the road in just a few hundred yards from where they exited onto the paved road stood a small cottage that looked like something out of a children's fairytale book.

She could tell it was an old cabin that had been very lovingly maintained. The flower boxes were overflowing with blooms, and the flower beds that lined the little stepping stone walkway to the cabin door were obviously well tended.

"Who does your gardening?" she asked as they made their way to the stone paved porch.

"I have a neighbor who sees to it through the year, as this is only a vacation cottage. She's getting on in years though, so I may have to find someone else in the near future."

Jenny reflexively reached for the door knob, but Burt teasingly tapped her hand and shook his head.

"Nope, we're gonna do this right," he said, and without warning scooped her up into his arms. "Across the threshold. Something we didn't get to do before."

He pushed the door open with his foot and carried her into the sitting room, which was lighted on three sides with large picture windows. As he stood her back on her feet, he encircled her in his arms and kissed her earnestly, giving her that feeling that her toes were curling under her.

"Now '*that's* what I'm talking about!" he exclaimed as they finally broke apart. "My wife, in my digs, in my arms. It doesn't get much better than that."

And with that they both broke up into laughter, holding each other up until they finally collapsed together on the braided rug on the floor in front of the cottage door.

When they finally caught their breath, Jenny looked around her, still seated on the floor with Burt's arm snugly around her shoulders.

The only word Jenny could find for the space was '*homey*'. Handcrafted afghans hung on the back of what were obviously dual loveseats that were upholstered in brown velveteen fabric that matched the braided area rug between them. On the shelves that ran under the main picture window were a lot of books whose titles were very familiar to Jenny, classic authors who had taken up much of her childhood quiet times.

A small table and chairs that would seat four people was laid with an ivory tablecloth and a small centerpiece of pinecones and holly arranged on a crystal dish.

The curtains matched the upholstery on the loveseats, and in one corner was an overstuffed chair next to yet another bookshelf. You could see into the kitchen over a breakfast bar style counter. It was all in sunshine yellows and whites. Jenny could see the classic old-fashioned refrigerator from where she stood, complete with a pottery cookie jar on top.

Besides the swinging doors that led into the kitchen, there was only one other door, that Jenny assumed led into the bedroom and bathroom, unless....

"Does this place have an inside toilet?" she asked in mock trepidation.

Burt laughed. "Yes, my dear, wifey-poo, it is fully equipped. No treading pinecones on your way to the necessary. There is still an outhouse in the backyard, but it hasn't been used in years."

He stood and offered his hand to raise her up. "Have a seat at the dining table, and I'll get us something to drink. Then I'll set up the Cubes board and I'll walk you through the basics. Knowing you, it won't be long before you are beating the pants off of me at the game, but I don't mind a little healthy competition."

Jenny made an attempt to imitate Burt's infamous evil laugh and failed miserably, which made Burt laugh as well. So far, she thought, this was going really well. In the entire time they had been married, admittedly only several months, they hadn't done anything remotely fun or romantic other than their interactions with one another either at the pool in their dreams or in the little house on Infinity Loop.

Getting away like this was such an awesome treat that Jenny could hardly believe they were really here. She almost wanted to pinch herself to prove it was all in real life and not in one of her nightly mental wanderings.

Burt returned with two frosty bottles of root beer. Jenny had thought it remarkable that this was also his favorite drink. They were constantly finding things they had in common that they had never realized over their short courtship.

He carefully set out two coasters and sat across the table from Jenny, invoking from his MDP a worn cloth bag, lumpy with its contents.

From the bag, like a magician pulling a rabbit out of a hat, he pulled a rolled-up piece of cloth and a pile of small, cubed blocks about one inch square. The blocks were each painted in the primary colors of red, blue, and yellow and were inscribed with symbols that Jenny immediately recognized from Lizzie's description of the game in her journals: the infinity symbol, a rectangle that represented a gateway, and a circle that represented the gatekeeper or agent necklace that every representative of the Alliance always wore.

There were also occasional keyhole-shaped icons, but they were not as frequent as the other three main icons.

"Okay," Burt said, finally, after unrolling the piece of cloth that was evidently the game board. "We'll take turns putting the cubes into this box," he said, taking a cube shaped box out of the bag. He scooped the cubes from the table back into the little bag and shook it vigorously. Then he emptied the cubes from the bag into the box, occasionally jiggling the box until the cubes were all nicely fitted inside.

He then put his hand over the open top and turned it upside down onto the center of the game board. He lifted the box, careful not to disturb the blocks from their places in the newly formed cube, which was four small cubes across and four high.

As Burt then explained the rules of the game, Jenny recalled her aunt explaining the game from back in her agent-training days, and she caught on quickly. As they began to play, she realized that they had never played any game together before and knew that this would be something they would now do together as often as they could, not just because it was a fun game, but also because it now held some romantic meaning for them both.

By the time they had played several matches and Jenny had managed to finally beat Burt soundly twice, Burt's stomach rumbled and they agreed it was time to clear the game away and get something to eat. Burt promised her that afterwards they could watch the sunset from a great vantage point.

Since they had come to the Merced via Elizabeth's awesome ability to transport from anywhere she knew to anywhere anyone else knew, Jenny assumed they would be on foot. But after they ate and cleared up, Burt led her to a neat little home-built shed behind the house. He opened the double doors and, lo and behold, there was a double seated scooter, complete with matching helmets!

"This little guy won't get us up some of the steeper climbs, but it's perfect for where I'm going to take you." After helping her don her helmet, being sure that the strap was snug but not uncomfortable, he mounted the scooter, gesturing her to climb on behind him.

"Put your arms around my waist and hang on!" he told her with a wink.

The little scooter was evidently electric because the engine made almost no sound at all. They buzzed down the long gravel driveway out onto the highway and away they went. Once again she found herself wondering if this was all as real as it seemed.

The road was curvy and she could see it was well maintained, with few potholes or other bumps to maneuver around. They hadn't gone far when he pulled onto a side road that took them to a bridge spanning a narrow area of the river.

He stopped the scooter and helped her off, took off his helmet, and laid it on the seat. Jenny did the same. "No danger of anyone swiping the scooter or our helmets. No one really comes here much; and even then, the folks out here are as honest as they come. During certain times of year when the tourists are climbing all over the place, it's a little different. But this is off-season, so we don't need to worry about it."

They walked out onto the bridge, and Burt led her to the side that was now facing the sun, which was already low on the horizon. They just stood there, leaning on the railing, and quietly taking it all in, with no sound but the burbling water flowing under the bridge. As the sun continued to sink, the sky turned orange and purple around the edges. The direction they faced showed the outlines of the mountains that surrounded the area, and it looked like the tips of the mountains were on fire.

Finally, the sun disappeared behind the mountain range, leaving behind it a glow like pale roses that reached up into a sky deepening into shades of indigo. The entire time they were silent, not even communicating in mind-speech. It seemed almost irreverent to disturb the silent dance of the heavens as the sun seemed to dance quietly beyond their sight.

Jenny could understand why ancient astronomers posited that the sun revolved around the earth. It most certainly felt as if it was the sun moving beyond their reach and that the earth upon which they stood was immovable.

When the first stars started to appear and before the rising of the moon, it was nearly pitch black and the wondering couple still stood in silence, now looking up into a sky unpolluted by the light of the human populace. The veil of stars that now appeared was breathtaking, bringing to mind sparkling diamonds strewn across black velvet.

This was one of the things Jenny had most missed about no longer going on hikes with her hiking club. Moments of awe and the wonder of creation filled her memories just as a warm fire in a fireplace filled a room with comfort.

Burt's arm lay across her shoulders, and at this moment she felt safer and calmer than she had felt in a very long time.

"I really needed this," she sent softly, still reluctant to disturb the sounds of nature around them. The water of the Merced burbled happily beneath them. Somewhere near where they stood, an owl hooted.

"I had hoped it would be good for both of us to get away for a bit," he also sent mentally, not completely breaking the comfortable silence, tightening his arm in a one-armed hug. *"You've earned it, no doubt about it. Shall we go back to the cabin? Or do you just want to hang out here a bit longer? Remember we have three 'glorious days and nights,' as they say in the travel brochures."*

Jenny chuckled at this. Aloud she said, "Do you have any idea how much I love you? You make me laugh and you make me feel safe and cared for. Not to mention that you are deadly handsome... just sayin.'"

He laughed at this and then kissed her again as the moon began to rise over the lowest mountain peak.

Jenny had never known any three days to pass both so quickly and so slowly. They hiked through woods and over mountain trails, took photos of themselves together, courtesy of Burt's little bot, in front of famous mountain views like Half Dome and Bridal Veil Falls, and in general just spent time together, something they had not had the opportunity to do since their wedding, which now seemed so very far away, even though they hadn't even had their first wedding anniversary yet.

Elizabeth showed up promptly at the end of the third day. "No issues, I assume?" she asked cheerfully, looking at the two lovebirds with a bemused smile.

Burt popped back with his endearing cocky grin, "Nope. And I don't expect there to ever be any, as most people on Planet Earth don't even know this place exists; and the ones who do are too busy just enjoying the scenery to care about a couple of newlyweds enjoying the fresh air."

Elizabeth nodded and put a hand on each of their shoulders. In a moment they were standing once again on the patio of the little house on Infinity Loop.

"Time to get to work," Jenny said with a sigh. And indeed, she didn't know how true that would be. Even with her nightly mental visits to various dimensions as part of her Gatekeeper duties while they had been away, she was behind on just about everything.

Chapter 2: Vena's Dilemma

"What's wrong with you idiots?" she shouted at the room in general. "Don't you get it? We've got the power, if you just had the guts to go on with the plan. Maybe it's time to remove the chaff from the wheat; maybe it's time to erase some of you from my life... or yours!"

Her generals and aides cowered before her. That felt good. She liked to think that they followed her out of absolute adoration and loyalty, but deep down she knew better. She had created herself as a power to be feared, revered, and obeyed. But her frustration grew as she realized that of those three, *revered* might never come, or at least, as she told herself, not until she conquered the multiverse and put every being under her direction and control.

Her parents, still immured in the dungeons, or "'guest quarters,'" as she had taken to calling them, were cowed, but not convinced that she was the ultimate power and must be obeyed without question.

Her plans continued to move forward, but slowly, ever so slowly. She fumed that, if everyone had done their part, she would have had ultimate domination of the multiverse by now. True, she hadn't foreseen the interference of the Dimensional Alliance and that snit of a so-called Gatekeeper and her clever machinations, but now, if Vena's minions would only follow through more carefully in the tasks she had given them, she could almost taste victory well in her grasp.

"Well?" She purred, dropping her voice to the quiet tones that almost always preceded someone's inevitable destruction. "What have you to say for yourselves?"

In the dead silence that followed, she scanned their faces, most of them paralyzed in trepidation. Some of them had developed facial tics that seemed to be activated only in her presence. Good. That was very good. They would obey, but unfortunately, she would first need to make an example of at least one of them. Maybe if she just let them stew for a bit? The impact would elevate considerably, she was sure. It would give her time to decide which of them least deserved life.

"I will consider it," she continued in that soft ominous purr. "You are dismissed. You have one interval to consider how much better you will serve me in the future. At that time, the least productive of you will suffer the consequences. The rest, I may allow to continue in service in my glorious presence."

None of them spoke a word, shuffling as quickly as possible through the door behind her, only just barely avoiding pushing and shoving one another to exit as fast as they could without triggering another outburst from her, which undoubtedly would be deadly.

She smiled to herself as the last one rushed out behind her and began to hum a silly little tune her mother had sung to her to calm her when she was a child, something about dancing in the flower beds.

She no longer danced or did anything so frivolous. She was much too important for that. She called out to a waiting servant. "Attend me," she said, and whirled around to exit the way her generals and aides had gone, her servant following as close behind her as she could without treading on the train of her royal robes.

She walked down the mirrored hallway with satisfaction, glancing from side to side at her own magnificence, reassuring herself that she still looked regal and somewhat intimidating. No one attending her in her palace would dare to dress in such finery or to imitate the flowing black and silver hair braided on the side in an intricate weaving to keep her hair from her face. After all, she would never consider depriving any of her subjects from gazing into the huge violet eye beautifully centered on her smooth forehead. She considered it her most notable feature and loved to focus it on a groveling petitioner with either what might appear to be compassion or what was definitely intimidation.

She thought of herself as formidable and was certain that her subjects agreed with her.

She entered the empty throne room and regally positioned herself on her ornate throne, finally looking down upon the servant kneeling patiently before her, awaiting her command.

"Well?" she said, intentionally inserting a tone of impatience into the question.

"It is done, Great One." The servant knew better than to speak in low tones. Vena hated whispering except when she herself did it for effect. "Mi successfully fooled the linkling they used to vet the applicants. She is currently awaiting her training to begin."

Vena suppressed a grin. At least one thing was proceeding according to plan. This, might even be more important than any of the assignments she had given to her generals. This was her opportunity to infiltrate the most essential and private workings of the Dimensional Alliance, dratted interfering busybodies that they were.

If it hadn't been for the Alliance, she would have conquered the vast majority of the dimensions by now, enslaving the people and pillaging their resources to add to the wealth of her empire and make the Inseni the final word on every aspect of intelligent life everywhere in the multiverse.

"This is good news," she replied. "For this you will receive an extra ration and perhaps a new blouse. What do you say to that?"

"You are too kind, Great One."

"Indeed, sometimes I think I am. Send in my Chief General, please. You are dismissed for now. I will notify the Household Steward that you deserve a treat for your diligence."

Vena had many servants with differing duties. The Household Steward was her most necessary and most irritating since, if she disposed of her, it would throw the entire palace into chaos. She alone knew and understood all the intricacies of what it took to run something so vast as the main palace of the Inseni Empire. And Vena suspected that the woman knew this and sometimes took advantage of it—but never blatantly, as that would force Vena's hand and she would suffer the consequences.

As if he had been waiting for her summons, General Nakka strode into the throne room and immediately bowed and kneeled before her, waiting for her to acknowledge him.

She allowed him to wait a bit in silence as a slight punishment for their current lack of progress.

"Rise and report," she finally said crisply, letting her impatience and disgruntlement show on her face as well as in her voice.

He rose, his deep brown eye looking directly into her violet one. "There have been... um... developments in some of our conquered territories...."

Vena snorted at the word *conquered*, as she was certain that if they were truly conquered there would have been no "developments."

He cleared his throat and continued. "Many of the populations we had thought as pacific and easily manipulated have started to express their dissatisfaction in subtle but effective ways, and we can't figure out how they are doing it."

"What do you mean you can't figure it out?" she growled, her eyebrow dipping dreadfully over that one violet eye. "You each have an eye, don't you? What are you doing on those planets: hanging out at a local pub and swilling the local brew? Are you befriending the locals? Are you *in* with them? Maybe fomenting a little bit of a supposed rebellion yourselves? Maybe you want your own little planet to rule and dominate?"

He put up both hands as if to fend off a potential blow, not that she would have stooped to dirtying her own hands in such a disgusting manner.

"No, Great One. It's just that things have been disappearing in the camps. Weapons have been coming up non-functional, and even food has gone missing despite heavy overlapping guard shifts and over-the-top security measures. The odd thing is that it happens when there are no locals anywhere in the camp or even close to it. And it isn't just on one planet, but now several dozen planets seem to be infected with this new menace."

He bowed his head and returned to his obeisance on one knee before the throne.

As she looked down on him, she felt her inward temperature begin to rise. Like the House Steward, she couldn't afford to eliminate this general. He not only knew too much about the intricacies of the actions of the troops, but he had always been loyal and diligent in the past.

"Please, Great One," he said, without raising his eye to hers. "Please, forgive. We are expending every effort to discover the cause of this issue. In the meantime, we are also watching the native populaces carefully to see they do not step out of line. This issue is not limited to a single dimension. It appears to be spread across a couple dozen dimensions, almost like a virus or plague."

"Hmm.... I will consider your plea for mercy, but I do expect better results, and soon. We cannot create our final push to conquer the Alliance until we have our current domains under proper control. Do you hear me?"

"Indeed, Great One. And I obey."

He waited quietly for her dismissal, and she deliberately let him stay there for a few minutes in that humble posture before finally saying, "Very well, don't disappoint me. Meet with your underlings right away, and make sure they understand my displeasure. I expect results."

He simply nodded, stood, saluted, and turned on his heel, striding purposefully, but not overly fast. However, she suspected that once out of her sight, he would practically run to find his support staff to arrange to fulfill her commands. He had always done so.

He was getting old, she realized, since he had been a young lieutenant when she was a teen. She had made him her general immediately following her coup of her parent's regime, especially since he had been one of her main supporters at the time.

She sighed. Now that she had the wheels turning on her major offensive, which she had confided to no one but her little spy, she would have to wait. She hated waiting. Maybe it was time for her to oversee the accommodations she would soon make use of, very soon she hoped. She really didn't treasure the idea of heading down into the dungeons any more frequently than she had to, but it was a necessary part of her strategy to finish the pesky Dimensional Alliance cretins once and for all.

Chapter 3: The Affairs of Dragons

Bob finished looking over the specs for the next batch of bots that would soon be coming off of the assembly line. The improvements in this next generation of bots were a direct result of the tests they had recently done in Sanglarka. In addition, all the current bots would soon be receiving a significant upgrade. He loved doing what he now did for the Alliance.

Technically he was an agent, the agent's necklace permanently around his neck, the little infinity symbol that dangled from the chain practically invisible to anyone who didn't know what to look for. He almost never reached up to touch it these days, but in the beginning, he had often touched the little symbol just to reassure himself this all just hadn't been a dream or the work of an overactive imagination.

In all the years of his career in the sciences, nothing had been as satisfying and mind-blowing as what he was doing for the Alliance. Working with the Alliance scientists, one of which was a dragon of all things, was beyond anything he had ever hoped for as a scientist on Earth.

His experiments in robotics and AI had been ground-breaking on Earth. But since his enrollment as a certified agent in the Dimensional Alliance, his horizons had expanded far beyond anything he could have previously imagined. The advanced technology he had been exposed to had triggered new levels of understanding, and he was now developing robots and AI applications that were beyond anything any scientist on Earth had even begun to explore or, for that matter, anything the current techs in the Alliance had imagined.

He hummed as he transferred the report to the other scientists through a closed network that was not directly connected to the Alliance communications network, which the Alliance Council felt was very likely compromised and accessible to their enemies.

He had hoped to never be engaged in warfare again, but in this case, he knew he couldn't have kept himself apart from it for any reason. Not only was Earth vulnerable to the machinations of the Inseni to dominate the multiverse, but uncountable dimensions and their occupants were threatened, many of which had already succumbed to superior numbers and weaponry.

The Inseni had been careful in their initial incursions to target only those dimensions that were pacific and less likely to revolt at their invasion or, in relatively few cases, those dimensions from which they could acquire technology the Inseni didn't have the capacity to create on their own.

They called their scientists "wizards" and were convinced that they were creating spells and great magics to find out how the tech they captured worked, what it did, and how to replicate it. None of their 'wizards' were native Inseni, but instead were those they had captured from the planets where they got the technology in the first place.

The unfortunate scientists, threatened with the torture or death of their families and friends, acceded to the Inseni requests. Bob had been given the opportunity to work with several of them since the revolution they had created on Peril's world, and he realized that they had been deliberately dragging their feet as they were given assignments and even had sabotaged the tech they were creating in small ways as their own way of resisting the Inseni. However, they had been careful to never give the appearance of anything but obedience to their Inseni masters in order to protect their families and friends.

Bob could relate to that. He had a similar motivation for what he now did for the Alliance, not that the Alliance would ever do anything bad to his family or friends, but that the Inseni were an impending threat to his entire planet. He remembered listening to a recording of the broadcast of "War of the Worlds" in school and hearing of the panic and odd reactions of those who had originally listened to the live broadcast, thinking they were listening to a live news report.

Earth, he reflected, was definitely not ready for an invasion, friendly or otherwise, and he trembled to think how some of the governments of Earth might react, some of whom might potentially decide to support the Inseni in their dreadful plans to completely control every aspect of intelligent life on every planet and dimension in the multiverse.

He looked up, startled out of his reverie by a loud, "Harumph" from Cornelium, the dragon scientist who ran the lab. Bob realized he must have been very deep in thought if he hadn't even heard the dragon come through the main door from the castle.

The lab was part of that castle, high on a mountain peak, actually dug into the side of the mountain wherein resided many dragons and the seat of the local government. They were just a dragon flight away from the nearest Alliance dimensional gateway. Bob had gotten used to flying "dragonback," as he called it. There were several young dragons who happily volunteered to ferry various Alliance agents between the castle and the gateway.

"Something?" Bob queried to the huge dragon scientist who had nearly miraculously sidled up beside him at his lab table without him noticing.

"Just this. I hear Burt got a bot recently?"

"Yes, I thought it was about time he had a companion to match Lizziebot, under the circumstances."

"Hmm.... And it never occurred to you that I might like a robotic assistant?"

"But you have a lab assistant, don't you?"

"Ah, yes, but that's beside the point. I can never have too many assistants, especially these days. When are you going to make a bot for me?"

"Oh, that's simple. I can just upgrade the programs for one of the bots we have coming off of the assembly line later this week, add in our science records and anything else you'd like to see your assistant help with."

"Excuse me? I don't think I heard you right." the dragon huffed, eyes pinning like an irritated bird. "I don't want a humanoid assistant. I want a draconic assistant. It doesn't need to be as big as me, but I want it to have all the features of a full-blown dragon, as you like to call our kind."

Bob was more than a little taken aback. He knew that Cornelium was a bit of a curmudgeon, but he'd never noticed any self-centeredness in him before. He tried hard to keep his face passive, not revealing this amusing turn of events in his expression as he asked, "Any particular color?"

At this, Cornelium chortled, a bit of smoke trickling out of one nostril. "Okay, I get it, Bob. But seriously, why do you create robots that look similar to humanoids? Because you feel comfortable with that conformation, right? And you know and understand the function of the various limbs and parts of a humanoid body. For me it is the same. I want a bot that functions in ways that are familiar to me. Is that fair?"

"Indeed, I understand," Bob replied, still trying to keep the amusement out of his face and voice. "I'll need some specs from you..." and he trailed off as Cornelium punched a button on Bob's computer terminal and a report in English scrolled across the screen.

"Will that do?" he asked, somewhat smarmily. And they both broke out in laughter that filled the lab, creating various reactions from the other scientists on their team. Cornelium waved them away when some of them appeared to have decided to check out what the disturbance was all about.

"Merv helped me with it, but we didn't want to disturb you until you had finished the upgrades on the current bot battalion on the assembly line," he admitted gruffly.

Bob laughed a full belly laugh, bent over, and slapped his thighs. When he had calmed down, he panted, "Disturb away, my friend. You'll get your special assistant, I promise you. Looks like you've done half the work for me already." He wiped the laughter tears from his cheeks. "Never had any idea you thought these robots were anything special, just something I cooked up in my thinker," he said, blushing and tapping his head.

"We both knew you'd been working night and day on these upgrades, but when I mentioned my idea to Merv, he said, 'Well, bloke, you won't know until you ask. Tell you what. Why don't I tinker a bit myself? You tell me the specs you want, and I'll put together some code as a starting place, so Bob won't have to start from scratch.' So I agreed and that's what he came up with.

"I don't know anything about computer code. I do the theory and come up with the concept, but my assistants have always followed up with the coding. I do understand the basic principles of programming, but it was never my interest. And this whole Inseni's-conquering-the-multiverse thing seemed to come from nowhere, and it's past time we got it dealt with. I know we're already maxed out on truly necessary projects. Don't put anything on the priority list on hold to do this."

Bob nodded and thought, *Nice dragon,* and almost shook his head at the idea of voicing that out loud.

"I'll keep that in mind, Cornelium. I do appreciate a new challenge, though, as you well know. I may lose a little bit of sleep over this, but I won't let anything go wanting because I'm thinking about it.

"The AI programming can be tricky. Understand that the bot can't do anything we haven't imagined for it first. They do have learning systems built into them, but they are still just fancy programming. Although lately, I have been wondering about Fidget and Lizziebot...." He trailed off, once again somewhat troubled by what he had noticed in the actions of the two bots he had initially created.

"Good," Cornelium said, with a satisfied smirk on his dragon face. "Now we'd better get back to work before Merv comes in and thinks we're socializing, as I kind of got on him about that the other day, and I don't want to give him anything to use against me for next time." And he chuckled that draconic chuckle that always made the hair stand up on the back of Bob's neck.

You would think by now, he would be used to it, but he still thought back to all the dragon tales he had enjoyed in his youth. He continued to be in awe of the opportunity he had been given to be part of the science team for the Alliance. It had fulfilled dreams he hadn't even realized he'd had. Of course, the idea he would one day be working in the lab of a dragon scientist had never occurred to him; and if it had, he would have ignored it as the fantasy of his imagination.

Lately he had begun to realize just how real it all was, as he had been introduced to many of the other dragons in the castle, as well as the humanoids that coexisted with them on this planet. Like every being he had ever met, the dragons he had become acquainted with were unique individuals with differing personalities and desires.

The main topic of discussion these days in various gatherings he had attended when time permitted was, of course, the Inseni situation and how it impacted not only their own planet but the entire Alliance of dimensions. They had discovered that at least a few dozen of those had double gateways, the Alliance one that they had known about and the Inseni portal they had not realized was there until Inseni troops came pouring through it.

It was a concern, not only because those particular dimensions were owed protection by their Alliance allies, but also because it set up the questions: Was it possible that every dimension that had an Alliance gateway also had Inseni portals? And how would that impact their strategy on how to protect the more pacific and less developed dimensions within the Alliance?

That wasn't even counting the issue of Inseni-dominated dimensions that had been previously unknown to the Alliance, which made them wonder if there were also Alliance-type gateways in those dimensions that had simply not been discovered yet.

Bob realized he shouldn't have been surprised that not all the draconic races on the planet nor the humanoid species agreed on what tack the Alliance should take on the issues involved. Some basically had been persuaded to "live and let live" or "let nature take its course" by certain factions that appeared to be led by Liliath's brother, of all things.

Others were militant to the point that they thought the Alliance should completely wipe out the Inseni as a people to eliminate the threat completely. Of course, this was completely against all Alliance policies, and definitely against anything Bob would agree to be part of.

Finally, there were those who went along with the Alliance's policies. Thankfully, at least in Bob's point of view, these were still in the majority, but Gighil's viewpoint seemed to be gaining momentum. He hadn't recently been on-planet, having taken up residence, for the time being, at Alliance headquarters to be near the action, so to speak.

Bob was grateful that his part of this conflict was small, even if it was significant. He was in no rush to ever return to military life. He was fascinated by the concept of a different kind of warfare that, at least on the Alliance side, was focused on doing the least possible damage and preventing the loss of life or injury to the combatants on both sides.

As he returned to his work, his eyes occasionally strayed to the programming still displayed on one of the monitors over his table. He was sure Merv had done a good job, probably having consulted with the computer specialists on his team, but he was itching to go into the code and see how he could improve on it and where he could take it. *By jingo,* he thought, *I'll bet I can add a few little surprises that neither of them thought of.* And he went back to his priority project with his head buzzing.

Chapter 4: Passing It On

Jenny smiled as she added a few new outfits to her MDP. She knew it didn't much matter what she wore when she was training her newest recruits for the mental communications team, but she also knew that these people were "noticers." They responded sensitively to their environment and reacted to their senses in a way that was different from that of your average person.

Liliath had been very careful in her research to find candidates who not only had the mental capacity to learn these new techniques but also had certain personality traits that lent themselves to being trustworthy, considering the sensitive nature of what they were attempting to accomplish.

Jenny still heard her mother's voice in her mind, clear as a bell: "Jenny, you only get one chance to make a first impression." It would have been easy to discount her mother's wisdom. She was one of the most cheerful, optimistic, and fun-loving people Jenny had ever encountered, and yet her long list of lifetime accomplishments was impressive. She had led many organizations and businesses over the years, and she had skills that would have surprised anyone who didn't know her well.

So, she dressed and packed based on her mother's wise advice, realizing that she had a certain status in her position as Gatekeeper and needed to live up to that.

She remembered clearly her first meeting with Miriha, the previous gatekeeper, and how impressed she had been with Miriha's overall appearance and the confidence and kindness that seemed to radiate from her. She hoped sincerely that she could replicate that in her own way, and that she would never make the Alliance sorry they had given her this incredible responsibility.

She heard her bodyguards laughing about something in the living room and smiled. They were a lot like siblings as they didn't always agree, although they tried to keep those disagreements private. But most of the time, they laughed and joked together like good friends do, even though they took their duties seriously. Sometimes they were so serious about it that Jenny had to admit she found it somewhat irritating.

She finished her preparations, took a last look at her hair in the dresser mirror, and went out to find them playing a game of cubes, Mynn and Lyra seated on the window seat facing each other, with the cubes board between them, and Nona evidently refereeing the match. They immediately looked up as Jenny entered the room, even though Jenny knew she hadn't made any unusual noise.

Chidwi, seated next to Tidbit just behind Lyra, hopped down from the window seat and leapt happily up onto Jenny's shoulder. Jenny was constantly amazed at how light the little linkling was. Her fur was soft against Jenny's neck as Chidwi patted her cheek, the linkling equivalent of a hug.

She continued to be impressed by her bodyguards' constant vigilance where she was concerned. She felt confident that she could depend on them in whatever circumstance they found themselves.

"We'll be leaving in a few minutes. I don't guess this is like a video game that you can save and pause?"

"I was just about to finish destroying Mynn," Lyra retorted with a wicked grin. "Give me five minutes."

Mynn growled. "She doesn't know what tricks I have up my sleeve. I agree. About five minutes should do it."

The three of them, each from a different dimension, had adapted quickly to the time constraints of Earth, even though their own planetary times were considerably different than what they experienced here. Of course, they each were certified agents of the Alliance, which meant that their internships before certification had taken them to disparate dimensions, where they had each served for months in various environments and cultures.

Jenny just nodded. Then, mentally shaking her head once again at the incredible experience she had landed herself in, courtesy of Aunt Lizzie, she went into the kitchen, where Lizziebot was cleaning up after their lunch.

"I'd like you to come with me," she said to the bot. She had become so used to having the AI powered robot that Bob had built for her, that she had begun to think of her more as a friend than a construct. The AI had originally been programmed by Lizzie herself but had since been improved and augmented by Bob's own research and upgrades.

Lizziebot could use mindspeech and was directly connected to the Alliance communications network. She also stored nicely in Jenny's MDP. Lizziebot also hosted a couple of Nanoites, all part of the Alliance's plan to overcome the intended domination of the dimensions by the Inseni.

Lizziebot replied in Lizzie's voice. "Of course, Jenny. I should be finished in here in the next few minutes unless this is an emergency?"

"No, the girls are finishing up a game of cubes at the moment, so I'll be back when they are done."

"Yes, Jenny. I should be finished by then."

Jenny still felt a little awkward about how much mundane housekeeping and other chores Lizziebot did for her. The idea that such an amazing piece of technology was being used to wash dishes and clean house seemed a complete waste. Although Jenny did, of course, use her for all the high-level tasks she was created for, she had to admit it sometimes made her feel a bit guilty to see her washing dishes or folding clothes.

Bob had scoffed at this. "Let her do whatever you need her to do. Consider her more as an assistant than anything. Fidget has always done simple things for me as well. They are tools, even though sometimes it is easy to think of them as sentient. I don't suspect that they have feelings to get hurt or offended. I do admit, however, that sometimes Fidget surprises me with how 'human' he seems."

Jenny had heard what he said, but often got the distinct impression that there was a lot more to these bots than Bob had originally intended or expected.

She sent out a mental message to Burt. *"I'll be leaving soon for Tarafau's place. As we discussed, I'll be training some new candidates for the mental communications project. If you need me, that's where I'll be. Hugs and kisses."*

He mentally sent back hugs and kisses and Jenny once again marveled at her unique marriage to this amazing man. They seldom got to spend time together, especially time alone, but they both were committed to their duties and each continued to hope that this would be a temporary situation, at least until they had resolved the issues with the Inseni. And she smiled to herself, remembering their little honeymoon trip.

She heard a hoot of laughter once again from the living room. Mynn was dancing excitedly in a circle, her arms in the air. Lyra was sitting in front of the cubes board gazing in puzzlement at the stack of cubes on Mynn's side of the board.

"I don't know how she did it! I was winning and I was sure of it! Next time...."

Mynn hooted again her high-pitched laugh. "Yeah, next time.... There's always a next time."

The three of them all laughed at this, and Lyra cleared the board and stowed it into her MDP. "We're ready," she declared with a sigh. "Grab Lizziebot and let's get out of here."

Jenny returned to the kitchen and sure enough, Lizziebot had finished there and went easily into the MDP where she would commune with the Nanoites that lived there. It appeared to Jenny, although she knew that this was a construct and not a real person, that Lizziebot actually enjoyed her time with the Nanoites.

She knew the Nanoites, who were definitely sentient beings, enjoyed Lizziebot's company. "What a strange life I've stumbled into," she thought as she led the way to the gate office.

The black cat that had been lazing on one side of the window seat trailed behind them. Tidbit walked through the office door; his black tail held high like a banner. As the door closed behind him, he transformed into a tall, bald, muscular black man in colorful robes native to his planet. Now he was Tarafau, Jenny's guide and adopted parent.

Tarafau's family had officially adopted Jenny as one of their members near the beginning of her journey as the Gatekeeper for the Dimensional Alliance. Jenny always looked forward to visiting there. There was a catch, however. There were no Alliance gateways on their planet or even in their dimension, as far as anyone had been able to determine.

However, Tarafau's people had a unique talent for being able to transport themselves and others across dimensions without the use of a dimensional gateway.

"Ready?" he asked the group looking at each of them in turn. They all nodded.

He put one hand on Jenny's shoulder opposite of Chidwi and the other on Mynn's, and the gate office faded from view. They found themselves standing in front of Tarafau's domed home. Moments after he removed his hands from their shoulders, he faded from view and then returned with a hand on Lyra's and Nona's shoulders.

All three of them had come with Jenny, leaving the security of the Los Angeles gateway to the technology the Alliance had installed on the property and to her new neighbors who just "happened" to be Alliance agents.

Bob had assured her that her property was the most secure place on Earth, and she could believe it. She was constantly amazed at the technology at her fingertips as the Gatekeeper for the Alliance. Even tech that was top secret within the Alliance had been installed in various places on that property. She had every confidence that there would never be another incident like the one where she and her bodyguards had fought three large alien thugs in her living room early on in her time as the Gatekeeper.

They entered the house and found Amenia in the basement kitchen and family room that was not visible from the street.

She stopped what she was doing, evidently beginning preparations for their lunch, and rushed over to give hugs to everyone, ending, of course, with Tarafau, her adored husband. That hug, unsurprisingly, lasted a bit longer than the others, Mynn finally clearing her throat in embarrassment.

As they broke apart, arms still around each other's waists, Amenia sent, *"Welcome, one and all. Your rooms are ready for you, and our candidates will make their appearance this evening. I knew you would probably like to have lunch at the Apex, so I am starting supper preparations now. I'm nearly done and then we can all head over to the Apex. I know Tarafau would love some roasted bud crawlers, and the girls might enjoy a short shopping trip.*

"It occurred to me that this might be a great way to relax our minds before we get to work."

They all nodded their heads in cheerful agreement. At Tarafau and Amenia's home they all used mindspeech to communicate, considering all the distinct languages they used natively. This was common in the Alliance and made communication so much easier.

They soon set off, walking, as was the native custom, down the path between houses that led to the city. As they topped one of the rolling hills, the Apex came into view. It was an incredible pyramid that dwarfed any of those ancient structures on Earth. Its sides had indentations running from the second floor to the top. Jenny knew that each of these indentations served as a staging place for multiple hydroponic gardens and that the glasslike appearance of the sides of the pyramid were actually solar panels.

At the very top of the Apex was a point that glistened like a multifaceted jewel. Within that level of the Apex was a complex energy-generation plant that used not only solar power but also a magnification system that generated extreme heat for thermal power.

Jenny was in awe that a culture that seemed, on the surface, very pastoral and ordinary had created a structure of such high-tech magnificence.

As they walked, they passed beings that were each very different from Tarafau and Amenia. There were five intelligent species on Tarafau's planet, some with wings, some with fur, and even a race of humongous spider-like creatures, who Jenny had found to be kind and extremely intelligent. They often greeted them as they passed, as Tarafau and Amenia were well known and respected in their community.

The long walk was pleasant, as all of them were in good shape, and it was almost no time before they found themselves entering the ground floor of the Apex. Jenny knew that there was also an extensive basement that was devoted to hydroponics and the cultivation of the amazing bud crawlers that produced something similar to a chicken's eggs, that were considered a delicacy by Tarafau's culture.

The ground floor was dedicated to shops, gathering places, and entertainment of various kinds, including music, dance, and even interactive plays that had no stage but wove amongst the crowd, engaging them in the production.

They stopped first at a food stand that featured roasted bud crawlers and sat to eat in an area where a group of musicians were performing local folk songs.

Afterwards, Tarafau excused himself to go talk to some of the officers on the local area council, as governmental offices were all established on one of the floors above. Amenia took the girls around to the various shops, and then they explored the crafts halls in the two levels above.

They all found something fun to purchase. There was no local currency, but Amenia got bonus credits for hosting Alliance guests, so she purchased something for each of them. For Nona, a colorful swishy skirt. For Mynn, a belt made entirely of tiny beads that were in a mountain-like pattern. For Lyra, a silky scarf in blues and greens that fell like a waterfall from her shoulders.

Jenny declined getting anything for herself but enjoyed the delight of her bodyguards. She had noticed that even on Earth they loved to go shopping. They went out with her on a fairly regular basis to malls or the farmer's market, keeping up the charade that they were just college students renting out Jenny's garage apartment.

During the entire shopping expedition, her mind kept going back to the things she would need to teach to the fledgling communications candidates and intensely feeling the responsibility resting on her shoulders. The time in the Apex was a nice break, and she understood Amenia's thought that this would relax them and help them to prepare for the days ahead, but Jenny still couldn't shake off all the things racing through her mind.

During her stay she would still have to perform all her regular duties as Gatekeeper, including her responsibilities for the effective and secure transfer of sensitive information across the dimensions. These she literally could do in her sleep, as that was often the only time she had available to accomplish everything necessary on any given day.

She knew it was a good thing to reward her bodyguards in simple ways like this. Amenia was right to try to get the next two weeks started on a light note. As much training as Jenny had been given in controlling her mind, she would have expected she would be able to stay focused on just having a relaxing time with her friends, but she knew that she spent so much time focusing on the needs of the Alliance that it could never be very far from her thoughts.

They returned to the house, their packages already speeding ahead of them in the unique underground delivery system the Daringi had devised to keep their roads free from most vehicular traffic. So, they laughed and chatted and teased back and forth even after they had trooped through the house into the back garden and flopped with contented sighs into the chaises that surrounded the firepit about fifteen yards from the glorious miniature forest at the back of the spacious yard.

Chidwi had not accompanied them to the Apex, even though she could have easily gone with them with her reflection turned on. Linklings were loved and respected by the local populace, and she generally was fawned on by most of the people they met, especially the children. However, for now she preferred to spend time with her tribe, her family, the linklings who lived in the grove behind Amenia and Tarafau's house.

Jenny had paused in the door that led from the kitchen into the yard to ask if Amenia needed any help, but before she could utter a word, Amenia had just smiled and shooed Jenny out the door. *"Spend some time with your friends and the linklings,"* she had admonished her. *"We will have guests soon enough, and Tarafau has finished all our preparations. There will be time enough for you to get back to work."*

And with a fierce hug for her "adopted" daughter, she gently steered Jenny out the back door and closed it softly behind her.

The girls were already chattering away, having fetched their new treasures from the delivery box. They were now admiring them and comparing their purchases.

In Amenia's case, she was a well-known counselor for people who on the one hand simply wanted to improve themselves or on the other were struggling and needed help to get over a crisis or some difficulty in their lives.

In Tarafau's case, he was also a liaison for the Daringi with the Alliance as well as being a certified Alliance agent, playing a double role to aid both his own dimension and the Dimensional Alliance in the pursuit of peace and protection of those who needed it.

They each were credited for their hours of service in their respective positions. Jenny had often thought this was a truly fair way to trade: hours for hours, with no profession getting a larger part of the pie, but only being awarded for their time and effort in any project.

As she settled down in her usual place on a chaise facing the grove of trees, she was delighted to see a troop of linklings scampering towards them, hooting, and cooing their melodic vocalizations. They actually all spoke to one another and all other beings they communicated with in mindspeech. The sounds they made generally corresponded to their moods and emotions at any given time. When disturbed, they gave out an earsplitting howl that reminded Jenny of an emergency siren on earth.

But now they were all crooning their beautiful linkling song in complex harmonies, never out of tune, but completely spontaneous. In Lizzie's time she had discovered that they could anticipate another's melody via their ability to read minds. Lizzie's linkling, Ynni, had participated in their spontaneous concerts under a tree at Alliance headquarters, to Lizzie's continued amazement.

Now, looking at the tribe of linklings sporting gleefully before her, Jenny once again pondered how many unexpected twists and turns had led her to her current adventure, and she would never take for granted her aunt's generosity in leaving her this legacy.

She was drawn out of her reverie as Amenia gently touched her arm. She then realized that they had visitors, obviously the new candidates for mental communication training.

Next to Amenia stood the three new candidates, all obviously from Gi's home world, as had been the first three. There was no dancing this time. That had already made the point that these beings were exceptionally gifted mentally. Jenny knew that not all the beings on that planet were mentally gifted, but when they were, it was genetically passed down.

"These are, Mi, Nu, and Za," Amenia sent, pointing to each of them in turn. One of the things that she had learned about their culture was that most of them looked very similar and that once again she might have a bit of a time trying to tell them apart.

"Welcome, each of you. I'm looking forward to getting to know you all, and I am sure we can all do some good together. I understand we'll be eating first and then retiring to the work room to get started. Thank you for volunteering for this opportunity."

They nodded practically in unison. Jenny was used to this, as it seemed that in their species, if they inherited the ability to use mindspeech, they also inherited a certain amount of mental empathy and could sense each other's feelings and anticipate their responses. It wasn't quite like the linklings' ability to read minds, but it was close enough.

As promised, Amenia served up an excellent meal of roasted bud crawlers and her amazing vegetable stew, topping it all off with a fruit concoction that was pudding-like with little pieces of several of the native fruits suspended in the cream. It was one of Jenny's favorite desserts ever, except maybe her mom's gooey brownies hot out of the oven.

They chatted about mostly inconsequential things in mindspeech, as there were now several different languages in play. The convenience of mindspeech was that they could eat and talk without worrying about speaking with their mouths full. Jenny chuckled to herself at the sometimes-unexpected benefits of her newly acquired skills.

And now all were satiated, including the linklings for whom Amenia had provided a few large platters of fruits and vegetables. Jenny had been amused to discover that Tarafau and Amenia got a special dispensation in credit hours for taking care of the linklings who had been adopted joyfully into Daringi culture.

It was considered an honor to be chosen by one of the little creatures to be linked for life. Amenia had told her that not long after the little colony had been established in their yard, a number of dignitaries and various well-known contributors within the local community had visited them; and to their surprise, some of them had been chosen, much like Lizzie and Jenny had.

When she had asked Amenia why she and Tarafau had not bonded with one of them, she had said that the linklings had adopted them into their tribe as protectors and caregivers, and a further bond was evidently not necessary.

Now that they were full, the linklings returned to their grove to rest after such a feast, and Mynn, Lyra, and Nona started clearing away the leftovers, aided by Tarafau. Amenia led Jenny and Mi, Nu, and Za into the work room. It would be a serious two weeks of hard work for all of them, but it would be worth it if it took more of the burden of communications off of Jenny's already full plate.

Chapter 5: The Bouncing Wizard

Vena stomped down the mirrored hallway, not even seeing herself reflected on either side. If she had seen the look on her own face, even she might have been intimidated by it. Her awful scowl sent servants scurrying about their tasks with added zeal, not that she noticed them.

Time was flying by, and she didn't feel like she had made much progress towards her goal: the ultimate domination of all dimensions now protected by the Alliance. It seemed to her that it should have been obvious who was more qualified to reign in the multiverse. After all, with her plan, all beings within her dominion would have been subject to control, to order, and they would no longer be burdened with the necessity of making decisions they were ultimately unqualified to make.

She knew that under her rule the multiverse would finally know exactly what they should do and would do it or face the consequences. She would have order. She would have domination. There was only one thing standing in her way, and she would see it eliminated or heads would roll.

She entered the stairwell at the end of the corridor and headed down to the next level. It wasn't quite the dungeon, but it was below the level where all important things happened in her fortress. The wizards who had been subjected to her reign early on were much too far below her to have any place in the areas of the fortress where anything of any importance happened.

Nevertheless, she knew she needed them. She sighed regretfully. She really shouldn't have eliminated so many of them. In a fit of temper, she had slaughtered five of them a few moons back. Of course, that had meant she had also had to eliminate their families, who she had been holding captive. After all, no sense in keeping people around who had a reason to rebel against her rule and were taking up needed resources. That would have been foolish indeed.

The three remaining wizards had been suitably cowed, so it hadn't been entirely wasteful. They had become much more diligent in the time since. Nevertheless, she really hated having to deal with them, as their magic was something she really had no control over and little if any understanding of what they could and could not do with their spells and incantations.

She entered their lair, or so they called it, with distaste, but she knew her regular surveillance was necessary to keep them on task; and their contributions were critical to the success of her plans.

They were gathered around a table, scrutinizing what looked like some type of blueprint regarding one of their many projects. They had explained to her that the symbols and drawings of each of their projects were necessary for their spells to work properly and must be very exact, lest the magic fail to work properly on demand.

Once their spells were properly in place, the magical items they created would work for the lowliest soldier, but she was under-impressed by the crawling pace of the creation of each of these magical objects, especially when she felt that, as she regretfully admitted, they were essential to the final success of her intention to dominate the dimensions.

Somehow, she felt magic must be some kind of instantaneous gesture or just the right words, instead of all this "planning" and drawing and mumbling among themselves to accomplish anything.

As she stood for a moment in the doorway, taking in the scene, one of them looked up from the drawing in front of them and tapped each of the others firmly on an arm.

As they all looked up, they went down on their knees, next to their chairs, heads bowed.

"Great one! We honor you!" they exclaimed in chorus.

"Yes, yes! Get up, you worthless worms, and report!" She almost hissed the mental sending, despising that she couldn't use regular speech with these sniveling creatures. But they each were from separate dimensions and didn't even use vocal speech with one another.

The shortest of the three was the head wizard, and he came forward, wringing his hands and bobbing up and down as he came. He was a hideous creature, two green eyes (two!) and long greying hair braided on either side of his face. His name was Rajed, and he barely came up past her waist. Typically, he tended toward what she considered unseemly enthusiasm, and she could barely stand to be in the same room with him for more than a few minutes.

"Oh, Great One! I was about to send you a message," he began, taking a quick glance up into her eye. He blanched, seeing the impatience and anger in her face. None of the surviving wizards had forgotten the results of her last disappointment. *"We are excited to announce that the communication spells are complete."*

He held out his hand to one of his fellow wizards, who immediately came up to him and put into his hand a small rectangular box with some knobs on the base of the rectangle. There was a small flashing green light above the knobs and what looked like woven material taking up the remaining area of the face of the rectangle.

"You see?" he asked expectantly. *"As we promised. It will transmit a voice to a receiver at the portal. The receivers at the main portal in the palace will transmit that voice to a private receiver we have established in the war room. With your permission, we will also install another receiver in your personal quarters. This will allow you to speak directly with your officers on every planet where we have a portal. We can have the entire magical spell in place and the receivers running within days—with your approval, of course."*

"Of course," she replied smugly, as if she had expected nothing different from this lowly worm. *"How soon can you complete this project?"*

"We are prepared to start immediately, Your Greatness. We will do the initial installations today and then begin to install them at each of the prime locations in your realm. We will need an escort to go through each of the portals, of course, and permission to leave the palace."

"You shall have it. We are pleased. Proceed with your plan. I will want frequent reports, and you will need to demonstrate the use of these magical devices for me and for my generals as soon as they are installed. Are we clear?"

"Very clear indeed," the little man responded, now bouncing on his heels, an annoying habit he had. He was always bouncing, nearly dancing at every step. She had done all she could to oppress him, hopeful that it would work

the bounciness out of him, but he persisted in cheerful optimism despite all her best efforts.

"*Then get on with it. Your childrens' next meals depend on it.*" And she swept out of the room, sneering at how easily these tools were cowed to her will.

Chapter 6: Into the Fortress

"So, what do you think?" he asked, pivoting before the mirror on the back of their bedroom door.

Jenny cocked her head and then surveyed him from his head to his toes. "And what exactly is this supposed to portray? You look like a very poor, very unsuccessful beggar. I'd toss you a coin, but you'd probably spend it on strong drink instead of a hearty meal."

Burt laughed in delight. "Ah yes, exactly what I'm going for. I need to look decrepit and down on my luck. Maybe even deliberately so. I actually know a few pretty wealthy bums in L.A. I followed one surreptitiously from his favorite corner one time. He walked with a terrible limp until he got to a parking lot, looked around to see if anyone was watching, and proceeded to get into a late-model sports car and drove off.

I had watched him the entire day. I guesstimated he made about six hundred dollars or so in the nearly six hours he had spent on that corner with his little cardboard sign. Now I know," he said, holding up both of his hands as Jenny began to object, "that not every beggar you see on the street is running a scam, but you never know. And you know I love your generous heart, my Jenny. Don't stop giving, anytime you get a chance."

Jenny shook her head. She knew her husband had seen a lot more of the world and the many dimensions than she had, but it still surprised her at some of the things he had done.

"So, what exactly are you going to be attempting in that get-up?" She asked, intentionally ignoring his implications that maybe she was a bit too softhearted.

"Oh, you know... hanging out staying unnoticeable and checking out the lay of the land, so to speak. There have recently been rumors that some of our earthling friends are beginning to catch on that something isn't quite right. And, you know, a lot of it is just the typical conspiracy theorists looking for attention and counting up their social media "likes." But it seems that there might be something stirring that may be a concern for the Alliance. It's kind of boring, actually, but I've been doing this for a long time.

"Especially in the current crisis, the last thing we need is to have to deal with someone discovering a gateway we don't know about, or figuring out that something is afoot based on recent abnormalities, like the huge planetwide power outage not all that long ago."

Jenny nodded. Even now she remembered how her dad had been involved with the cleanup of that situation and she had found herself confiding in him, startling him with her mental abilities for communication and getting his promise not to reveal what she and the Alliance were doing. She was confident that he would keep his word, but she also realized that many top-secret organizations were even now still trying to figure out what had happened then.

She knew that Burt didn't think of what he did as anything special, but she clearly remembered the day her dad had thrown his newspaper across the living room in anger. What had set him off was a reporter who, when speaking of the heroic acts of a man in the National Guard who had saved many lives in the wake of a local disaster, referred to him as "a common soldier," meaning he was a low-ranking soldier.

"There is *no such thing* as a 'common soldier'!" he had exclaimed. "Every man or woman who raises his or her hand to take the oath to lay down their lives in support of the cause of freedom, knowing they may possibly someday make that oath a reality, is extraordinary and deserves respect!"

He had fumed about that for over an hour when he took pen in hand and sent a scathing letter to the editor of the paper, which they published with an abject apology by the reporter, who later was relegated to the social page, covering weddings and funerals.

Burt was so unassuming and casual about what he did, but she knew that, nearly every time he went on assignment, he was taking a risk. He recognized the same about her role in the Alliance.

Between the two of them, they knew they needed to treasure every moment they had together. Jenny was not in denial about the precarious nature of her position in the Alliance. She knew from past experience that there was a perfectly good reason for her three bodyguards, as much as she would have preferred not to put them in danger.

"So, do I look enough like a vagrant, or should I add some pungent aroma?" he continued, wearing his adorable cocky grin.

"I think we can do without the aroma part," Jenny put in, tilting her head to one side and taking it in for effect. "So, when do you leave, and do you know how long you'll be gone?"

"This should only be for a couple of days. It's more for reverse-psychology propaganda than anything. I'm gonna be spreading 'little green men' rumors to make certain people basically a laughingstock. We're hoping that it will end up on social media and make those who are inciting action towards eliminating the 'aliens' from Earth quiet down. If we make it less *War of the Worlds* and more "Toto, I've a feeling we're not in Kansas anymore," we can take a deep breath and move forward."

Jenny knew he was right. She totally agreed with the Alliance's assessment that Earth wasn't ready to deal with the idea of extraterrestrials already living on the planet. One more reason that Tarafau, aka Tidbit, still had to do his 'cat impression,' as Burt called his transformative powers.

Tidbit raised his furry head from his paws from where he was sprawled on the window seat, as if he had read her thoughts.

"Will Elizabeth be transporting you, or will you use other means to get where you're going?" he sent, his ears pricked forward.

"I'll be heading out in 'normal' clothes from L.A. Airport and changing when I get to D.C.," Burt replied in mindspeech. *"I understand Elizabeth will be taking a break at home while I'm away. Of course, she is on standby. All I have to do is to let my new little bot know I need her, and he will contact her via mindspeech, via Jenny. I am beginning to think maybe Elizabeth should have her own bot as well, but I think Bob has his hands full at the moment."*

"Speaking of which," Jenny added, *"I need to get back to Amenia's, as I need to finish doing the training for my new communication specialists. I told them I would only be gone for a couple of days, and my time is up. Tidbit, are you ready?"*

Burt snatched her around the waist, his fake beard tickling her shoulder as he kissed her thoroughly. When she caught her breath, she laughed and kissed him back.

Tidbit stood up on the window seat, stretched languidly and hopped down, the tip of his tail twitching.

"How much longer will you be at that? Should I go get the girls?" he sent with a tinge of amusement in his mind voice. *"Or I could finish my nap?"*

Jenny and Burt broke apart with a laugh, and Jenny patted at her mussed hair.

"Really, Jenny, please be sure to meet me at our place tonight. There is something we need to discuss."

He looked so serious that Jenny's smile faded. "Is there something wrong? Something you haven't been telling me?"

"No, but it's a decision I need to make and I need your help, since anything I do these days must take your needs into account."

"Hmm, that sounds serious."

"It is, but not scary serious, just something we need to talk about, okay?"

Jenny nodded and hugged him one more time and pecked him on the cheek. "Let's go," she said as her bodyguards entered almost on cue from the hallway. Chidwi leapt onto her shoulder with a happy chirrup and patted her cheek. The girls simply nodded and turned on their heels towards the entrance to the gate office, Tidbit bringing up the rear, his tail held high behind him.

As they entered the cozy office area and the door closed behind them, Tidbit melted into his native shape and was now Tarafau. It had become somewhat routine, to Jenny's continued amazement, for him to place a hand on the shoulder not occupied by the linkling and another on Mynn's shoulder. They melted from the office to find themselves in front of Tarafau's home.

He released them, faded away for only a moment, and then Nona and Lyra faded into view directly in front of them. Tarafau grinned, his fangs one of the few things that let you know he was alien.

"I can smell the roasted bud-crawlers from here," he sent waving them to follow him as he strode up the pathway to his front door.

When they proceeded down the spiral staircase into the family room and kitchen area, Amenia was there wiping her hands on an apron. With a glowing smile, she welcomed each of them, extending two hands to grasp theirs and then threw her arms around her husband and kissed him soundly before withdrawing and sending in mindspeech, *"Supper is waiting for us outside. I just sent it out with Mi. She has been so helpful during her stay here, and I must say she is progressing much faster than her friends. Not that they are slouching at all, but Mi just seems to have an inborn knack for mental communication. I think you will be pleased by their progress."*

"Thank you for all you have done to make that possible. I wouldn't have even known about my trans dimensional communication talent if it hadn't been for your mentoring."

Amenia put an arm around her shoulder for a sideways hug as they exited into the sunshine. This was a blooming season, so the edges of the yard were a riot of color, like a beautiful frame to the vast lawn of clover-like ground cover. Jenny imagined it would have been fun to run on with her bare feet, as it looked soft and probably warm from the sun overhead.

She always felt, in this place, that she was surrounded by astounding beauty and understood why Amenia took such satisfaction from working in the garden that edged the yard. Overhead, the rings of moons and asteroids that orbited the planet were like jewels against the nearly teal sky. The groves ahead towered majestically, similar to the tall aspens on Earth that Jenny had always admired.

As they walked toward the grove, Jenny could hear the contented cooing and chirruping of the linklings who had established a colony there. It was a soothing sound, and Jenny smiled as Chidwi leapt down from her perch on Jenny's shoulder and scampered ahead, calling to her tribe with chirrups of delight.

Her bodyguards trailed behind her, knowing from experience there was no danger here; but ever aware of their duty, she could almost feel them from behind, looking pointedly in every direction, ready to spring into action at the slightest hint of danger to Jenny.

Amenia had set a table on the rack over the fire pit that had been designed for that use. It was laid with what many might have considered a banquet, with all Jenny's favorite foods from this planet. The girls, standing behind her, oohed and aahed with delight at the generous spread. They didn't need to be coaxed when Amenia gestured for them to begin to fill their plates.

As Jenny took her filled plate to her usual chaise facing the grove, she noticed the three new communications specialist candidates exiting the house and heading in their direction. She paused before seating herself, waiting to greet them.

She was impressed with how they carried themselves with grace and confidence and gave each of them a one-armed hug, balancing her plate in the other hand.

"I am so glad to see you three. I hear good things about your progress and hope the Alliance can soon give you your assignments. Your aid in this project will mean a lot to many people you will never meet, but will hopefully ensure their safety and will allow me to do more for the Alliance than I can currently do."

They nodded and smiled and then turned to the table to get their food. Jenny knew she might never be close to these young women as a companion and confidante, but she already liked each of them and knew she could work with them easily and with confidence that they would do their jobs well.

Once they were all seated with loaded plates, Tarafau gestured for a moment of silence before they ate. Jenny had been surprised to discover that nearly every dimension had a version of "giving thanks to the Creator of All Things." Of course, each culture had its own name in their language for this, but it always seemed to translate in mindspeech, at least for Jenny, and as she had learned also for her Aunt Lizzie, as "The Creator of All Things."

To the delight of all assembled, the linklings then emerged out of the grove and began to cavort in a kind of dance. It didn't have any real choreography to it, but it was obvious they were dancing to some music none of the rest of them could hear.

Afterwards they came over to greet the little dinner party and were rewarded with fresh fruit and vegetables that Amenia had included in their little feast. They sat encircling the group, except Chidwi hopped up beside Jenny on the chaise.

"Many new younglings," Chidwi confided to Jenny. *"The tribe grows and is happy. Chidwi is glad to be here to see them all."*

"You miss them, don't you?"

"Yes... and no. Chidwi is happy to visit, but I can't imagine staying here and how much I would miss you, if we couldn't be together. We are linked in ways I can't begin to tell. My heart is with your heart, my Jenny."

Jenny couldn't think of words big enough to thank Chidwi for that sincere sending, directly from Chidwi's heart. Chidwi reached up with one tiny hand and patted her cheek.

Tarafau stood from his chaise. *"And now let us clear up, as there is work yet to do. We can leave the fruit and vegetables out for the linklings to finish."*

They all immediately stood and begin to clean up the leftovers to carry back into the house, Tarafau lifting the large pot of stew, and each of them returning to the house laden with plates, utensils, and bowls. Chidwi jumped to her perch on Jenny's shoulder, not wishing to trail behind, and the remaining linklings set about distributing the leftovers among themselves with delighted chirrups and hoots.

Jenny could sense some mental conversations weaving in and out of the group as they went and during the washing up and putting away of the remains of their feast.

Finally, Amenia shook out her cooking apron, hung it on its hook at the kitchen door, and turned to the group. *"Now that we are all rested and fed, let us adjourn to the workout room. All of us will be needed for this initial session."*

Jenny noticed that her bodyguards looked a bit disappointed at their inclusion. She knew they had been looking forward to a trip to the Apex.

"We'll all go to the Apex in a day or so," Amenia said, noting the sad faces. *"We'll go when we have earned the outing. I promise you it will be worth your time."*

Nona sighed and the other two nodded, and they all trooped down, including Tarafau.

After they had dutifully seated themselves in a meditation position on the mats in a circle, Chidwi jumped down from Jenny's shoulder and stood behind her, one small hand laying on her shoulder and her tiny body close enough to warm Jenny's back.

Per Amenia's instructions, they all closed their eyes and relaxed, breathing in complex patterns each of them had been trained to do in early agent days to enter the state of a REM trance.

In their interdimensional mental session the night before, Amenia had briefed Jenny in the specific procedure she would like to follow with this group. So, Jenny gathered each of the minds in the circle, carrying them with her into her mental fortress.

She introduced her bodyguards to the gate guardian, who lowered his staff and raised the portcullis to allow them entrance. She could sense the awareness of her bodyguards in this alien environment. They were on alert even in her mental world.

Here in this place, no mindspeech was needed, as basically they were all already joined in their minds, so when they spoke to one another it would be as if they were using vocal speech. Although each of them would speak in their native language, it would be received by the others in their own tongue as naturally as if they were all speaking one language.

"We will be meeting first in the communications center and then perhaps in at least one other building on the town square. Please follow me." And she gestured and, without taking a single step, they were all at once in front of the double glass doors that led into the communications space.

Jenny could see that her guards were a bit unnerved by what might have felt to them like magic. She tried not to laugh as she told them, "In here we can do things we might not otherwise be able to do in a physical space. You need not fear. You saw the guard at the portcullis? It is the only entrance, and only the people I have vetted can ever get in here."

"As far as you know," Lyra said with furrowed brows. "Many have considered themselves safe before with supposedly trusted friends and in supposedly safe places." She raised one brow as if to say, "Remember?"

Jenny couldn't help but blush at this reminder. She had trusted Sam as her very best friend and had been bitterly betrayed by her. She had thought herself safe in her own home and had been attacked by burly minions of the Inseni. She nodded in acquiescence.

"You're right," she admitted. "I won't take your service lightly. Continue to guard me so I can continue to focus on my tasks with confidence."

She turned to the rest of them. "So far you have learned how to contact people with mindspeech across dimensional space. Our next task is to learn how to project images simultaneously with our mindspeech transmissions. Come with me."

She strode into the video broadcast studio, a visualization that had led her to finally be able to project images of herself along with mindspeech, including the images of others, so they could do a visual conference call, as Burt called it.

She then proceeded to introduce her candidates to a foreign concept, the idea that you could transport moving, speaking images across long distances. While her bodyguards had been exposed, to their delight, to television in their little apartment over her garage, the three candidates from Gi's home planet didn't have that kind of technology. They were a mostly rural people, and none of them had ever seen a television set or experienced a movie or anything like it.

So, true to the nature of this space, she was able to demonstrate, using the cameras with her bodyguards as the actors on the set, how a camera worked. She was amused to see the reaction of her students. She had grown up with this technology, but she remembered clearly the story of her grandfather buying the first color television in the neighborhood. Neighbors would slow down as they walked by the large picture window in the living room, hoping for a glance of the television, in awe that you could have what amounted to a movie theater in your home, with lifelike colored images moving across the screen.

For the first time, these three young women got to experience seeing moving pictures projected onto a screen with the synced sounds of the voices of the bodyguards in front of the camera as they discussed what they wanted to check out in the Apex this time, as you could never see it all in a single day.

"You must be able to picture your communications as a complete package of both visual and audible sendings. This will require some practice, but, after seeing your progress, I am sure you can do it. Your predecessors have managed it, and this will allow us to have group discussions and conferences, as well as visual demonstrations, across the dimensions, and it will give us a clearer idea of events as we try to assess the conditions in other places."

They all nodded seriously. Some things were just much easier to show than to tell. The multiverse was vast and diverse, from the planetary conditions to the beings who lived there. Being able to communicate in this way would be the equivalent of interdimensional travel without a portal.

"So, for now, I will demonstrate by taking us all to visit my friends in Sanglarka and Puerto Rico on Earth. You will be able to see me make the connections with them and will experience how the three-way connection almost seems as if we are in the same room together.

"Bringing you all along is simple, as I already have a mental connection with each of you." She led them from the control room into the studio where there were already chairs for each of them.

As the situation room of Sanglarka faded into view, she couldn't help but smile at the sounds of delight and awe from her guards and the training candidates. She had gotten used to this by now, but it helped her remember her own amazement the first time she had pulled this off.

There before them were Lova, Arvid, and two people Jenny hadn't met yet, the newest agents from Earth who were in their early training before going to the Alliance agent training center. Two young women and a young man with expressions of excitement and awe on their faces.

"Hello, Lova! Thanks for arranging for our little demonstration here. Hey, Arvid! Wish I could be there for some of your spicy sugar cookies and mulled cider."

They both grinned.

"I thought it would be good for our new recruits here to get a taste of what they're in for in the coming months," Lova replied with her usual welcoming smile.

"Let me know when you figure out how to send cookies via your little tricks," Arvid said with a sardonic smile in his deep gruff voice, "and I'll bake you up a batch right away."

Jenny laughed. "Okay, let's bring on Switzerland, shall we?"

She paused and sent a thought via the connection to Adelle, the leader of the science team and gate guardian for the Switzerland gate.

The scientists there were a mixed batch of earthlings and some humanoids from various dimensions in the Alliance. Unlike Cornelium's lab, which was often visited by various configurations of beings, they had to be careful just in case someone on Earth got wind of this very unusual observatory high in the Swiss Alps. It had been built by the Alliance long before such things were considered commonplace.

Any Earth scientist would have been astounded at the technology available in this particular observatory, from its advanced telescopes to the many projects throughout the complex. Like Sanglarka, it was far away from any earthly transportation. The only way to get there without a gateway would have been by helicopter.

Just like the Sanglarka planning room, the breakroom of the lab came immediately into view. At this point, those in Jenny's communications video studio were joined on two sides by the Sanglarka group and the Switzerland group. Both of the groups joining this demonstration were used to conversing in this way, but Jenny's students were suitably awed.

"Each group will please introduce themselves to the rest individually. And you three," she said, turning to her students, "need to pay attention. These introductions have a purpose. You will be able to contact any of these individuals in this way once you have completed your training. Knowing who you want to speak with is key."

All nodded solemnly; and as Jenny pointed to each one who appeared to be in the room with them, they each spoke their name and title clearly. The young women were obviously focused, and Mi even mouthed the names as each was spoken. Jenny could see why Amenia was impressed with the young woman. She obviously took the training very seriously—not that the others weren't being attentive, but something about Mi was just slightly different.

Jenny had often been accused by her fellow students in school and even in college of being a teacher's pet and a "brainiac," but she enjoyed school so much that learning was a delight to her. Mi, however, seemed to be really working at it in almost a somber manner.

Once they had all gone through the exercise, they took turns showing the rest of the group something related to their particular role in each place. Jenny thanked them all and, with a thought, both of the Earth groups disappeared from the studio.

"Now," Jenny said with a smile to the three serious young women seated in their own semicircle in the studio that only actually existed in her own mind, "this is what we will be learning how to do at this phase of your training. Once all three of you are competent in this section, you will be ready to be assigned to your various posts. We will adjourn from here, and then we can have a question-and-answer time out in the backyard."

They all nodded seriously, and at once all of them were back in the workout room, seated in a circle. Neither Tarafau nor Amenia had spoken during their mental trip, but Jenny knew they were there as much as to lend Jenny authority and credibility as anything else.

Inwardly, Jenny sighed. It was going to be a very interesting two weeks.

Chapter 7: Burt's Dilemma

Burt sighed with relief. It felt so good to be out of the rumpled unkempt guise he had taken on for the last week. He had been surprised as a new agent when he had learned how rumors actually spread. He had always thought it was people of power who created the gossip chain that influenced large groups of people, but he had discovered in his training that more often information spread most quickly among the common folks.

So, during the day he dropped in on conversations on city streets, coffee shops, and parks; dropping some well-chosen words about the government cover-up about UFOs and how some of those "aliens" were actually getting government assistance and college scholarships, using honest citizens' hard-earned tax dollars.

In the evenings, he retired to the little flat he had rented and went online, invading various chat groups and sending out some cleverly faked videos on the various video platforms.

All this was designed to create more suspicion of the government than of the aliens themselves. Each message was crafted to imply that, if there really were aliens, they wouldn't need government help and that the likelihood that they would want to take over the world was pretty slim. After all, if they could make spaceships that could travel so far, wouldn't they be able to have everything they needed without any help from "puny earthlings"?

He felt it had gone well. He had already heard what might have been considered echoes of the rumors he had planted in some circles that surprised him. Some of the various channels that carried conspiracy theorist messages were even beginning to repeat, sometimes nearly word for word, the messages he had sent out.

He had posed as a former government employee, down on his luck and now reduced to asking for handouts.

The conflicting messages, aliens asking for a handout on the one hand and aliens' not needing help from anyone, had started some fearsome debates, none of which could be settled in any meaningful way, hopefully forestalling any action on either side to look further into any slips by the Alliance.

But now a more difficult prospect lay ahead of him. He had met Jenny's parents, two really nice folks who had immediately begun to call him their "son-in-love" as opposed to son-in-law. He had enjoyed some great talks with Mr. Japhet since their wedding and now felt comfortable around him.

He had admired this stalwart man and his dedication to serving his country and in other capacities, one of which was a weekly volunteer position at a local foodbank.

Burt had been impressed with Ed's attitude even towards those who had at one time been his enemies while he served in the military. He had discussed this with Liliath and with Lova at Sanglarka.

He knew that at one point Jenny had, in desperation, revealed her role in the Alliance to her dad and had sworn him to secrecy. True to his word, he had never revealed this, even to his wife.

One of the things Burt had been wrestling with lately is his split responsibilities between doing his usual agent tasks and caring for Jenny, who was at constant risk as the Gatekeeper. He knew that she was being guarded by some very competent bodyguards and that there was more defensive tech around her than any ruler in any country on Earth had ever had.

But every fiber of his being quivered with the thought that she might again be captured and subjected to pain and potentially death by her captors. She had gone through so much already. His beautiful little wife was capable with a quarterstaff and could hold her own one on one, most of the time. It was that "most of the time" that bothered him, that and because it was unlikely that most of their enemies would bother with a quarterstaff.

All agents were trained with the quarterstaff, as it was the one weapon that would go through a gateway without setting off an alarm. And the purpose of the staff was strictly for self-defense.

He wanted to be with her. He wanted to be by her side. Recently, Tarafau had taken him aside. He too was separated from his wife more than he would like. He stood there, towering over Burt as he did with most of the beings he interacted with.

"Burt, I have something I want to talk to you about, but for now, I would appreciate it if you didn't mention it to Jenny. Until I get it cleared with Liliath and the council, I don't want to get her worked up about it. I have a feeling that she will be of mixed emotions about it."

Burt had nodded solemnly, almost afraid of what might be coming.

"So, this is the thing. I think that Jenny may have graduated from the need of my instruction and guidance. You also have proven yourself worthy of respect and trust. I would like to propose that you are an appropriate guide for Jenny. Just as Luz is the Guide for Juan in Puerto Rico, it seems appropriate for you to be Jenny's guide. It would mean most of your other agent duties would be given to another, preferably an earthling.

"If we were to attempt to replace you, we would want someone with the maturity to act wisely in every tense situation and be able to be a trusted agent. Currently, none of the Earth agents in training are yet seasoned enough to take your place."

"Wait a minute," Burt had replied, grasping Tarafau's massive upper arm. Against the huge muscles and the blue-blackness of Tarafau's arm his hand looked puny indeed.

"Two things, if I understand you right. You want me to be Jenny's guide. I must give you an absolute 'yes' to that request. Secondly, you need an Earth agent candidate to replace me. Is that right?"

"Indeed, Burt. You have understood perfectly and by the look on your face I am guessing you know such a person?"

"I think I do. I know you haven't met Jenny's father, but it is clear to me that she gets her courage and ability to focus instead of panic in a bad situation from him. She gets her optimism and work ethic from both parents, and they have brought her up to act in integrity. The point is," he continued when Tarafau raised one eyebrow as if to say, *"and…?"* *"her dad is not only tested and tried in combat, but he spent about half of his army career in army intelligence. He has been trained in most of the things we learn in agent training.*

"It's true that he doesn't have Alliance training, but he would be up for it, I know he would. I know he's not a youngster like most of the agents in the Alliance

start out as, but I honestly believe he would jump at a chance to help Jenny, by coming into the Alliance."

Tarafau's brows knit together and he closed his eyes. From experience Burt knew that this was how he reacted to new and unexpected information. As was his way, he was contemplating deeply before he spoke.

"If we were to try to recruit him, how do you suggest we do it?" he finally replied.

"I suggest we let Jenny contact him and bring us into the conversation. He has already experienced mindspeech that one time with Jenny during the world-wide blackout awhile back. I know he promised Jenny not to divulge any of this and the reasoning behind it. He would agree not to say anything to anyone even if he declines the offer."

"What about his wife? It would be nearly impossible to keep it from her if he decided to become an agent."

"Her? She looks adorable and sweet on the outside, but she was a military wife nearly the whole time they've been married. She understands him very well, from what I've seen already. I think she would fall right in with it."

Tarafau nodded solemnly. *"I can see you have already given this some thought."*

"Well, not the part where I'm Jenny's guide, but I have sometimes considered that Ed Japhet would be an asset to the Alliance in whatever capacity they used him. He has real-life battle experience and isn't afraid of tech. He knows how to play it 'under the radar,' so to speak, and he is about as trustworthy a person as I've ever met."

"I feel you are right. I have met him, though he won't remember it as I was Tidbit at the time. My first impression was that this was a man who could be depended on. I listened in as he spoke with Bob about his military career and got the sense that he was not bragging about it, but stating his experience as fact.

"However, how do you think Jenny will feel about all this? It's a lot to put on her all at once. I know she is currently busy, training the next set of mental communications specialists, but will she accept our conclusions? To be honest, she doesn't have much of a say in any of it, but the last thing we want to do right now is to distract her from her current tasks."

Now, as Burt reclined on a chaise in the back patio of the little house on Infinity Loop, he found himself wishing that this evening's meeting wasn't going to be at the little pool beside the Merced River as they generally did when Jenny came to visit him in his dreams. He really wished it could be a face-to-face meeting so he could hold her hand in his as he spoke to her.

Of course, he could do the gesture in the mental world where they met so often, but there was no sensory input of warmth or the tightening of his grip when he was being emphatic, or the little hand squeezes that were their own private code for *I love you*. They had developed that early in their relationship and it was fun to be able to say this to one another without anyone else being any the wiser.

Now, even though he had ordered out take-out for himself from their favorite Chinese restaurant, he was almost anxious to get to bed to get this over with. He wasn't entirely sure what Jenny would think of all this, but he hoped she would be glad to hear it.

It occurred to him that perhaps he shouldn't tell her the entire thing. Maybe, just the part about her dad would be good. The rest should probably come directly from Tarafau or Liliath.

He invoked DAT out of his MDP. He was glad that Bob had created it for him. DAT not only made a very efficient little butler but played a mean game of cubes. Burt had thought he had gotten used to being alone in all his assignments and hadn't minded much being a bachelor. But since he met Jenny, every minute without her put him slightly out of sorts.

"What can I do for you, Boss?" DAT said immediately when he had appeared out of the MDP in what Burt wanted to think of as a magic trick.

DAT had picked up "Boss" from Fidget, he was pretty sure. He didn't correct him, however. He thought it was kind of cute.

"Well, DAT, the delivery guy will be here in a few minutes and I would love it if you would set the table, just for me. I'm not having guests today. It's just the two of us, and I thought I might be up for a game or two of cubes after supper."

"Sure, Boss." And the little bot turned and headed into the kitchen, calling over his shoulder, "Paper or regular plates?"

"Let's forgo the paper plates this time. You don't mind doing the dishes, do you?" he quipped to DAT. He knew DAT wouldn't get the joke.

"No, Boss. I will gladly do the dishes," the bot replied, as Burt had expected. Bob had told Burt to watch for eventual development of a personality in the bot, but so far, it just took commands and obeyed as expected.

The plate and fork for his lone meal was barely on the table when the doorbell rang with his food.

He sighed as he helped himself to his favorite dishes out of the little carboard containers. Another meal alone. Hopefully, if all went as planned, he would eat more often with his sweet wife.

After finishing his meal and several intense games of cubes, he finally retired to his empty bed. He did his breathing exercises to allow himself to finally drift off to sleep.

After a few nonsensical dreams in mixed dimensions, the little pool near the Merced River faded into his view and on the stone by the edge of the pool sat Jenny, typically dangling her feet into the water. She had complained that it wasn't quite the same in the dream state, since she had now been there in person, but the main thing was that in this mentally constructed place, he could see her and she him.

"How did your assignment go?" she asked, patting the rock beside her to indicate that he should sit as well.

"Oh, you know, the usual. I think I left a lot of people a lot to think about beside 'aliens among us.' But I'm done with that for now, although I may soon have a new assignment...."

"Oh? Nothing too dangerous, I hope."

"Actually, it could be quite dangerous, but I can handle it, I think."

"So... tell me about this 'not so dangerous' assignment. Where will it take you this time?"

"Actually, I'm not entirely sure. I think it depends a lot on where you'll be spending most of your time in the future."

"Do you know something about my future travels that I don't know then?"

He cocked his head with that sly, cocky grin she had grown to love so much. "Well... actually, I may be as much in the dark as you are, but let's just say our future assignments will probably coincide more often than not. Tell me, do you like having Tarafau as your guide?"

"Of course I do, but I am somewhat sad he doesn't get to spend more time with Amenia. They are such a cute couple and she obviously adores him. She told me lately that if he wasn't my guide, he would probably be serving on the Daringi council in some position or another. She feels her people could use his wisdom and levelheadedness these days."

"I'm sure they could. Rumors are that there have been some disagreements lately as to the extent of their involvement with the Alliance. After all, they have no gates that they are aware of, nor do they have any particular needs. Both Tarafau and Amenia are concerned the council may decide to withdraw their aid from the Alliance, if something doesn't change."

Burt fidgeted beside her. This was, of course, one of the reasons the upcoming changes would make sense, but he still wasn't sure how Jenny was going to react to it. Oh well, nothing for it but to plunge ahead...

He cleared his throat, then wondered distractedly if he was actually clearing his throat where his body lay in his bed.

"So, this is the thing I needed to speak with you about. It has two parts, and I got elected to tell you about it. I don't know which part will be more difficult for you, but bear with me."

Jenny looked up into his eyes, her own eyes wide with concern. "They're putting you on a permanent assignment somewhere?"

"You could say that. The first part of this is that the council agrees with Amenia, that they need Tarafau working in the Daringi government to curb some of the more radical suggestions that are being made about their relationship with the Alliance." And he held up his hand to forestall the obvious question in Jenny's face. At that point, he realized that he needed to press on regardless of his earlier reservations about telling her all.

"Since, as the gatekeeper, it is requisite for you to have a guide always at your side, they felt the most logical choice would be... well... me."

Jenny's countenance brightened, but there were still questions in her eyes. Nevertheless, she let him continue.

"This would be a permanent assignment, and it would require me to go with you wherever you go, whatever you do. What do you think so far?"

"Are you kidding me? What do I think? Well, of course I think it is amazing and I can hardly wait! Silly goose, what did you think I would think?"

And she threw her mental arms around him and gave him a hug that neither of them could actually feel.

"But wait... there's more!" Here he paused and took a deep breath. "It's about your dad."

"My dad? What do you mean? Has something happened to my dad?"

"No, Jenny. Your dad is just fine, at least he was the last time I talked to him. It's just that the Alliance would like to bring him on as an agent, to basically replace me. And that they feel like both of your parents should undergo agent training."

"But they're old!" she exclaimed and then ducked her head in embarrassment. "Please don't tell them I said that."

"I won't. But they aren't as old as many who serve, and both are physically fit and healthy. Typically, they would be considered middle-aged, not ancient.

"The majority of my assignments don't really involve anything dangerous, and your dad did serve in intelligence in his army days. He knows how to think on his feet and he may possibly even become a liaison between the Alliance and Earth at some point. He has the skills and the smarts for it. And people tend to respect him."

"Have you already spoken with him about this, then?"

"I didn't want to do that until I spoke with you. So, what do you think?"

"My first thought is, he'd jump at the chance. He's been champing at the bit ever since he retired. And a cause like this would attract him like an ant to a picnic. But even then, on second thought, do I really want my family involved in all this? I just don't know...."

"Well, I understand your feelings, but you know time isn't on our side at the moment. And it wouldn't have to be long term, just until we've settled the score with the Inseni and restore some kind of peace to the multiverse." And he shook his head and grinned again. "No big deal, right?"

Jenny sighed. Burt was right. If this had been a real pool, she would have been tempted to push him in, just to allay some of her frustration. It was a good solution. Her dad was already well-trained and could get through the agent school in a few weeks with a little special attention from the instructors. Her mom would bump along as she had always done, like the faithful wife she was. Neither of them would complain, and both of them would not only see the necessity but would be eager to help.

"And they would be stationed on Earth? No one the wiser?"

"I suggest a summer home in Laguna Beach, close enough to have access to the L.A. gate, but with no obvious ties to any of our operations. It isn't like the Inseni aren't already aware of them, as they have visited the house on Infinity Loop a few times. The Alliance would foot the bill, and they could still travel easily to San Diego when they wanted to."

"You're right, of course. So how do you want to do this, and when?"

"I thought we might just decide to drop in on them once you get back from your current assignment. We haven't visited with them for any length of time since the wedding."

"Mom and Dad will be happy to see us both, I'm sure. Okay, we'll plan on it. When will they switch you to the Guide position?"

"Soon. I think when you come back from this training you're doing, we'll be making a trip to Alliance headquarters, and they'll brief us there."

"Then, I guess we'll just see what happens. It would be nice to be able to be together all the time. I do worry about you, you know...."

Burt shook his head and laughed so hard that tears streaked his cheeks and he had to hold his belly. "*You* worry about *me*?" he finally choked out. "Do you have any idea how much *I* worry about *you*? Silly girl. Of the two of us, I am never in the kind of danger that seems to be around every corner where you are concerned. Why do you think they have upped security four times in the past six months?"

Jenny wondered if he had tears running down his face in his sleep. If so, his pillow would be wet when he woke up. "I actually don't worry about myself much these days. After all, with a guide and three bodyguards, someone is going to have to either be very brave or very foolish to attempt anything..."

"Or very intent and persistent. I really feel like somehow the enemy has gotten the idea that you are the 'key,' if you'll forgive the implication, to the whole struggle with the Alliance. As if, when they captured you or worse, they could then conquer the Alliance without resistance."

"That's not the case, of course, but they probably have no idea about the backup Gatekeeper or anything about her," Jenny said, her eyes narrowed in thought. "And nothing they would do would coax that information out of me. Not even my communications specialists know anything about that, and I'm not about to tell them."

Burt put an arm around her reflexively, knowing that neither of them could feel it. "None of us doubt your courage and commitment to the Alliance, but the one thing I've learned as an agent for the last several years is that you never really know what's out there, and almost nothing is as it seems."

She looked up into his face. "We both need to get some real sleep, my darling Burt. See you tomorrow night?"

"Wouldn't miss it for the whole multiverse."

Chapter 8: Mixed Signals

"How do you do this again?" Vena asked, her brow furrowed, and her mouth twisted in what she was sure was a lovely yet intimidating snarl.

"Just twist this dial... er... um... this round thing with the markings on it. And then push the button on the receiver..." and he thumped the receiver with his finger for emphasis. *"Then just say something, and in a minute, you will hear someone reply. The dial... this round thing, is how you choose who to speak to. See the chart? It has the markings for each of the dimensions where we have installed units near their portal.*

This portal," he pointed at the portal next to them, fervently hoping she wasn't getting impatient with his explanation, *"is connected to all the units shown on the chart."*

Vena and Rajed stood together on a broad, covered veranda that had been built around the portal that was in the center of her majestic fortress. She disdained the idea that she needed instruction from this lowly wizard, but for now, she wanted to keep this lovely toy to herself; and, in order to maintain her superiority, she needed to continue to appear all-knowing.

Of course, her generals would eventually have a unit of their own, but for now she wanted to bask in the power of instant communication with the lowly ones who had been named overseers of her domains.

Their stewardship definitely left something to be desired, and she hoped that this tool would allow her to keep a closer watch on the fools. Of course, this was nothing compared to what she would soon have access to.

She was impatient with the whole process of getting the little twit, Mi, trained by that prat, Jenny. She knew it was necessary, but she felt like she was so very close to having the crucial last piece to the puzzle of how to finally defeat, demoralize, and destroy the fools who so arrogantly called themselves the Dimensional Alliance.

Therefore, she obediently followed his instructions, peering at the scroll with the markings on it. Selecting one of the more important posts in the network, she spoke forcefully into the receiver.

"Post Alpha, report!"

There was some fuzzy crackling, and then a barely recognizable voice emanated from the receiver.

"Reporting, Your Greatness. How may I serve you today?"

Her snarl turned into a haughty, small-mouthed smile.

"With whom am I speaking? I wish to speak with General Quilk."

"I am he, Great One. I have been awaiting your communication, not stirring from this spot since the receiver was installed."

"Well, that is a waste of time on your part. In the future, you will station a watch person at this post at all times who will have instructions to fetch you at once when I call. Do you understand?"

"Yes, indeed, oh Great One." She could almost hear the prostration in his voice.

"This was a test. Keep the unit powered at all times." She knew that evidently these units used a mysterious power that must be fed to continue to make the stations continue to run. Each of them had been equipped with a device that a man would sit upon and by pressing pedals that rotated a wheel would induce the spell that would give these devices the magic necessary to do what they did. In her case, in another room two of her servants were constantly rotated to power her own device, but she didn't want to smell the odor of their sweat as they did so.

The servants slept in shifts and only took breaks for the necessary. Even then someone took their place for the minutes it took for them to relieve themselves. Other than that, they even ate while pedaling.

She could tell Rajed was feeling much too pleased with himself. The nerve of the little wizard! After all she had done for him and his fellow wizards. She had been inordinately patient with their slow progress. This was no more than should have been expected. They were wizards, after all.

So she cut the transmission by pressing the little button again and scowled at him.

"The sound wasn't very clear." Although she had to admit to herself it was working better than she had hoped. Not that she would ever tell him that. *"And all this dial twisting and button pushing. Couldn't you have made it a little less onerous?"*

"The magic is complex; and in order for non-magical beings to operate it, it has to be done this way. Otherwise, you would require a wizard to be at each station, and at present, um, we are a little short." He obviously didn't want to mention exactly why they were short several wizards after her last explosion, but he didn't lower his eyes.

It still seemed deplorable to her that these beings sported extra eyes. With her one, very proper eye, she gazed back at him.

"Hmph. Well, if it's the best you can do...."

"We would never dare to do anything but our best magic for you, Your Greatness."

"And you say you will be able to place one of these in my private quarters?"

"Indeed, after we have enough of the magic cord to extend from this device, you will have one for your private quarters and also one for your strategy room."

"And you say you can hide the cords, or at least make them inconspicuous?"

"Per your orders, Great One."

"Then, carry on. The guard posted at the entrance to the veranda has orders not to allow anyone besides you and your fellow wizards to enter without my express permission. I expect you to be present at our next meeting in the strategy room to train my generals. You may withdraw."

Rajed bowed and turned for the entrance, almost dancing across the polished stone floor in the bouncy walk that seemed to be normal for him.

Now, she thought as he exited through the gate, *I will* have order. *I will have control and I have only to wait for that twit, Mi, to complete her training and that* thing... *that, that* creature, *will be vanquished and victory will be* mine*!*

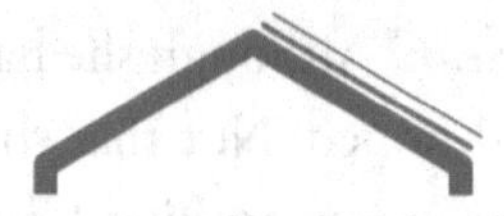

Chapter 9: Dragon Train

Bob rose early. Today was the first day of a weeklong tour of the scholastic institutions and labs of this planet. Cornelium and two dragon assistants would be flying him, Merv, and Anela from the heights, where the main governmental seat resided in the massive palace dug into the mountain peak out to their first stop, the academy of science.

There, beings from all over the dimensions came to study and research various scientific disciplines. It was considered a high honor to be invited to participate in the various projects sponsored by the academy.

Bob dressed carefully and stored Fidget with his Nanoite inhabitants and Xihu, his current Mookookie companion, in his MDP, along with his laptop and some of his favorite snacks for the journey.

The first leg of the trip was going to be a short one, as they were only heading down into a nearby valley, nearly as he could tell, about a thirty-minute ride dragonback.

There was a rap on the door. "Come in, Merv," Bob called out as he donned a hooded sweatshirt. The ride might be a little chilly, considering the altitude they would be flying from.

Merv entered, a grin on his face. "G'morning, mate. About ready, are you?"

"Yep. I've checked everything off of my list. I have to say I continue to marvel at the convenience of the MDP. No luggage... not even a backpack, for a weeklong journey, and I don't even have to go through security to get onto my flight. Ignatius even has a habitat inside the MDP. Fidget is taking care of him. He didn't want to be left behind. He told me he wanted to see what other winged creatures there were on this planet, after he heard Cornelium describe some of the wildlife we might encounter on this trip."

They both laughed at this. Although Merv was definitely not from Earth, he passed nicely for a British earthling and even had a legal passport to allow him to travel on Earth-bound airlines, something he found "quaint and rather amusing, old chap," as he had told Bob on one occasion.

You'd never guess from looking at him now that he had once been Merlin, from the Arthurian legends. He stood there in jeans, a t-shirt, and tennis shoes, a hooded sweatshirt slung over one shoulder.

"Well, let's get on with it, then!" he exclaimed, clapping Bob on the shoulder.

They strode down the hallway to the large reception room that led into the tunnel carved from rock which opened out on the other end to what might have been considered a hangar, as it was from here that the dragons came and went, sometimes taking passengers as the need arose.

The cavern was huge and high ceilinged, much like the giant hangars that housed large Earth aircraft. The opening to the outside had enough clearance for a 747 aircraft of Earth to have easily launched from there, but Bob couldn't even imagine the Earth pilot who would have the courage to try it. No runways here. Just a sheer drop into what almost appeared to be a bottomless gap between mountains.

Cornelium and his two companions were there with attendants neatly strapping the specialized saddles to their backs.

"Ah, there you are. Anela was about to send someone for you," Cornelium sent in his gruff mind voice.

Anela stepped from behind the smallest dragon and waved. *"Glad you made it. We will be leaving in just a few minutes. I see you brought something warm to wear while we're flying. You might also want a pair of these."* And she threw each of them a pair of goggles that reminded Bob of the old airplane pilots who used to necessarily sport goggles and a scarf around their necks.

These were easily adjustable, and Bob and Merv soon had theirs on. Within a few minutes, as Anela had predicted, they were each astride a dragon, Merv on Cornelium, Bob on a dragon named Shackle, and Anela on a dragon named Slyd.

As each of their passengers grasped the handles on the saddle that were made for that purpose, each dragon in turn stepped to the opening and plunged out, wings snapping wide to catch the air currents.

Bob took a deep breath as he felt Shackle's great leg muscles bunch beneath him and the great push as Shackle sprang out into the open air. Bob knew this would never get stale or mundane for him.

They first plunged downwards and then, gaining speed in a long glide, Shackle began a steady stroke of his wings, soon catching up with the rest of the wing. They flew in a V formation, Cornelium taking the lead as the largest of the three.

Though this wasn't Bob's first trip dragonback, he still thrilled to the nearly disconnected feeling. There was nothing between him and the sky and the drop below but the warm back of the dragon he rode; and although he somehow thought he should be just a little bit afraid, instead he gloried in the rush of the wind as they sped along past the sentinel peaks around them.

This part of the planet was like taking the Swiss Alps and multiplying them both in height and area by perhaps ten, Bob thought. He'd seen maps, of course, but nothing compared to experiencing it in three dimensions.

Shackle didn't seem to be the talkative sort. Other dragons he had ridden with had actually been very happy to carry on a conversation, but Bob didn't mind. This gave him the opportunity to contemplate what they were about to do.

He, Bob Reid, humble earth scientist and inventor, was going to hobnob with several groups of scientists renowned across the dimensions for their skill and intellect. He wondered what in all creation he could possibly contribute to such a high-level network. Not to mention he was buddies with Merlin, of all people!

He blessed fervently the day he had moved across the street from Lizzie Japhet and their friendship that had finally resulted in this incredible opportunity. He would have given anything to thank her for all she had done to enrich his life. Yes, she had been old when she passed and had lived a long and exciting life, but he would never have had all the adventures he had experienced since Jenny and Burt let him in on their secret of secrets.

Now here he was, having boarded a dragon as if it was just another ordinary day and not the least bit unusual. He couldn't stop grinning.

They were heading through a long trough between two chains of mountain peaks. The spaces between each of the mountains wasn't broad enough for any settlements, so they saw no sign of habitation. Merv had explained to him early on that a number of refugees of various races had settled this planet, due to their getting stranded from their home dimensions, having gone through gateways accidentally long before the Alliance had been formed and the gateways had been networked together and protected from accidental entrance by creatures and beings who were unaware of their existence.

"At that point," Merv had explained, "it was like someone slammed the door and locked it. Many had been stranded, because there was no way at the time to figure out where they had come from initially. The dragon folk, among others, welcomed several races to colonize the less used parts of their world, as it is large.

"Actually, you've probably noticed that you feel like you've put on a few pounds since you've been here. The opposite is probably true. The gravity is simply more powerful here because of the size and density of the planet. Since dragonkind generally inhabit the high places, with only a few exceptions, there was plenty of room for settlements on various continents and islands, as well as on the plains and in the deserts you will see when we make our tour."

Merv had explained that there was a dwarf-like race similar to Arvid and Ingot called the Frini, whose city they would visit first. There was also an aquatic race that inhabited the two huge oceans on the planet called the Onui. The ones Bob was most anxious to meet were a pixie-like winged race called the Nolm, although not the minute mischievous creatures out of fairytales. They were about the size of a grade-school human child and were known for their studious and curious nature, very clever with technologies and gizmos.

The Frini, who were hosting their first visit, were scholarly and tended towards the study of herbology, healing, and chemistry of various kinds. Merv had informed him that this place was a kind of retreat for scholars from across the dimensions, and he would soon encounter some of the beings he had considered myths and legends. They were aware of Earth and earthlings, and Merv said he was looking forward to seeing their reaction to Bob as much as he was looking forward to seeing Bob's reaction to them.

The ride was peaceful and the view spectacular. After a while, the scenery began to change. The mountains weren't quite so tall, and the spaces between them began to widen. Just ahead, Bob could see a huge space opening out as they got to the end of the mountain range.

There was a large stretch of what was obviously farmland with well-tended fields, orchards, and vineyards. From this height, it looked like a beautiful patchwork quilt. Beyond that, he could see the city and caught his breath at the sight.

"This must be how Dorothy felt when she first saw the Emerald City," he mused. "Not at all what I expected."

Some of his awe must have shown on his face because he heard Merv chuckling. He was turned in his saddle, looking behind him at Bob with glee. "I was waiting for this, old boy," he called behind him. "I know how it took me the first time I saw it. Spiffing, wot?"

Bob could only nod, with no words to describe how he felt at that moment. The city was round. That was the only way he could think of it. There were no corners that he could tell, and there were several of what could only have been called skyscrapers emerging from the center.

Many of the buildings were actually see-through domes, no need for windows, and the many floors were clearly visible through glass or plastic from the outside. Within many of the rooms, beings of various configurations were busy at different tasks.

At the center of the great circular city was a cylindrical building, taller than all of them. Like the domes, the outer walls were transparent. The effect was that the entire city sparkled almost blindingly in the sunlight.

Various beings walked on walkways on the side of broad avenues, and numerous vehicles moved almost silently along many streets which were laid out in concentric circles throughout the city. The thing that stood out for Bob, what made it almost magical for him, was the fact that this was not the loud, clamoring noises of what he thought of as a large city.

The silence was what a friend of his would have called *deafening*. As they got closer, Bob would have expected, if nothing else, the sound of voices. But evidently, mindspeech was the common "tongue" of these residents who were so very diverse.

They glided down in a spiral towards a large grassy area, one of several, spaced around the edges of the city, which seemed to have been placed there mainly to accommodate the dragons entering the city to drop off passengers.

However, they didn't land there, simply dipping a wing in salute to several beings below who were waving at them.

Instead, they soared back up to a wide opening at the top of one of the large skyscrapers. The opening was tall enough that the passengers didn't have to duck their heads to enter. The inside resembled the large cave in the side of the mountain that housed the castle that held Cornelium's lab.

They were greeted by humanoid attendants similar to those who lived in the castle.

"Ah, here you are," a young woman sent with a welcoming smile. *"On time, as usual, Cornelium. And we welcome our guests. Please dismount, and we will attend to your friends. Their saddles will be cleaned and stored here, ready for your return trip. Cornelium, your usual suite is prepared, and the additional apartments are ready for your companions."*

She nodded to Bob, Merv, and Anela and beckoned to them to follow her. She was tall, nearly as tall as Merv, and her long periwinkle blue hair hung nearly to her waist in an intricate braid pattern. Her skin was almost mahogany in color, and her eyes were deep green. She moved with grace and confidence before them, taking Anela by the arm.

Bob recognized that this wasn't anything new for Anela or Merv and that he shouldn't be surprised these people knew Anela and that perhaps some of them were even friends or maybe even related.

"I am Benia, by the way. I will be your escort and guide," she sent back to Bob and Merv.

Merv grinned at Bob, and Bob couldn't help but grin back. *"Now your adventures truly begin, old chap. As Burt would say, 'You ain't seen nothin' yet!'"* he sent privately to Bob. And he slapped Bob congenially on the back.

Bob pretended to stagger at the blow, and they both laughed at Merv's private little joke, but inside Bob couldn't help but wonder, a little late, what he had gotten himself into.

It was true, he had expected to see a variety of alien beings, but what he hadn't expected was how many of them were generally humanoid. Indeed, there were varying skin colors and configurations of facial features, but most of them had two legs, two arms and the body parts you would expect in any human gathering.

The types of clothing also varied in how much they covered and in the wide range of colors and fabrics, from animal skins to gauzy, flowing robes and some that resembled nothing more than the frontier clothing of the 1700s on Earth.

Some beings were obviously male or female, and then there were those he wouldn't have had the courage to try to define by gender.

As they passed various labs, most with glass doors that allowed them to peer inside and see individuals busy at various tasks, Bob had to smile. Even here, scientists seemed to need a specific type of environment to do their work, and these labs felt familiar to him. He could tell that he would fit in well with this group.

The halls they wandered down were wide and the ceilings tall enough for Cornelium to pass through with no problem. As such, Bob had to admit, if only to himself, that he felt very small and somewhat insignificant. After all, who was he in such company? Even on Earth he hadn't made a huge splash in the scientific community.

True, he had his share of discoveries and inventions to his credit, but most of his work had been done for large corporations on hush-hush projects that the company ultimately took credit for.

Most of his best work, if he was honest, had been done since he was accepted into the Alliance network; and he felt sure that once again, his best stuff would never be acknowledged by the scientific communities on Earth.

Had he been the kind of person that needed the kudos of his associates, he would have felt slighted and probably underappreciated.

Nevertheless, he also knew that he wouldn't have traded his life with anyone else's. *Look at me,* he thought as they continued to move through the vast complex, *hobnobbing with my fellow "wizards" on a planet in an entirely different dimension and hanging out with people who are used to technology that would blow the minds of any of my fellow scientists and inventors on my home planet. Who'da thunk this was ever even possible?*

He chuckled to himself and noticed Merv gave him a sidewise glance. *"What's so funny?"* he sent privately.

"Just thinking how we're just casually striding down a hallway that my compatriots from home would have considered a complete fantasy. If I was ever al-

lowed to tell any of my companions back in the labs on Earth about any of this, they'd put me in a looney bin or tell me I should write a book."

Merv grinned. *"You're probably right. If they ever decide to write about you, however, just be sure they get your name right... Merlin, indeed."* And he shook his head with amusement.

Suddenly, Cornelium slowed and stopped in front of a huge door at what appeared, finally, to be the end of the corridor. Sure enough, he opened the huge glass door in front of him, ducked slightly and beckoned the rest of them to follow him.

Bob barely held back a gasp. He felt like he had just entered scientist heaven. Before them spread a vast laboratory with various areas obviously adapted to different types of beings to allow scientists to work together, each with their own tools and equipment.

Cornelium strode to one corner of the huge room, nearly the size of a football field. As they passed the various areas, some of the scientists glanced up from their work, but didn't seem to be at all curious to see the three humanoids and their huge dragon guide. They had left the other two dragons at the entrance to the facility, where they had immediately rushed off to a different part of the complex to see to other tasks.

This corner area was obviously made to accommodate large beings. In addition to two other dragons, there was what seemed to Bob's eyes to be a troll or an ogre, as well as a being that anyone in the Pacific Northwest would have immediately identified as a Sasquatch.

This group immediately ceased working on their projects and turned to Cornelium, who presented his human companions. *"You know Anela and Merv, of course, but this is Bob, a human scientist and robotics expert from the planet Earth.*

Bob, please greet Gorl," and what Bob in his head thought of as a Sasquatch bobbed his head in acknowledgment in Bob's direction, *"... and Flun,"* now the ogre nodded his head at him, *"... and Marl."* And this time the dragon tilted his head in greeting.

"I am honored," Bob managed, not sure what else to say. *"Your complex here is amazing. I don't think we have anything on Earth that begins to compare."*

Marl nodded. *"Even within the Alliance, a campus of such magnitude is rare. We welcome you, Bob, from Earth. We have heard many good things about you from Cornelium. You have taken much of our own technology and improved upon it. We look forward to spending the day with you in a meeting of the minds."*

"Thank you, Marl. I am not sure how much I can add to what you have already done, but the essence of science is curiosity, and I admit there is much I hope to learn from you. Cornelium has planned a whirlwind tour of several facilities, but I hope in the future we can spend much more time together."

Heads nodded, and Bob could feel their approval. In his entire career, as a scientist and inventor, he had never experienced so much acceptance and lack of ego in his peers before. It was as if these scientists had advanced beyond pettiness and were all eager not only to share, but to support and encourage one another.

"So, what are you working on at the moment?" he continued into the silence that followed.

Cornelium pointed to Gorl. *"Gorl has a project I think will interest you."*

Gorl nodded his shaggy head. *"It involves a power source we had initially thought impossible, based on light. Not solar power as has been used in cultures all over the dimensions, but light captured and stored in a new way."* And with that, Bob's adventure began, and he found himself wondering over the next several days if it was possible for a person's brain to explode from too many new ideas which seemed to sprout endless new trains of creative thought.

Chapter 10: Snarls

Liliath paced her apartment at the top of the Alliance headquarters building, her coloring shifting constantly from cool blues and greens to intense reds and purples, as her thoughts roiled.

She was certain that her predecessors had probably had their share of challenges in their respective terms, but she was baffled at what to make of the sudden upsurge of conflict and contention among the various representatives of the member dimensions in the Alliance.

She knew there were few issues that were presented in council where there was unanimous agreement among the representatives, but these days it seemed that few things were presented without vehement arguments and high emotions on the part of the general council.

Her brother wasn't the only agitator, either. Even the Daringi representative kept bringing up objections to numerous proposals, which was surprising, as in the past they had nearly always been adamant supporters of the high council's suggestions.

All she and the council wanted, at this point, was to come up with solutions to the increasing incursions by the Inseni without it coming down to dimension-wide conflict and potential cataclysm. Every new meeting by the general council left her feeling this way—torn and both intermittently angry and anxious for the success of their efforts to stop the Inseni in their tracks.

In frustration, she went to the balcony and leapt out into the open sky. She didn't even pick a direction but just soared up farther and farther until the air grew thin and the buildings below looked like specs on the ground below her.

Now she breathed deeply and pumped her wings fervently, putting distance between herself and her cares. Now maybe she could think. Now maybe she could reason this out. The warm air rushed by her, and the scenery below was almost a blur as she sped away.

She tried to remember the more peaceful days with Ingot at the head of the Alliance, but realized that even then, there wasn't always peace or universal agreement. Although at the time the Alliance had been mostly united in their efforts to conquer what they thought was a Grogan incursion, the conflict had resulted in his death and the incapacitating of the other high council member, leaving Liliath unexpectedly in charge and having to choose two new councilors.

The other two were helpful and tried to be encouraging, but when it came down to it, in the future, whatever came of her time in office as the High Councilor of the Dimensional Alliance, would be put to her blame or commendation. At this point, she was feeling it would be to her blame, as she was struggling to see how to unite the Alliance and ultimately conquer the Inseni to stop their incursions once and for all.

She realized she was now hovering over the agent training center, where she had served for years as an administrator and advisor for the instructors who served to train potential agents for the Alliance. She had taken great satisfaction for what they had accomplished over the years and still felt a surge of pride when she thought of some of the amazing agents they had produced over time.

She remembered how reluctant she had been to leave that position and fill the post of second councilor to Ingot. But Liliath had always been one to serve where she was called, and Ingot had been very persuasive. He had just come into office preparing to serve his five-year term, after having spent five years each in both the second and first councilor positions for the chief councilors that had preceded him.

Liliath had been serving her first term as a second councilor when the disaster that had taken Ingot's life and horribly wounded the first councilor had thrust her into her current position as chief councilor, a position she had never aspired to in the first place.

Now, here she was, feeling woefully inadequate and so very tired of the ongoing conflict and contention that seemed to infuse the Alliance on nearly every level. She couldn't imagine what Ingot would have done in her position and shuddered to think what would have happened if her brother rather than herself had been elevated to chief councilor. Either way, it was her problem now, and she needed a clear head to deal with it.

It wouldn't do for her to allow her emotions to overcome her reason. But she found herself more and more frequently wanting to flame something, anything, just to release the tension she was feeling.

She realized she was circling above the training center and focused on what she saw there. Agents were going to and from classes, some training out on the main training ground, doing the various workouts designed for various beings. She smiled to herself; All seemed peaceful and familiar there, something she hoped she would always be able to count on.

She found herself wondering if this conflict would resolve during her term as chief councilor or if she would hand this mess over to one of her current councilors to resolve, in their turn.

No! She would not, could not, burden another being with this dilemma. Her determination hardened, and she noticed that some of the agents in training had noticed her circling above and had begun to point at her, drawing the attention of their fellows.

"Enough of this!" she chided herself fiercely. "Get back to work, you ninny! You haven't been this wobbly since you cracked the egg. Stop vacillating and move forward. You know what you need to do, if you'll only admit it. Now, do it!"

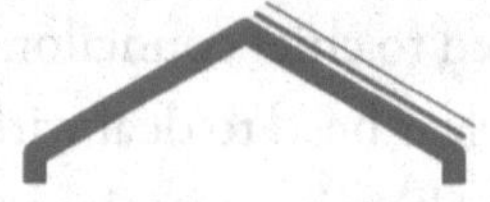

Chapter 11: What Goes Around...

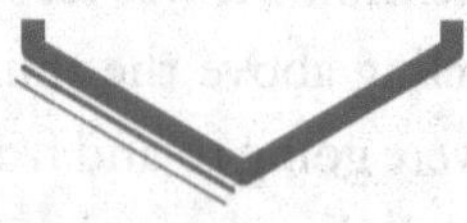

Vena stood expectantly before her generals, waiting for the answer she knew was not going to come.

"Well?" she asked, her brow raised ironically. *"What progress have you made? What do you know now that we didn't already know? What action have you taken that will move us forward? I want* answers!*"*

She saw them cringe and wanted to hit them for that. What kind of cowards had she assembled? These were supposed to be men of war, men of courage and fortitude. And what did she have before her? A band of shrinking, cowering idiots, without an original thought among them. Silence.

"All right, then. Let's say the reports we are receiving via our magic listening devices are accurate. Name me one resource, one bit of magic, or information we have acquired, that will be of use in the coming conflict. You have three sunsets to come up with the answers I seek or I will begin to... thin... your numbers and replace you with more suitable, productive leaders. Am I clear?"

They nodded as if it was rehearsed, in complete unison, not one of them uttering a sound and not one of them meeting her glowering eye.

She turned and swept out of the room, down the long, mirrored hallway and down a long ramp that led to the stairway into the dungeons.

She needed to vent, and that was the one place where she could do so without actually stepping on her own toes. She knew she needed every one of those wretched generals if she was going to succeed in her aspirations, and so she needed something or someone to take her frustrations out on. What better than the prisoners justly held in the depths of her palace?

She frowned at her own foolish generosity in seeing to it that her prisoners had mostly adequate food and other luxuries like blankets and basic hygiene requirements. (The latter had been mostly for her own benefit, as she couldn't stand the stink otherwise.) She didn't want them to feel like they were safe and living in luxury. It would defeat her purpose.

At the same time, most of them were hostages to assure the continued performance and loyalty of her minions: the servants, soldiers, and wizards who provided the services necessary to her dominion and control of the beings in the vast reaches of her kingdom.

As a result, the extent of the dungeons was almost more than the upper reaches of her fortress, extending from below the palace and, in some cases even beyond the reaches of the walls of her fortress.

She took great pride in the fact that the climb to and from the dungeons didn't tire her or challenge the limits of her strength, unlike many of the beings who served her. She grinned at the memory of others panting behind her as she moved briskly up and down the long ramps that connected the dungeons to the palace above.

There was little light here, an occasional glow-light spaced several steps apart, but this was no issue for Vena, as her eye adjusted easily to the dark. Darkness was actually more comfortable to her than the blinding light of day whenever she traveled in her kingdom in her comfortable carriage. She only drew the window shades, however, whenever they were traversing the countryside, with no peasants to line the streets bowing in adoration.

She would not have deprived the wretches of her glowing presence, even to her own discomfort.

But here, in the confines of her dungeon, she could bask in the darkness and revel in the lack of harsh and overwhelming light.

By the time she reached the upper level of the dungeons, now far below the palace, she had calmed to a certain extent... a good thing, as she knew that if she had not settled down, she might have done something unfortunate that would have negated the value of the hostages and lost her the loyalty of her indentured servants.

The guard at the barred gate bowed deeply as she set her key to the lock and let herself in. The keys at her waist jingled pleasantly as she strode around, reminding her that only she had access to every room, locked box, and hidden passage in her fortress.

She went directly to the first barred door and peered in. Her parents looked up; and unlike the other prisoners, her parents looked directly into her eye with neither pleading nor horror. She still didn't understand it, how they could look longingly and lovingly at her when she looked down at them in utter loathing and disrespect.

"So, Mother, how comes your current work of art?"

Her mother sat at a large loom, a project of many colors before her. Leanna's tapestries were famous throughout Vena's kingdom, selling for huge sums to the various nobles who attended to the serfs, seeing to it that the vast majority of their profits, wares and the best part of their foodstuffs made their way to her fortress.

Her father, on the other hand, was working with pen and ink, transcribing another of Vena's proclamations that would be circulated throughout her kingdom, being shouted on street corners and in market squares to be sure that no citizen was ignorant of her laws and decrees. None of them could ever claim ignorance.

But only a chosen few of her subjects could read or write, those few who were allowed being constrained early on in their lives to apprentice to scribes. These were those whose job it was to enlighten the populace to the proper way to live their lives under their enlightened and obviously more intelligent ruler.

He did not look up again from his work, and neither of them spoke to their daughter. They were well aware that any wrong word would earn them either a suspension of rations for a day or more or a session with the royal enlightener, whose persuading methods were not only more than uncomfortable, but from time to time exceeded their bounds with occasional fatalities.

She had absolutely no regrets. They had always thought themselves better than she was and wiser, an unfortunate error on their part. She couldn't allow them loose in the kingdom spreading misconceptions about her and her intentions.

After getting no answer from her mother, she proceeded to the next cell, smirking at the two miserable creatures who immediately bowed themselves to the stone floor upon taking in the glory of her countenance blessing their lives. They were of little consequence, parents of her general-in-chief.

She peered into cell after cell, with each of the occupants responding similarly to her presence. Then, finally at nearly the crossroads of corridors she came upon the cell she had been looking for.

There, huddled together were the wife and children of her chief wizard, Rajed. The woman did not prostrate herself, but merely gave a token nod of respect and gathered her children behind her, like a mother hen gathering chicks beneath her wings. She waited there in silence, taking care not to look directly into Vena's glowering eye.

"So, Letha, your husband has saved your life, or at least the life of one of your remaining children, again. You are fortunate he cares for you so much. Of course, you realize you and your spawn are taking up valuable resources I could more effectively use for my other servants. Deleting one or more of you would be helpful, if not for the cooperation and results achieved by your husband. I strongly suggest you continue to encourage him. He will be allowed to visit with you later today, after he has completed the tasks I have set for him."

Letha only nodded, her arms continuing to spread behind her and in front of her children.

Vena huffed and spat on the floor beyond the bars and turned down the right-hand corridor beyond the cell.

On either side of the long passageway, she noted that the various prisoners huddled in the far corners of their cells, being careful not to look up at her. Her mouth twisted into a grin of contempt. They were all below her notice in every possible way.

Finally, where the corridor dead-ended in one last cell, on the right-hand side, she stopped and peered into the dismal, dimly lit place where she stored the parents of Mi, like forgotten barrels in a storehouse.

Unlike the other prisoners, they looked directly into her eye with neither pleading nor horror. She wasn't quite sure how this could be possible, as she had been careful not to treat them with any more consideration than any of the rest of her prisoners, only giving them an occasional treat of an extra meal or water to bathe in or even some extra glows to give them some more light, whenever Mi completed or exceeded the tasks she had been assigned.

"Mi has been certified by the twit Gatekeeper and has insinuated herself into her confidence. As a result, you shall have an extra ration. If she succeeds in the next step in my plan, you may even be graduated from prisoner to servant. Do not presume on my generosity, however. Any disruption or unruly behavior on your part will result in oblivion. Do you understand?"

"Yes, Great One, we understand," the husband said as they both nodded solemnly.

Vena harrumphed and turned on her heel. Now to get back to work. Jenny would be hers, and she would be the master of all. It would happen.

Chapter 12: Tied in Knots

"It won't be long now," Lova sent with a grin. *"You can't know how convenient this way of communication has become; and as you expand your network of trusted mental communicators, we're feeling like we can do so much more. All the other gate guardians agree that it has been life-changing to not even have to visit via the gateways to the other gate guardians in order to relay important, sensitive information."*

Jenny was trying very hard not to be impatient, even though she knew that things were progressing much faster than she had expected. She just wanted to be done with all this and to have life settle down into some semblance of normality. Not that her life would ever be normal, she admitted. However, by the end of the day, at least one part of her life would now get better.

Today the official change-over from Tarafau to Burt as her guide would take place. This, of course, meant that there would be little need for their nightly meetings at the little pool in Burt's dreams. She had enjoyed this even more since she had been able to actually visit this spot on the banks of the Merced River with him, but she admitted that it wasn't the same as having him by her side.

She did worry, however, that perhaps Burt might begin to find "tagging along" with his wife as she fulfilled her role as the Gatekeeper boring, considering the intrigue and adventure he normally found in his role as an Alliance agent.

At first, she had hoped that this might mean she would no longer need her bodyguards, but Burt had disabused her of that notion. "Considering how much trouble you are able to get yourself into at any given time, I don't think having the girls around is a bad idea at all. Just think of them as cousins who have come to stay, permanently."

Jenny had acquiesced reluctantly, but she really did wish she had more "alone time" with her husband. However, when it came down to it, some was better than none, and the girls were pretty good at staying in the background when Burt was around; unless it was gathering for a meal or a workout, they tended to stay within earshot without being obvious.

Jenny had resigned herself to the fact that her role as Gatekeeper required some adjustments in her lifestyle. She remembered the guards at the entrance of Miriha's office complex and the various so-called servants who were constantly available for Anela. It was all part of the job. There was an obvious risk to this position, and she would just have to deal with the inconveniences that might cause in her life.

And, as if her thoughts had conjured them from thin air, all three of her bodyguards entered the gate office.

"So, is he due soon?" Lyra asked, the other two looking expectant.

"Yes, Lova just told me they were sending him off in a few minutes. He should walk through the door any—" and once again, as if she had waved a magic wand, Burt stepped through the door from the gateroom.

He waved jauntily to the girls and grabbed Jenny up from her chair and threw his arms around her in a fervent hug. Then turning his head to wink at her bodyguards, turned back to her and kissed her thoroughly.

"Just doin' my duty," he remarked as they drew apart with another grin at all of them. "Double duty, it seems, now. So, let's go grab a root beer and kick back in the patio. We need to decide how we're going to move forward with this."

"No argument from us," Mynn retorted as the three women turned on their heels in unison and headed out the office door into the hallway.

Burt turned back to Jenny. "This is going to be great!" he exclaimed, his eyes twinkling and his look mischievous. "I finally get to hang out with my wife, and I'm getting paid to do it! How did I ever luck out?"

Jenny laughed with him, and her worries of the moments before faded away. He had that effect on her. He could make even the most difficult moments seem almost carefree. She was sure he felt fear like the rest of them. He only dealt with it differently. From the stories from his childhood, he had shared with her on their Merced getaway, she realized he had not had it easy. Both parents had passed in his late teens, and he had pretty much been on his own ever since.

He hid his fear with humor and a self-confident, almost childlike attitude. Outwardly, even though he was in his latter twenties, he seemed not much more than eighteen or nineteen years old. But she knew he was a deep thinker; and, according to all the Alliance members who knew him, his skills as an agent, diplomat, and intermediary were unmatched even by agents with years more experience.

They strolled out to the patio arm in arm. Evidently Burt's suggestion had been taken seriously by the three bodyguards who were already placing root beers out on the patio table all around. And apparently Lizziebot had also set out a plate of Arvid's famous spicy sugar cookies, which, from the aroma they had inhaled as they had passed by the kitchen, were right out of the oven.

"I put in my order ahead of time," Burt explained, seeing Jenny's look of amazement. "That little bot of Bob's is beginning to come in handy, since he is connected to the very private bot network. Did you know about that? Evidently, now that we have Nanoites installed in each of the bots, they can go completely outside of the Alliance communications network and their connection is faster than anything the Alliance has available."

Jenny just shook her head, somewhat bemused at the continual progress of the Alliance's combination of tech, science, and community that they were able to leverage in ways she would have never thought possible prior to her time as a guardian and now as the Gatekeeper.

As they sat, Burt raised his glass of root beer. "A toast!

To the Gatekeeper and her continued success and safety!"

The other three raised their glasses and they all clinked before each of them took a big swig of root beer and reached for one of Arvid's cookies. Burt took two, offering the second one to his wife with a little bow.

"Oh, come on, you four!" Jenny retorted. "I'm not that big a deal. Mostly, I feel like a relay station for the Alliance. True, we now have six in the mental network; but other than that, what have I accomplished?"

"Well, you'll be able to do a lot more soon. We have a breakthrough in process, top of the top-secret projects going on right now, that may relieve you of the necessity of being the switcher for the network, and you'll only have to deal with the issues that relate directly to your responsibilities. Won't that be nice?" Burt said with a wink and his trademark cocky grin.

"Okay, so, Mr. Official Guide of the Gatekeeper, what do you have for us today?" Jenny quipped in return.

"Well, it goes something like this: Bodyguards will continue their usual shift patterns, even when I am on the premises, which should be most of the time, at this point. Tarafau is taking over agenting with his amazing daughter, Elizabeth, on his home planet as their home base, except when they are hanging out here or at Sanglarka.

"Two new earthling agents will be handling the assignments I usually take care of, after some extensive training by me. They still lack quite as much experience as I have, so they will be checking in with me from time to time via their own little bots, kindly supplied to them by our friend Bob. This way I can communicate with them instantly without the tedious use of the network, a gateway, or the need to have Jenny run interference.

"Sound good so far?" he asked with one raised brow, looking from face to face.

All but Jenny nodded solemnly. She just gave him that ironic "Really?" look and he grinned and continued.

"Now that Jenny's students have graduated and been stationed at their various posts, Jenny will have more time to work with me on some strategies as to how we can contact the various dimensions where the Inseni have established outposts. We need to figure out how to infiltrate the native populations and basically start the same process we did to overthrow Peril's dictatorship."

"And if we need to travel?" Jenny asked dubiously.

"It is true, we don't have Elizabeth on tap at the moment, but we will be issued a Daringi in a week or so, assuming it gets approved by the Daringi council. Admittedly, they have become somewhat recalcitrant about additional participation in this particular Alliance project."

Jenny winced. She had heard that a number of the various Alliance member dimensions were beginning to be split into factions concerning their current dilemma. Some wanted to just "let sleeping dogs lie," so to speak, and simply concentrate on securing the gate system to prevent any further incursions. The majority, however, tended towards the more humanitarian posture of the Alliance Council towards rescuing those dimensions that were currently being terrorized and dominated by the Inseni.

If she was honest with herself, she could see both sides of the issue and hoped with all her heart that the conflict with the Inseni didn't actually make things worse than they already were.

"And my dad? Where does he come in with all this?"

Jenny was afraid of the answer, as she knew her dad would join up as an agent in a heartbeat as soon as he knew what was at stake.

"Ah, well, that was next on the agenda. You and I, two sweet little newlyweds, are going to go visit Mom and Dad and have a little chat."

Jenny couldn't help herself. She rolled her eyes.

"Just like that? How do we explain our entourage?" she asked, looking meaningfully at the girls.

Burt stroked his chin. "I don't' guess we can pass them off as unknown cousins, considering your dad's penchant for family history, at least not as your cousins. I was thinking instead of bringing them along in our MDPs."

The three women sat up straight in their patio chairs as if at attention. "Really?" Mynn said, her eyes alight.

"Really." Burt agreed solemnly. "I am getting both of them set up inside like really large RVs... cooking facilities and the whole bit. You each will even have your own bedrooms in each space and robotic assistants. You may find yourselves spending more time there than you might think. Jenny and I have a number of trips that will be happening over the next few months, and it would make me feel better if you were close."

"And a television?" asked Lyra, who was particularly fascinated by soap operas and sitcoms since Jenny had installed a television in their little garage attic apartment.

"And a big screen television with all the channels." Burt agreed jovially. "A large stock of your favorite foodstuffs and all the little comforts you've gotten used to. You'll have instant communication with us via the bots, and whenever we holler, you can come to the rescue. How does that sound?"

"What about workouts?" Nona asked, and the other two nodded.

"Workout facilities will be provided in both our MDPs. The workers will be arriving any minute now to work on them. In the meantime, we can expect to leave in the morning. These guys are fast and efficient. Mine is mostly already set up, and Jenny's will be the one they'll be working on the hardest. You three will take turns between my MDP and Jenny's, with two at a time always in Jenny's. Got it? You can create the schedules yourselves."

Three heads nodded in unison and three grins told Jenny that this new adventure was totally to their taste. What a thing to spring on her like this! She hadn't had a clue.

"I don't suppose I get any say in this?" she inquired ironically. She already knew the answer.

"It was the only way we could figure out how to let you do the traveling we are going to have to do over the next few weeks. You said you were getting bored holed up here with nothing to do but relay messages. Well, now that you are freed from all except the most top-secret communications, you have the time to get to your other duties, including some formal training.

"By making you more mobile and by keeping your schedule apparently random, the likelihood of an attack will be minimized, and we can keep the Inseni guessing, since the word is out that you are high on their 'most wanted' list."

"Okay. It makes sense, but by no stretch of my considerable imagination did I ever think I would become a bed and breakfast for a group of bodyguards."

And they all raised their glasses once again and toasted a new adventure in the multiverse.

Chapter 13: Homecoming

Jenny had never been so nervous about going home to visit her parents. Admittedly it had been a long time since her last trip home, and that had been just after she had graduated from college, before she had started her "adulting" life. Her mom had helped her furnish her little one-bedroom apartment near the college campus while she had still been in school, and so, although she was pretty sure nothing had changed much at home, she was still a bit uncomfortable about what they were about to do.

Burt had assured her, that if her dad decided not to take the Alliance up on their offer, he had been given permission to use his little mind-wiping device to clear both her parents' memories of the purpose of their visit, and even her dad's memory of her contact with him during the worldwide power outage caused by the Inseni, what now seemed like ages ago.

Jenny knew the technology was pretty specific and that no significant memories would be erased. She had seen it done a few times now with potential agent candidates and felt confident that it had no ill effects.

Nevertheless, she found herself also wondering how her bodyguards were doing in their new home. They had loved what Burt had done inside the two MDPs for their benefit. They had even gone so far as to say that they would just as soon use the MDPs as their permanent new "barracks" instead of the little apartment above Jenny's garage.

Evidently the facilities the workmen had created, with the help of their robotic companions, had been excellent and very high tech. Jenny had been amazed at how quickly they had finished the job.

So it was, that she and Burt drove down to San Diego via route 101, also known on some stretches as Pacific Coast Highway (PCH), Highway 1, or "the king's highway." The drive was pleasant, watching the many little ocean towns fly by. They stopped in at a seafood restaurant for lunch, and it seemed in almost no time, considering the pleasant company, they had driven into her mom and dad's driveway, to the place where Jenny had grown up.

Her mom had tried to throw her arms around both of them, but short as she was, she succeeded only in choking them both with her arms extended around both of their necks. Her dad shook Burt's hand firmly and enthusiastically, then slapped him on the back. Burt pretended to be knocked over by his father-in-law, and Jenny and her mom laughed. Then her dad grabbed her in a bear hug, and Jenny almost squealed like she had done as a young child.

They marched into the living room. "You'll be spending the night?" Her mom asked hopefully.

"We'll see," Jenny responded carefully. "If Burt gets a call from work, we might have to drive back tonight. But, we both got a break and thought it was about time Burt got to see where I grew up."

Ed chuckled. "Getting the grand tour, are you?" he said, with a knowing smile. "Well, we're glad you're here. Mom's fixed a nice snack, and you can relax after your long drive."

"That sounds amazing," Burt agreed. "I remember the spread she made for our wedding day. I've been looking forward to it."

Jenny's mom blushed. "That's kind of you, Burt. It's just a nice salad and a sandwich bar for now. I've got a roast planned for supper."

Burt sniffed the air appreciatively. "Ah, just like my mom used to do. We were tantalized by that slow cooking roast for hours before it was finally served. And is that home-baked bread I smell?"

Jenny watched her mom swell with pride, looking up at her son-in-law with delight. "This one's a keeper," she said with an elbow gently into Jenny's ribs. "I always knew you'd get a good one."

Jenny couldn't help but grin up at her dad. Even though, thanks to his older children, he was a grandpa and gray was creeping up his temples, he was as strong and agile as a forty-year-old, and his mind was sharp. She always knew she could depend on him for his good advice and support whenever it was needed.

They sat down to make-your-own sandwiches and salad, and finished with brownies still warm from the oven. In other words, heaven, at least as far as Jenny was concerned. They even had her favorite, iced root beer, and

Jenny could tell by the satisfied look on Burt's face that it suited him just fine as well.

As they ate, they chatted about inconsequential things like the local soccer team that her dad was coaching, and their latest findings in their family history. Jenny was fascinated to learn that they were related as cousins, five times removed, to George Washington, and Burt remarked that he thought perhaps there was a famous outlaw from the wild west in his own family tree.

After they all helped her mom clear the table, Jenny joined her mom at the kitchen sink, drying the dishes while her mom washed, something she had often done as a kid. Meanwhile, her dad and Burt went out into the backyard so her dad could show off the most recent additions to his vegetable garden.

Jenny had the feeling that Burt was also getting a dose of her dad's awful dad jokes, not to mention a generous portion of advice on how to be a good spouse and eventually a father.

She had noticed that neither her mom nor dad had mentioned potential grandchildren, for which she was grateful. She wasn't sure that either she or Burt were ready for that yet, at least not until they settled the issues with the Inseni.... And she had to laugh to herself about that, as if it was just one more thing on her checklist and not confronting one of the major powers in the multiverse.

Afterward they gathered in the living room, dad in his recliner, mom in what she called her reading chair, the basket containing her most recent crocheting project next to the comfortable overstuffed chair that Jenny so often pictured her mother in whenever she thought of her.

Jenny and Burt sat side-by-side on the loveseat that faced both chairs, holding hands. This felt so right to Jenny, so far outside the usual stress of what they had devoted their lives to recently, that Jenny almost wished that the two of them were just a newly married couple enjoying time with Jenny's folks, with nothing more on their to-do list than the two of them working at a regular day job.

She held back a sigh of regret, but instantly realized that she would have never met Burt without the Alliance and was grateful for the chain of events that had brought her to this point, regardless of the outcome.

She had originally introduced Burt to her family as a travel guide for international executives, which easily explained why he wasn't home much. They were impressed and always interested in his travel adventures, although Burt was careful to emphasize that he was under a nondisclosure agreement with the various companies he worked with.

Her dad understood the importance of keeping confidences, as much of his military life had included time with the Army security agency, so they never asked for too many details.

Jenny, on the other hand, had kept up the pretense of writing for companies where her name was never mentioned or credit given, but as she had assured her parents that there were benefits, a regular salary, and travel involved, they seemed to have come to the conclusion that she finally had a "real job," and that they could relax their concern for her future.

Besides, she also had a husband with a good job, something that was a relief to them, considering the culture of their time. They knew, their "little girl" would be cared for, regardless of her personal income.

She chuckled inwardly about that. They had no idea the resources she could draw on at any given time. The little house on Infinity Loop only scratched the surface of her good fortune, financially at least.

She exchanged a nervous glance with Burt. Was it time? She sent, mentally, *"So are you going to do this, or is it up to me?"*

"I've got this, Jenny. Relax. It's going to be just fine."

Burt then did something that surprised her. He reached out mentally to her father. *"Sir, can you hear me?"* he sent.

Jenny recognized his use of the word "sir" to address him when he had previously been using his name Ed or dad and once again she admired his skills as an accomplished diplomat.

Her dad stopped in mid-sentence, as he had been relating one of his own adventures during Desert Storm.

His eyebrows shot up and he looked at his wife, noticing that she was still listening attentively to this story that she had heard many times over the years.

She looked back blankly. "And?" she prompted, as if she might finish his sentence for him.

"Umm, just a moment," he said, holding up a hand to stall his wife.

"Excuse me, but I think, young man, you have something you need to tell us; and I think we need to hear it right now." The tone was stern, as he might have used when speaking to a member of his platoon.

Jenny knew this tone of voice, having experienced it many times in the course of her youth. It brooked no compromise. It was a demand, pure and simple.

Burt, to his credit and to Jenny's relief, didn't falter or take offense. He looked straight into his father-in-law's eyes. "Jenny and I have something important to share with you both, and I had hoped that would get your attention."

Her dad sat up a little straighter and her mom leaned forward in expectation. Jenny was sure she was hoping for the announcement of an impending grandchild and felt a little embarrassed that this might disappoint her, but she made no move to interrupt.

"Hmm. Go ahead, then. Let's hear what you have to say."

"Well, sir, I have to confess that Jenny and I haven't been completely honest about what's been going on with us, and I know that you already know part of this, so I'll cut to the chase, with apologies to Mom and a plea for patience on her part.

"As you are aware, Ed, Jenny has been involved, since receiving her inheritance from her Aunt Lizzie, with so much more than ghost-writing for a mysterious company. Her travels have been much farther than any place on this Earth, and her responsibilities have been much more essential to the well-being of everyone on this planet."

Her mom gave a quiet gasp, but her dad simply nodded for him to continue.

"The thing is, there is so much more out there than we had considered possible, and this universe we live in is one of an infinite number of dimensions wherein live beings of all types, many of which are beyond our imagination.

"There is an organization called the Dimensional Alliance that oversees interdimensional affairs among consenting cultures. They are the stewards of a network of interconnected dimensional portals that allow instantaneous travel from one dimension to another.

"Here on Earth, there are a dozen known portals of this type that remain, for the most part, a complete secret from the general populace. Jenny's house happens to sit on one of those. At some point, we will be happy to allow you to see this for yourself, but for now, will you take me at my word?"

Ed simply nodded somberly and then turned to Donna with an "it's going to be all right" look.

Burt nodded and reached for Jenny's hand with a little squeeze. This was going better, so far, than Jenny had hoped.

"So, what you both need to know is that your daughter is a very intrinsic part of the Alliance, as she is known by her title as *the Gatekeeper*. She is responsible for keeping the entire network secure and running at optimum efficiency for all the dimensions, as well as being the liaison between the various Gate Guardians, whose job it is to keep their own dimensional gateway available to their own people, as well as maintaining security to prevent unwanted incursions into a particular dimension.

"These are nearly overwhelming responsibilities. But your daughter is significantly qualified to do this, as she has some previously undiscovered gifts. She has the ability to communicate mind to mind over the boundaries of dimensions, as well as person to person."

For some reason, Jenny realized that now was the time.

"It's true, Mom and Dad," she sent to them both. *"I can speak across long distances, as long as I know the person to whom I wish to speak. I learned to communicate mind to mind in my Alliance training, but the ability to do this across long distances, including across dimensional boundaries, is highly unusual."*

Her mom's mouth formed a small *o* and her eyes brimmed with tears.

Jenny got up and knelt by her mom's chair, her arms around her, and just held her for a moment while her mom cried.

"It's okay, Mom. I know this is a big shock..." she began, but her mom cut in.

"I always knew there was something special about you," she said, wiping her eyes and looking into her daughter's face with wonder.

"You always were so good with communicating, knowing what to say or what to write in a way that touched people's hearts."

"Then you believe all this?"

"Jenny, you've always had a wild imagination, but I've never known you to lie, at least not deliberately. I'm sure this has been very hard to keep from us. But I notice your dad doesn't seem to be very surprised about all this." And she looked significantly at her husband, who shook his head solemnly.

"Besides, I can't deny what I've just experienced. Beats the heck out of cellphones, I'll tell you!" And she laughed nervously. "So, why now? I am sure we could have gone along blissfully ignorant, like the rest of the population of Earth. And am I to guess that this is top secret, and we can't tell anyone else about it?"

Jenny and Burt nodded in unison. Then Burt spoke up, as Jenny continued to kneel by her mother's chair, willing her mother to feel her strong, supportive emotions.

"Mom and Dad, we did give you this information for a reason. You see, I have recently had a change in my position as a diplomat and ambassador for the Alliance and my new position is to guard your daughter and support her in her role as the Gatekeeper. And as such, this leaves my position open, at least temporarily."

He looked directly into the blue eyes of his father-in-law, and Jenny knew that, although she didn't think he was communicating mentally, they were relating on a much deeper level.

"You want me to come out of retirement and fill your youthful shoes?" was all he said, but Jenny could feel an underlying excitement in the question. She knew that he often missed his life in the military, but she also knew he had retired more to be with his wife and give as much to her as she had given to him during all his time in the service of his country.

"Actually, we want both of you," he said, and smiled as Mom gasped once more beside Jenny. "You see, you will need to go through some training and the new position will need the skills you both have. "You," he continued nodding at Donna, "will have the opportunity to explore your own hidden talents, as there are those among us who think that Jenny gets her own gifts from both sides of your family, not just from her Aunt Lizzie.

"You would both undergo training, starting at Sanglarka, an Alliance outpost in the mountains of Sweden, and then in the Alliance agent training center 'in a galaxy far, far away.' If you accept this calling, you will want to sell your home here with the cover story that you are retiring to an epic retirement community in, I don't know, maybe Arizona or Laguna Beach?" And he laughed at that. "Don't worry, we'll think something up. Maybe something more like a worldwide genealogy tour, unfolding the epic tale of your ancestral origins?"

Ed chuckled at that. "I see you may have done this before. Tell me, are you the one who recruited our Jenny?"

"No sir, but I'm sure glad someone did. It was actually Aunt Lizzie who had that honor. She had been stalking your daughter since she was in grade school. But I was definitely introduced to Jenny early on, in her term as the Gatekeeper. We actually met due to the curiosity of her neighbor. I believe you've met Bob Reid?"

"Ah yes... him too? Just how many agents of the Alliance are running around our planet without us knowing about it?"

"You need to understand, sir, that considering the current state of affairs on our planet, now is probably not the right time for them to find out about the Alliance. I think you, of all people, can recognize that currently the human race isn't quite ready to know that aliens are a reality and that we aren't actually alone in the multiverse. They're still arguing over whether or not the moon landing is a hoax, after all."

"You are probably right, son," Ed agreed somberly, "We can't even get along amongst ourselves. No need to add what many people would view as an additional threat. So, I am guessing this is less of an order and more of a request? What happens if we decline this adventure?"

"Well, sir, by this evening you would think we had all had our lunch and root beer and warm brownies fresh from the oven and had a pleasant conversation about Jenny's writing assignments and my travels.

"You would remember talking about family history and the latest crochet creations a la Donna Japhet, and you wouldn't remember any of this conversation. But you completely get to choose. The Alliance is very much against forcing any being to accept an assignment. One of the main reasons they were founded was to protect the rights of every being to choose how they want to live."

Jenny's dad nodded, his expression one that Jenny recognized. To her surprise, he was earnestly considering Burt's proposal. He turned to her mom.

"Well, Donna, what do you think? We've never been part of the same adventure before. I think we'd make a good team. How are you feeling about all this?"

She looked up into her husband's face, and Jenny could see the light in her eyes that often showed up when her mom was having an epiphany.

"I don't guess we are so old we couldn't give it a try. But what if we do try and we don't measure up, or they decide we aren't right for the job?" And Jenny was proud that her voice hadn't quavered, nor had she sounded at all afraid.

"Then," Burt put in, "You would find yourself back in your nice cozy house with a swell in your bank account, some kind of tax refund or something, without remembering a thing about it, but feeling like life continues as usual. But I have a good feeling about you two... and my feelings usually work out pretty well."

"Then, Ed, I think we should give it a try. I don't see the downside, although I'm sure there probably is one. There usually is. But no more than us just hanging out and going to an occasional family history conference. Besides, this way we can stay in much better contact with Jenny and Burt..." and then she paused, her mouth pursed. "But what about the rest of the family?"

"Well, you may have noticed that Jenny has been keeping in touch with you two on a regular basis? That happens because of some 'dastardly alien tech' that allows her to appear to be on Earth all the time, even when she is often not only off planet, but in a completely different dimension."

"What surprises me, is how fast you two climbed on board with this," Jenny said, not even trying to hide her astonishment. "Where are all the deep-dive questions and skepticism? You asked more questions when I told you where I was going to go to college."

"First," her dad said, holding up a finger, "I had already had a, shall we say, interesting encounter with you before this under very odd circumstances. Second," and another finger went up, "I've been having a hard time keeping all this from your mother, who was making some rather shrewd guesses. Third, and finally," and the last finger went up, "We're both ready for a new adventure, something we can do together.

"All those years I went off to various assignments for months at a time while she held down the fort and made all the necessary decisions, moved house at a moment's notice, and never spoke a word of complaint; don't you think she deserves some adventures of her own?"

Jenny sighed and nodded. She did understand, and she was proud of her dad for taking her mother's needs into account and giving her the credit she deserved.

"So," her mom piped up, "when do we leave, and what do we take?"

That was so typical of her mom, Jenny thought, always ready to take a practical approach to anything that was thrown in her way or any opportunity that presented itself.

"Well, you won't need much, just a few changes of clothes and any medications you take," Burt replied. "You can let your peeps know you're going on a cruise in the Fjords of Sweden and you may be out of touch for a bit. That's not far from the truth, and it should hold them while we get you set up with a good cover story and get you the initial training you need to make a final decision. Will that work? Catch a flight to L.A., and we'll pick you up at the airport. I'll pay for the tickets."

Jenny hugged her mom, who was now beaming with anticipation, and only now began to realize why Burt was such an effective liaison for the Alliance. He was a born salesman and knew how to close a deal.

Chapter 14: On Pins and Needles

Bob chuckled to himself as he worked. After a whirlwind tour of the five largest science communities on the dragon planet, he was only beginning to absorb what he had learned. It seemed like his life as an inventor and scientist on Earth was so far behind him now.

It had never occurred to him, in all those lectures he had given at various universities around the country, that what he was teaching was rudimentary, at best, in the bigger universe of science and its disciplines.

If anything, although he was recognized in some fairly high-reaching circles in the scientific community, he now knew that Earth, although more advanced than many cultures across the dimensions, was still in its infancy regarding many of the sciences.

Something that had also never entered his mind was that although most of the laws of physics and other areas of science were immutable, there were some variations that would have astounded his colleagues at home; and much of what he had thought was simple and logical had turned out to be much more complex than he had ever considered.

However, he also had discovered that many of his ideas and views about how to apply scientific principles were of great interest to the scientists he had met on his journey, and they seemed to agree with Merv that his different point of view was definitely worthy of consideration.

All in all, it had been a pleasant exchange of ideas and concepts, and now he felt fired up to move forward on the current focus of robotics. He had been surprised to discover that most cultures in the multiverse didn't really have a lot to do with artificial intelligence or any kind of mechanical servants. Even though most cultures had one form or another of manufacturing, not that many actually employed advance mechanics to perform tasks that

Bob had assumed were essential for the mass production of goods of various kinds.

Of course, Lizzie had taken advantage of the Alliance technology that was available to her when she programmed the AI that existed on Jenny's tablet, and it had been that very thing that had led to him completing his work on Fidget and Lizziebot.

And now, several Alliance agents and gate guardians had mechanical servants that used Bob's algorithms to imitate intelligent responses and learned new things as they were taught and exposed to new functions.

So, as he worked on this new and exciting project, he realized he was humming "We Are the Champions" and couldn't help pumping his fist high in the air as the last few commands were entered into the personal computer station with multiple screens provided to him in Cornelium's lab high in the mountain palace that was quickly becoming Bob's home away from home.

"Alert!" Fidget suddenly sent. Bob was again grateful for the bot's new ability to communicate mentally, something he still didn't quite understand. It had been programmed into every new robotic servant being currently used by the Alliance to overcome the language barrier when thousands of dimensions and their cultures had to be taken into account.

This was a signal announcing the arrival of Cornelium into the lab.

Bob hastily changed screens on the computer, as this current project was, at least for now, for his eyes only.

The dragon who stumped across the lab to stop by Bob's lab table huffed, as he stopped beside him.

"Grimp would like a copy of that 'periodic table' you were telling him about," he sent as he looked curiously over Bob's shoulder at his now innocuous screen. *"Been working on that production issue, I see. Those techs on the bot assembly line were commenting that they wish they had you full time in their plant."*

Bob hadn't blushed in a very long time, but he nearly did with such a compliment coming from Cornelium. The gruff dragon wasn't very free with his commendations.

"Thanks. I'll send it out in a minute. I was just wondering when that big convention may happen, the one they were discussing at our last stop. And will it be just the scientists here, or will others be invited?"

"We're still working out the details, for the moment. More than likely it won't happen until we get this issue resolved with the Insenium. I for one would like to get back to pure science instead of being engaged in this conflict, but I can see that even the scientific community will be threatened if we don't get this straightened out."

Bob nodded, and Cornelium nodded back and turned to tread over to his own part of the lab. It was kind of like going from a doll house to a regular one, comparing the difference in size and shape. Cornelium had been kind enough to create a "humanoid" sized area for those who had the privilege to work actively in his lab, a fact that Bob appreciated, since he had no desire to feel like a toddler in a highchair as he did his work.

He sighed and went to the files he needed to send to Grimp and realized he would have to wait to continue his other project until Cornelium was out of the lab.

Bob had been doing a lot of very-early-morning or very-late-night work on this project, but it wouldn't do to reveal too much too soon.

He barely got the file sent out when Merv popped in, looking rested and cheerful.

"Ahoy, matey, what's new?"

"Well, Merv, everything and nothing, as usual. And you?"

The "everything and nothing" thing had become a running joke, as nearly every day brought some new discovery, and yet the looming issues they were dealing with were virtually the same every day. Until this situation with the Inseni was finally resolved, a lot of their discoveries would have to be put on hold, unless it applied to the current state of affairs.

"Well, then, I think some good news is an appropriate topic for discussion. The final design for the mini bots has been tested and approved. We can move forward with it. The first run of bots will be delivered in a couple of weeks. Now I just need to get with our strategy team and make preparations.

"In that same arena, you should know that the transfer of the Guide position has been completed and the newlyweds will finally have some time together. Burt is an accomplished agent and will function well as the Guide for our dear Gatekeeper. I think it's something for the record books. Although there are Guardians who have spouses as Guides, to my knowledge there has never been the same situation with the Gatekeeper."

Bob smiled broadly at this. He had been concerned about Jenny, even with Tarafau as her guide. Tarafau was more than adequate protection under most circumstances, and his wisdom came from vast experience over hundreds of years. However, Burt was wise beyond his years and was one of the most accomplished agents in the Alliance. He was also not so arrogant as to think he knew it all. He would willingly consult with any of his peers and elders as he needed help to guide Jenny well in her position.

"So, all recovered from your trip, I see," Merv said, peering over Bob's shoulder at the specs scrolling down the screen.

"Well, we still do have a few things on our plate," Bob admitted. "I sometimes wonder what would happen if the leadership of the Inseni were to change somehow. Surely not all the Inseni care about dominating the multiverse. I mean, how does it even help them live a better life? It feels a lot to me like when Hitler tried to take over Earth. When it came down to it, it wasn't the German people who wanted world domination. It was down to one madman and his flunkies."

Merv gave a low whistle. "Well, mate, it's like this. You are a creator, a visionary, and most of all a kind person. You don't get the addiction that can come with power over the choices others make. Greed, pride, and narcissism are foreign to you. But, as you have witnessed, it isn't just a trait in certain human beings. Good and evil are both spread throughout the multiverse.

"Some beings feel like everything should point to them and that existence owes them everything they ever want, even when they already have everything they need to be happy and satisfied with their life. It is one of the great mysteries why this happens. It's one of the things I have studied in multiple dimensions, especially in Earth's early history.

"Don't twist your head around it too much. I still haven't figured it out. In the final analysis, it's why I'm on the side of the Alliance. The right to choose is important. Whenever a power interferes with that, especially within the ranks of the Alliance, we have to stand up for the principles we are founded on.

"We can't save every being in the multiverse. But if we can prevent the gateways from being used for the purpose of domination and power, then it is worth whatever we are having to do to prevent it."

He took a deep breath and exhaled in a noisy sigh. "And that's a longer speech than I've made in a very long time. I think the last time was probably sitting around a roughly made round table, a very long time ago."

Bob couldn't help but laugh and reminded himself again how ancient this being was that he dealt with in such a casual way.

And although he agreed with everything Merv had said, he still found himself anxious to get on with it. He knew they had to take each step carefully, but he also had nightmares that it would all be too little too late. How much time did they really have, after all?

But he didn't express these fears to Merv. He was very aware that the ex-"wizard" knew perfectly well what was at stake, and he wouldn't have been at all surprised to discover that Merv spent more than a few sleepless nights worrying over the timeline too.

Chapter 15: Above and Beyond

"Now you've done it!" Mynn exclaimed, covered from head to foot with trailing pond plants, now standing waist deep in the koi pond.

"You're the one who wanted to wrestle!" Nona said through fits of laughter. "I've been watching those gals on the Wrestling Channel, and I've learned a few new moves. Here's a towel," she added, fishing one out of her MDP, as Mynn clambered out of the little pond.

"Seriously? I think I'll need a shower after this."

"But not before you dry off. You don't want to leave puddles all over the floor on your way to the apartment. It's not like you can just take a portal into the bathroom," Lyra said, shaking her head at the two combatants. "I don't imagine it ever occurred to you that this kind of exercise might be more appropriate in the workout room?"

Jenny held her sides, still belly laughing at the interactions of her bodyguards. Honestly, sometimes they argued just like siblings, even though each of them was from a different dimension. In the background, she could hear chuckles coming from Windsong, something she knew the rest of her companions didn't get to add to the feeling of the comic antics of her bodyguards.

"Come on, you three," she said, trying and failing miserably to act like one of the sterner librarians she had known in her life. "Really, you'd think we didn't have more urgent things to take care of... like, I don't know... the inevitable doom of the multiverse?"

She had intended this as a joke, but despite Jenny's effort at being humorous, her bodyguards instantly were at attention, somber and attentive, as if something so hilarious had not been going on seconds before. That made Jenny laugh even harder, but her girls were so suddenly somber that she couldn't sustain it for long.

"We're sorry," Lyra offered, a look of pure contrition on her face. "We just got a little carried away."

"I was kidding… just kidding!" Jenny replied, now almost irritated. "It isn't like the three of you don't need an occasional break from all the worries of the multiverse we just happen to be a party to. That wasn't a reprimand. It was a joke. Gee whiz… nobody ever gets my jokes."

Burt strode out to see them all standing there, Mynn with pond weeds in her hair and draped around her shoulders and all three of Jenny's bodyguards looking chastised and solemn, and Jenny looking like a thundercloud. He stopped, bemused.

"Something?" he asked Jenny.

"Nope, just a little horseplay and three bodyguards with no sense of humor," Jenny grumped back at him.

"Well, bad timing on my part, I suppose, but there is something we all need to do. We can wait for Mynn to clean up her act and then we need to head out. I'll brief you all in the gate office. In the meantime, I could use a welcome-home hug from my wife."

And he suited words to actions and just held her for a moment.

"So, is this serious? What's up?" Jenny asked.

"Don't get too worried, kiddo. It's serious, but not devastating. We just have to take a trip. Since the girls seem to like their new digs in the MDP, we are all set up to make tracks and get some things done. Ted has been given a heads up that we may not be around much the next few months and he will be taking care of the grounds.

"Angela and Travis and the kids, as well as our grouchy friend on the other side of our driveway, will be watching for telltale signs of any mischief. For now, I know you already have your MDP packed and ready to roll, so it's time to get going."

"Well, haven't you just been a busy guy?" Jenny cooed with only a slight ironic twist to her words. She still wasn't quite used to Burt being around as much as he had been lately, and he had immediately taken a lot of things into his hands that were so often on Jenny's plate. On the one hand, she was grateful for the extra time it gave her. On the other—well, if she was honest, she was used to handling her own affairs; and up until now, the full implications of being a "couple" hadn't had a chance to sink in.

"Okay," she said. "So, we're taking both bots, of course. Anything else I need to consider before we meet the girls in the office?"

"Actually, we should be seeing a cab pull up any moment now, so you'd probably like to be out there to greet your parents. We're dropping them off at Sanglarka on the way out, not to mention doing a little business while we're there. And no, it wasn't on your schedule or to-do lists. I didn't think you needed to be bothered with the details. For once, let someone else take on some of the less vital tasks, will you? It's part of the reason I'm your guide instead of Tarafau, who has to be Tidbit while he's on Earth.

"He couldn't do a lot of things that were getting in your way of doing what you need to do. Trust me, your current workload is superhuman. I promise you to be more forthcoming in the future, but for now, just let me take a bit off your load, please?"

Jenny actually blushed. He was right, and she knew it. She needed to reduce her micromanaging. Before taking on the role of the Gatekeeper, she had gotten used to doing everything for herself. As a ghost-writer, she had spent hours and hours in quiet solitude doing her work. Now she was a part of a very intricate team, and she was going to need to adjust. That was all there was to it.

So, she hugged him back, sent a mental *"See you later,"* to the tree and the koi pond, and headed in to the living room where Lizziebot stood silently waiting for her next command. A thought took her then, that perhaps she might want to spend a little more time actually plumbing the depths of what Lizziebot knew.

Burt was right, of course. She really didn't have time to do everything she actually wanted to do, having been so seriously overloaded with tasks over the past few months. Maybe it was time for her to let go of some things that didn't require her personal oversight.

She watched Lizziebot fade into her MDP and turned as she heard an engine stop outside in the driveway.

"That will be the parents, I think," Burt announced.

Chidwi leapt to her shoulder from the back of the loveseat she had been perched on and turned off her reflection. Then, Jenny and Burt went out to greet them and to grab their luggage. Jenny hugged her parents, and they all trooped into the living room. She noticed that neither of her parents had seemed to feel Chidwi on her shoulder perch, and assumed, since they didn't yet know anything about her, that they just thought they felt Jenny's hair brush their arm rather than Chidwi's furry little arm.

"So where from here?" Ed asked, shifting his backpack travel bag on his shoulders.

"Not far," Jenny said, anticipating with delight what she was about to show her parents. And right at that time, the girls entered from the garage.

"Mom, Dad, allow me to introduce my bodyguards, Lyra, Nona, and Mynn."

At that point, she was proud of her parents who greeted these strangers kindly and without any expression of surprise or disapproval. "Nice to meet you," her mom said, shaking each proffered hand.

"Glad to see you are taking care of our daughter," her dad said, if a little gruffly. "All three of you at once, or do you take it in shifts?"

"It depends on the situation, sir," replied Nona with dignity.

Jenny could see the approval in her dad's eyes. He knew a professional stance and attitude when he saw it.

"Okay, everyone, follow us," Burt said, gesturing towards the hallway.

With obvious curiosity, her parents followed him through the door of what they must have thought was a closet in the hallway, since no room could possibly have fit there. Jenny had to admit she had to hold back a fit of the giggles when she saw the look on their faces, looking around the generously sized full-fledged office with a library, a desk, multiple chairs and even some statuary, where they had been sure only a closet could have existed. And they were only getting started.

Her mom just said, weakly, "Nice."

Her dad's eyebrows had shot up, but he said nothing. Jenny could tell his military mind was busy assessing the situation.

The girls came in from behind and closed the gate office door.

"All set?" Jenny asked.

"Roger that," Burt replied. "Girls?"

"We have everything we need between your MDPs and our own." Mynn replied.

"Set for what?" Jenny's dad asked almost sternly, as if he suspected a prank was being played on him. She knew he really didn't like surprises much.

"For this," she simply said and opened the gateroom door with an ushering motion at the group.

As they filed in, Jenny knew she would treasure the looks on her parents' faces for the rest of her life. She remembered with a bit of nostalgia her first time into the gate office and the gateroom, and she almost envied them for what was about to happen next.

She opened the Sanglarka door, and the sweet smells of the mountain meadow filled the hallway.

As her parents stepped through the rose-covered archway and the mountain vista spread before them, Jenny couldn't help but feel a warm pride in her parents. There were so many ways they could have responded to this, but they both just took in the scenery as if nothing all that unusual had just happened.

To be fair, they had been given a bit more of a heads-up than Jenny had that first time through a gateway. But even then, her mom was just gazing around in wonder, but without fear, and her dad, once again, was assessing the situation as if he had been on patrol in enemy territory... no fear or even suspicion, just the natural reflexes of a military man.

Lova, Arvid, and Elizabeth were there to greet them, and it was lovely to see her mom and dad be welcomed as honored guests.

"We have quarters arranged for your stay here," Lova said. "But before we go any farther, there are a couple of things we will need to do. Leave your luggage; it will be taken care of. Come with me, and we will take care of a few little details and then we will enjoy a friendly meal before doing the rest of our business."

They wandered up the path from the meadow, in through the double wooden doors, and entered the lodge. Lova escorted them back to the situation room between the library and the workout room. Jenny felt like she was home. She had visited here quite a bit mentally recently but hadn't been physically there in what seemed like ages.

Once inside, Lova gestured for each of them to be seated. Jenny's ever-vigilant bodyguards, however, simply arranged themselves standing behind Jenny and Burt's chairs. Lova sighed but didn't correct them.

"Welcome, Donna and Ed Japhet, to the Sanglarka lodge, the main Earth gate for the Dimensional Alliance. You are the third and fourth Japhets to grace our home, and we are glad to have you, if Lizzie and Jenny are any indication of what to expect from you.

Today you begin a very special journey, what some might call an adventure. Before we can begin your training, there are a few things we need to do and a few things you need to know. For example, Chidwi, please make yourself known to our guests."

Jenny stood up and faced her parents, who looked wary. She realized they were only just beginning to realize how big a deal this really was. So, when her mother gasped and her dad grabbed her mother's hand as Chidwi faded into view on her shoulder, she was glad that both of them had healthy hearts.

"Chidwi," Jenny said with what she hoped was a comforting smile, "is a linkling, a being from another planet. She is my companion, and we are bonded in a special way. She is a kind soul, and we spend almost all our time together. Chidwi, meet my parents."

Chidwi leapt down to stand before each of her parents and held out her tiny hand as she had seen humans do. To her surprise, her parents each solemnly and carefully shook the offered tiny hand, saying, "Hello, Chidwi." And her mom added in a hushed voice, "She's adorable."

"And she has saved my life more than once," Jenny added as Chidwi then leapt agilely from the floor back onto her shoulder perch.

"Now," continued Lova, "You will find that not everyone you will meet over the next several weeks will speak English. Actually, probably most of them won't, so we need to fix that." And moving closely in front of the two of them, she placed a finger on each forehead.

"Now you should be able to hear me address you. Please nod your head," she sent.

Bemused, they each nodded their heads.

"I know you have had communications from Jenny in this manner before, but here is what you didn't know. You can do it too. Please tell me your name, but don't use your mouth. Use your mind."

"*Donna Japhet.*"

"*Ed Japhet.*"

"*There, Donna and Ed, I'll bet you never learned a language that quickly before. Now, whether you speak the other person's language or not, you will be able to communicate. They will hear what you think towards them in their own language, and you will hear what they think towards you in yours. For instance, you probably had no idea that I am thinking at you in Swedish.*"

They all chuckled at that.

"*You can choose to speak to only one person privately or broadcast it to a group. You simply have to think of your intended audience, and they will hear you. If you are speaking privately, no one will hear you but your chosen person or persons.*"

"*In other words, I can dress down my wayward daughter privately or in front of a group?*" Ed sent with a mischievous smile.

"*If you so choose.*" Jenny sent back with an answering grin.

"*And this will translate into any language?*" Donna sent, catching on immediately that mindspeech was now the order of the day.

"*Yes, Jenny's mother person,*" Chidwi chimed in. "*Now you can speak with Chidwi, and Chidwi can tell you that Jenny is my good friend and that you were a good mother to her.*"

Tears welled up in her mother's eyes at this.

"*It is not for crying, Jenny's mother!*" Chidwi sent, somewhat alarmed at the emotion she had triggered. "*Chidwi tells you this for happiness making. Jenny is a good human and helps many, many people.*"

Donna wiped her eyes and reached out one finger for Chidwi to grasp in response, and Jenny knew that something special had passed between them.

"*Okay,*" Lova now continued in mindspeech. "*You should know that nearly all communications in the Alliance are conducted in mindspeech. That was stage one of your training. See? You're doing well already!*

"*Now we have a second thing. Please look behind me at the screen and you will now experience some things that are a lot like face time on a cell phone. You are about to meet the High Councilors of the Dimensional Alliance, who have some things to speak with you about before we can continue your training. After that, there will be one more thing, and then we can have lunch.*"

The screen behind her that seemed to appear out of thin air lit up, and there was the familiar, at least to the Alliance agents in attendance, face of Liliath.

This time, both of her parents gasped and then held very still. The screen was large enough that it nearly felt like the dragon was right in the room with them. Her two councilors, as alien as two beings could be, sat just behind her on the dais of what Jenny recognized as the private council room at Alliance headquarters.

"Due to security issues," Liliath sent, ignoring the two humans' first reaction to her appearance, something she had become used to, *"we must do this over long distance communication channels. Normally you would appear in person before the council. Lova, however, will be our proxy in this matter today.*

"Ed Japhet and Donna Japhet, please arise."

And without hesitation and obviously having gotten hold of themselves, they stood and waited.

"It is our understanding that you have accepted the assignment to become agents of the Dimensional Alliance on Earth to represent both the Alliance and your people for the remainder of your life. Do I understand that correctly?"

Both of them sent an emphatic, *"Yes!"*

"Then, do you swear on whatever you hold true and sacred to never reveal your association with the Alliance or its existence without express permission from this council and, without ever having to deny your own beliefs, to be true to the needs of the Alliance to protect the innocent and the safety of all its members?"

"I do," was projected in unison from their two distinct mental voices. The voices, which Jenny recognized from her childhood, were no less individual than their vocal speech, a function of mindspeech that never ceased to amaze Jenny.

"Then, I hereby authorize Jenny, the Gatekeeper of the Alliance, to issue you each a token of your new calling as trainees of the Alliance and Lova to issue you each an MDP, which she will teach you how to use in your impending duties."

Lova handed Jenny two agent necklaces with their little gold infinity symbol hanging from the center, and she solemnly fastened them around each of their necks, stretching on tiptoe to fasten her father's until he bent to make it easier with a daddy grin of pride at the station his daughter had achieved.

Lova held out an MDP bracelet to each of them, gesturing for them to put them on.

"Now," Liliath sent, *"I hereby claim you as agents of the Alliance, and commend you to your trainers. We will meet in person when your training is complete, to give you your assignments. Go in peace."* And before any of them could react, the screen went dark and faded away.

"Wow," Ed sent, wiping imaginary sweat from his brow, *"I feel like I'm back in the platoon being addressed by the company commander. And what—I mean, who was that again?"*

Lova smiled at his belated reaction. She knew how Liliath could affect even those who knew her well. She had actually been impressed at how calmly they had both seemed to take being addressed by a dragon.

"Liliath is the Chief Councilor of the Dimensional Alliance. Much like the president of your country, she rules for one term in that position, having served two other five-year terms in the first and second councilor positions.

"Unfortunately, she didn't even get to serve her entire first term as a councilor before both the currently serving councilors above her fell victim to an enemy attack. She will serve her five years, and the first councilor will rotate into her place and choose a new second councilor from available candidates.

"The system is designed so that no two councilors in those positions are ever from the same dimension. Typically, it will be years before another being from Liliath's dimension, for instance, will become a representative in these top offices.

"Every member-dimension of the Alliance is represented by two beings, one as the main representative, and one as a backup. Each dimension has its own requirements for their representation. In some instances, it is done by a planetwide vote. In other cases, it is a hereditary position. Any of them, at any time, could be called upon to serve as one of the high councilors.

"Does that answer your question? Consider it one of the first parts of your training," she concluded with a smile.

Jenny's mom and dad seemed to be speechless, at the moment, but both nodded their heads.

She then handed an MDP to each of them, instructing them in mind-speech to put them on.

"So, just one more thing before we go to the lunch Arvid has prepared for us. Ed, please remove your backpack. It appears to be heavy."

Ed immediately did so, and Jenny was somewhat surprised that he did not protest that it wasn't heavy at all, knowing his often-consistent masculine pride at being able to lift heavy things. He held it out in compliance.

"Touch your bracelet to the bag and think, 'Store this.'"

They all chuckled as he and her mom gasped at watching the bag seemingly crumple into nothingness.

"Now think, 'Remove backpack,'" Lova sent again.

Open-mouthed and with eyebrows raised, her dad and mom watched with awe as the bag once again was weighty in her dad's outstretched hands. He almost dropped it in shock.

"You can think 'Inventory,' and see everything that is stored in your MDPs. Both of you do that now."

Jenny rejoiced, watching her parents' eyes widen even more, knowing that they were seeing shelves upon shelves of stored items that were typically pre-stored in an agent's MDP before it was issued. She could already see her mom making a mental inventory and deciding what all she would want to add in there for their comfort and to allow her to continue to do her various crafts on her off times.

She also knew her father was thinking about how this would help in strategic situations and what things he would add from a purely preparedness standpoint.

"Now that we've covered the basics," Lova announced, bringing them all out of their various reveries, *"Let's eat!"*

With a grand gesture, she led them out of the room into the dining area, the long table already set up with plates and utensils and a long side table nearly groaning with Arvid's good cooking. Two types of stew, one with just vegetables from their greenhouse and the other with beef and noodles in a heavy gravy-like sauce, not to mention home-baked fluffy rolls; and for dessert, their choice of a strawberry cheesecake or Arvid's famous spicy sugar cookies.

"Don't stand on ceremony," Lova sent. *"Our guests go first. And once we've all filled our plates, we'll give thanks and enjoy full stomachs and congenial conversation."*

They happily did as directed, and after a moment of silence to give thanks, they proceeded to enjoy the great food and the mental conversations that wove in and out among them.

"One great thing about this mindspeech," her dad put in at one point, *"No one is going to fuss at us for talking with our mouths full."* And they all laughed, nodding in agreement.

Afterwards they all pitched in to clear the tables and put the food away, Arvid directing them, as Jenny's mom oohed and aahed over the wonderful cooking facilities while asking Arvid for his recipes. This made Arvid swell with pride. They all acknowledged Arvid's cooking abilities, but there was something about being praised by another experienced cook that seemed to swell him even more.

"Now, generally we do this before we eat, to work up an appetite, but today's ceremonies seemed more to the point. So, what we will do now, is show everyone to their rooms and you can change into something serviceable for a good workout. We'll take it easy this time since our tummies are all so full of Arvid's bounteous luncheon."

To her surprise, it was her mother who rubbed her hands together in anticipation of a workout. Jenny wondered what she would think when she found out it was a workout both mentally and physically and then with quarterstaffs.

But they all went to their rooms. Burt and Jenny were housed in Jenny and Lizzie's old room, and since the bed was very spacious, they couldn't complain. Mom and Dad ended up in Burt's old room, and the rest went to their usual places. Jenny's bodyguards, after a short discussion, declined Lova's offer of the room between and opted instead for their rooms in Burt's MDP, something that really raised her dad's eyebrows.

Jenny knew right now that her parents were going through some very quick mental adjustments and only hoped it wouldn't be too much for them, although she knew that each of them was made of pretty tough stuff, considering all they had been through together.

She knew her mom worked out regularly with an online Zumba class and her dad had always kept in shape, but she couldn't help but wonder what each of them would think of participating together in the Sanglarka style workouts.

Now, all changed into casual clothing, they headed downstairs to the well-appointed Sanglarka workout room.

Jenny was surprised to learn that her mother already knew about mindful breathing techniques and that her dad didn't pooh-pooh this as what he used to call "airy-fairy stuff." When they arose from their session, Lova praised them both for catching on so quickly to even some of the more advanced exercises.

Then, Arvid looked each of them up and down, assessing their relative heights, and walked over to the quarterstaff bucket and gruffly presented each of them with an appropriately sized quarterstaff.

Arvid was always the leader and instructor in this and was currently undefeated by anyone, including Tarafau in their occasional bouts after the general group workout. He walked them through the steps of the choreographed forms, all the experienced members of the group falling into step with practiced ease.

At one point, Jenny heard her mom's quick intake of breath as she sent to the group, *"It's just like a dance with sticks!"* which made them all chuckle, and one of Jenny's guards behind her actually missed a step.

Then, Arvid called a halt and they all stood waiting with their staffs at the rest position.

"Now we will split up into pairs and have some sparring matches. Jenny, you can spar with your dad, and I will spar with your mother. The rest of you match up however you'd like."

Jenny was a little alarmed at this announcement. Her mom was shorter than she was and, although she was spry for her age, Jenny could in no way imagine her sparring with anyone, much less Arvid. She could only hope that the reason for this pairing was so that Arvid could go easy on this grandma lady.

But she had no time to ponder this, as Arvid sent *"Begin!"* and Jenny realized that her dad had no intention of going easy on her. His eyebrows went up, however, when his roundhouse blow met her staff in midair and she countered with a pivot and a blow to his shins. He barely caught it with the end of his staff, and then they went into something that really did feel like a well-choreographed dance.

"Clack! Clack! Clack!" The room was filled with the uneven cadence of blow after blow being fended off around her and her dad, as they circled one another.

Jenny had learned early on in her training to watch the eyes of her opponent and so she was patently unaware of anything else happening in the room. The only thing that existed at this moment was her dad's face who was also watching her face carefully for anything that would give away her next move.

From time to time, she would hear an occasional grunt or exclamation as a staff made connection with flesh. The standing order in these sparring matches was that blows were pulled slightly to avoid doing any lasting damage. Jenny was very aware that these "puny sticks," as a troll had once called them when speaking to her aunt, could do severe damage when swung in full force.

Suddenly there was a furious flurry of blows from the match behind her, and she watched her dad's eyes widen, looking over her head. She thought this was a ploy, so she didn't check the circular blow aimed at his midriff.

He grunted and grabbed her staff, turning her to see what was happening behind her.

With her dad's hand resting on her shoulder, she realized that the cacophony of rapid blows was none other than her mother and Arvid. Arvid's eyes were wide as Donna advanced on him, he catching one rapid fire blow after another. When he finally countered with a blow towards her upper arms, she ducked under the blow and with a sweeping motion knocked his feet out from under him. He landed with a thump on his bottom and an incredulous look on his face.

The entire room broke into yells and applause, many of them thumping their staves on the floor. This had never happened before in this room. Arvid defeated! Jenny wished Tarafau could have been here to see this.

"I've said it before," her dad shouted to Jenny above the ruckus, "Never mess with the mama bear!" The note of pride mixed with laughter in his voice was unmistakable. Jenny turned to see tears of laughter running down his face, and then she noticed him clutching his side.

"Did I hurt you?" she asked looking up at him with concern.

"No more than I deserved, allowing myself to get distracted. I guess you and your mom just taught us all some important lessons today," he said with a one-armed hug. "You're really good with that thing. You could have taught some of my recruits a thing or two, I'll tell you!"

Jenny watched with glee when her mother held out a hand to Arvid, offering to help him up. To her surprise, Arvid accepted her hand and when he was on his feet grabbed her in a hearty hug. *"Well done! Everyone, this is what I've been trying to teach you! It's all about firm intent and absolute determination. She knew what she wanted to do and found just the right opening and took it. Well done, Donna! But, may I ask, who taught you to fight like that?"*

"I had three big brothers," she sent with what could only be called a wicked grin. *"They were all a bit afraid of me, to be honest. They taught me to wrestle as a bit of a joke but didn't find it so funny when I beat each of them at one time or another. Also, the quarterstaff isn't much different than a baton, and I was a 'twirler' in high school; even got a few awards for it."*

Arvid nodded, then held her hand up above both of their heads. *"Let this be a lesson to us all. Never judge your opponent by stereotypes or what you think you see on the surface. Donna has the ferocity of a dragon and the heart of a mother. Those two things obviously make a dangerous combination."*

They all cheered and one by one came up and either hugged her or shook her hand. Jenny sighed and shook her head. To think, she had been worried about how her mother would work out as an agent. Maybe she should have been worried about whoever might get in her mom's way out there.

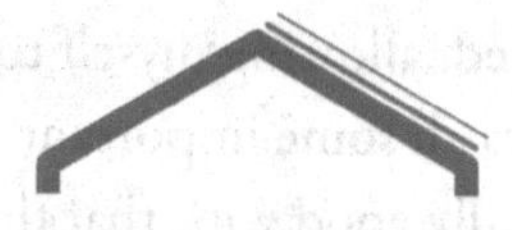

Chapter 16: Bumpy Roads

"It seems like just yesterday I was whining about being coddled and cooped up in that little house," Jenny murmured as she tripped on a small rock on the riverbank. Burt reached out a hand to catch her, and she let him help her without complaint.

They had left her mom and dad in the loving care of the crew at Sanglarka and had left from there to someplace Jenny had not thought to ever return to. They were now in what was left of Miriha's village. Most of the damage had been repaired by the returning refugees, but now and again they still came upon rubble.

Jenny hadn't been this far out at any point before Miriha's death. She had only visited twice before that, and now she found herself on a tour of what the villagers were currently doing to repair and renew the area around the town.

Burt was taking them on a reconnaissance tour of several areas that had been involved in the earliest infringement of the Inseni on various Alliance sites. When they were through here, they would be going to the Mookookie planet, to Noony's delight, and they would be checking out Sam/Engoza's planet as well.

There were, Burt knew, still some indigenous people there. The point of this exercise was to allow Jenny to get the big picture and to keep the Alliance up to date on what they found via Jenny's ability to communicate securely across dimensions.

They would be spending only a day or two at most at each location. After they completed their business here today, they would be returning to the house on Infinity Loop for the remainder of the Earth day, at which time they would be receiving their Daringi counterpart, who would be taking Elizabeth's place to give them ready and immediate access to both the odd travel destinations they had planned as well as a quick escape, if it became necessary.

According to Burt, on the Mookookie planet they would be meeting with the Mookookie council as well as the planetary council made up of the refugees that had been stranded on the planet when their own planets had been ravaged—and in some cases, destroyed—by their Inseni overlords. After their rebellion that had been staged by Jenny, Burt, and Elizabeth, with the help of the native Mookookie, they had formed a representative government and, as far as anyone could tell, the arrangement was working out well.

"So, do you think the linklings will return, now that all is peaceful here?" Jenny asked their native guide, Nulph, who would soon be installed as the new Gate Guardian for this dimension.

He seemed a gentle soul, but also very determined to make a difference for his people. He had explained in detail his work with the local town council and how they would be reaching out to the communities that hadn't been affected by the incursion of the Groga. He was grateful that the damage had been so localized and was very aware that the danger wasn't quite over.

Jenny had asked him about the linkling grove outside of town, as they hadn't seen a sign of them as they had come through to the town from the gateway on the beach.

"We are hopeful," he said, not looking at all hopeful, *"but we still are not sure where they disappeared to. We actually have begun to do choruses in the evenings that sound a lot like the cooing song the linklings used to sing in the grove outside of town. But so far, we have had no response."*

He glanced at Chidwi, who sat on Jenny's shoulder stroking her face.

"Chidwi is sure they will come," Chidwi sent to the young man. *"Chidwi hears them. They are far away, but they will come."*

Nulph's face lit up. One thing that all his kind knew was that a linkling would never lie.

"So, how can the Alliance help?" Jenny asked, hoping to distract Nulph from the linklings.

"We are actually doing very well with our own resources. We look forward to the reopening of the gateway, as we always enjoyed visitors from other dimensions, regardless of the Inseni's dastardly plans. We still mourn for the lost ones

of that time, but we know they are now in a safe place with good things to look forward to.

"But just as we miss someone who travels far away from us, we miss the companionship we shared with those who were destroyed by the Inseni. You can count on us to support whatever plans the Alliance has, going forward. We have felt the heavy hand of the Inseni and have no wish to see any other being under their thumb."

Jenny felt deeply for this kindly man. She could see his commitment to his people and to the Alliance, not only in his face but relayed by the mental connection made by mindspeech.

"There is one thing that would be very helpful," she sent. *"If you were willing to relay to the Alliance representative who will be assigned here anything you can remember about your experience with the Inseni... even the smallest detail could make a big difference in how we approach the task of eliminating their campaign of domination from the multiverse. We don't want to annihilate them or kill them. But we do want to keep them from ever being able to inflict their own will on the other beings throughout the dimensions."*

"I fail to see how one is possible without the other," Nulph confessed, his eyebrows furrowed. *"I don't see what means we can use that will eliminate the threat without eliminating those who are threatening."*

"I have a strong feeling that it isn't all of the Inseni, any more than it was all of the Groga, who are initiating these attacks. I think there is a force behind all this that must either be convinced to stop their deprecations or be constrained against their will, to protect the rights and the will of others." Jenny said, completely understanding how impossible this would sound to him, as it often did to her, when she was honest with herself.

The rest of the day was spent preparing for his swearing in as the new Gate Guardian. He would be receiving his key at Dimensional Alliance Headquarters later that day, and Jenny and Burt were his "ride" via the gateway on the beach and through the Earth gateroom.

By the time they got home after returning the new Gate Guardian to his home and unsealing the gate office, it was nearly time for their new Daringi companion to show up. Jenny found herself leaning tiredly against Burt as they sat on the loveseat in the living room.

"We've only got a few more places to go in the next two weeks, and then you'll get a kind of a break, as you will be attending a special training with Liliath regarding the full spectrum of your duties."

He chuckled at her answering snort at the word *break*.

"Well, at least you won't be climbing over rock piles or taking another tour of wreckage," he replied to her unstated objection.

She sighed. "I know, and I get it. I'll be glad to finally get a more complete picture of what I'm supposed to be doing. All I've been doing since I got this position is putting out brush fires and hoping I'm not messing it all up."

"See here, young lady," he countered in a stern voice, mocking her resigned tone. "You couldn't mess it up if you tried. You got handed the mess. You didn't create it. Even Tarafau and Liliath admit that you have done so much more for the Alliance than they had ever expected of you. Stop with the 'pity party' already!" And with that he kissed her soundly, breaking off only when a loud "Ahem!" sounded from the hallway behind them.

Her three bodyguards were entering the living room from the hallway, each with evident delight at having discovered the newlyweds "smooching," as her dad would have put it.

"We thought you should be reminded that your Daringi friend should be arriving any moment," Lyra said, snickering. "Wouldn't want to give him the wrong impression, would you?"

Both Burt and Jenny straightened up and Burt looked at his watch, which was more an affectation as anything, since his bot, DAT, would happily tell him the time mentally. He insisted on wearing the watch, as outdated as that was, since it had been his father's and one of the few things he had left to remind him of his parents.

At that moment, Jenny was struck by an unexpected thought. It began to be apparent to her that they were assembling a team with as many varied talents and abilities as any superhero association or questing party she had ever read about growing up. It surprised her that such disparate individuals could all be so firmly committed to their cause.

Throughout the multiverse, other groups were assembling, all dedicated to one thing: to rid the dimensions once and for all of the threat posed by the Insenium. It was becoming clear, however, that not all of them agreed on exactly how this was to be accomplished, and this worried Jenny.

How could they ever succeed in their endeavor if they couldn't be united in purpose and in agreement with the principles the Alliance espoused so firmly?

And yet, she could see both sides of the disagreement. She recognized that perhaps one of the easiest ways, if it could be called *easy*, would be to eliminate the threat entirely by wiping out the Inseni people.

That method would certainly require an ongoing conflict for a very long time, but, if successful, it would mean they would never have to deal with the Insenium again.

On the other hand, she admired the dedication of the majority of the Alliance to the concept of using as little violence as could be, and if it were possible, to actually bring the Inseni people around to become better neighbors and eliminate the threat by eliminating the mindset.

She was brought out of her reverie by a gasp from Mynn.

Fading into view in front of them all, was an apparently young Daringi man dressed in jeans and a t-shirt. Jenny had learned at her last visit to Amenia that a number of the younger generation of Daringi had begun to affect Earth styles, due to their exposure to people like Merv and Burt in the last few months. Both Burt and Merv had made appearances at the Daringi council to explain the Alliance's stance on the current Inseni issue.

All three of her bodyguards had responded immediately to this sudden appearance by putting themselves between the young man and Jenny.

"It's all right," Jenny sent to the group. *"We were expecting him. At ease."* She almost chuckled aloud that this military expression had come so naturally to her mind. Her dad had told her that frequently as a teen, when she got overly rambunctious or adamant about something.

The girls relaxed, but not by much, parting so that Jenny could see the young man more clearly.

"I'm sorry," he sent. *"I didn't mean to startle anyone. I was told this was the time on Earth I was supposed to be here. You were expecting me, of course."*

"Of course," Jenny agreed. *"My bodyguards are always alert and ready to react in any circumstance. By all means, have a seat."* And she gestured to one of the chairs across from the loveseat.

He did so, and then surprised them all by saying aloud, "Thank you. My name is Lucal, but you can call me Luc. All my friends do."

His English was slightly accented, much like Elizabeth's, similar in cadence to that of one of her Hawaiian friends.

"Where did you learn English?" she asked, glancing at Burt and her bodyguards, who were also obviously impressed at this unexpected skill.

"It is now being taught in the university, due to Lizzie and Elizabeth's influence. The Daringi have been very impressed by the earthlings they have met. When you became the gatekeeper and spoke so eloquently before the council, many of us desired to eventually come to your planet and meet the people who were having such a large impact on the multiverse."

Jenny didn't know what to say. She knew that the majority of the people on Earth were good people, but she also knew that due to cultural influences even in modern times, the Earth was not quite ready to join the Alliance. Until there was more international unity and less intercultural contention, this might be many years away yet.

The fact that other cultures in the multiverse had been positively affected by earthlings continued to amaze her.

But all she said aloud was, "It is good to meet you, Luc. We have made arrangements for you in the guest room of our house as well as a living space for you in our MDPs. Are you familiar with the current status of the MDP network and how we are now able to use them in the same way you would use a spaceship?"

He nodded, the elongated lobes of his ears swaying gently forward and back. "I was briefed by Tarafau himself before I left home. He told me about the bots, the Nanoites, and the Mookookie, as well as about my task.

"It turns out that I have a talent similar to that of Elizabeth, one of my mentors. I can take a set of place coordinates from a person's mind, even if they don't consciously know what they are. Like Elizabeth, if you can think of a place you have been and picture it in your mind, I can take you there.

"This is why I was chosen for this assignment, and I am looking forward to getting to travel the dimensions with you and your company."

"Great! Let's give that a test, shall we?" Burt chimed in with his usual enthusiasm. "I'm thinking of a place. Take me and Jenny there, then come back and get the girls."

Luc simply nodded as Burt and Jenny stood up, Chidwi leaping immediately onto Jenny's shoulder. Luc didn't even blink. He put a hand on each shoulder and before she could wonder where they were going, they were standing before the little pool near the Merced River.

Burt couldn't have chosen a more obscure location; and yet, Luc landed them right on the big flat rock next to the pool without hesitation.

Before either Burt or Jenny could say anything, he faded from view and immediately returned with all three girls in tow. He had placed one broad palm on two shoulders at once and one hand on another.

"Wow!" Lyra said. "I could get used to this. Where are we?"

"I don't know," Luc admitted. "Burt, where are we?"

"Just a little spot very few people on Earth even know exists. Well done, Luc! You pass the test. Now let's try one more." He looked intently at Luc, who nodded and once again placed a hand on Jenny and Burt's shoulders.

They faded into a place that was only familiar to Jenny because of reading her Aunt Lizzie's journals what now seemed ages ago. It was the training ground at the Alliance agent training center in a completely different dimension. There were beings outdoors, going from place to place, who didn't even blink when they saw Jenny, Luc, and Burt fade into being before them.

Jenny supposed they were so used to seeing and experiencing unusual things by now that it was becoming almost expected from one day to another.

He disappeared and he and the girls soon faded into view. Nona kept her composure, but Lyra and Mynn both squealed in delight.

"We're home," Mynn sighed contentedly. "It feels like it's been ages since I was here last."

"Okay," said Burt. "Let's go home. We have work to do."

Chapter 17: A Bug in Her Ear

Jenny's whirlwind tour of the different dimensional gates—encouraging the Gate Guardians and speaking with numerous councils and government organizations—seemed to go by in a blur. With the help of Luc and the support of her bodyguards, Burt had been able to get her everywhere she needed to go, and, in most cases, the important beings they needed to communicate with were already known by Burt, so he did most of the introductions.

Luc had no trouble deducing the various locations from Burt's mental sendings; and, so far, they hadn't had a single hiccup in their plans.

Jenny was grateful, however, to finally be home, even if for only a day or two, sitting out on her patio, just enjoying the California sunshine and listening to Windsong humming to himself.

One of the planets they had visited reminded her of a weeklong trip she had once taken to Seattle. It rained the entire time they were there. On another planet, the entire population lived underwater. Some were humanoid and lived in submerged village bubbles; others were naturally aquatic intelligent beings, reminding Jenny of manta rays.

Most of those they met were humanoid, although there were many who would have been considered mammals but for their extra legs or eyes. One was more reptilian, and another would have been mistaken for a very large insect on planet Earth.

All in all, it had been something she had never imagined, nor would she have believed it if someone else had told her they had been to such places and met such a diverse number of intelligent beings.

Now, as she closed her eyes and felt the warm sunshine on her face, she was grateful for this little refuge and was forcefully reminded that these respites would be few and far between in the coming days.

Nona and Mynn were quietly playing a game of cubes, obviously confining their conversation to mindspeech, and Lyra was inside Burt's MDP watching her favorite soaps. They had taken to splitting the three bodyguards up so that both Burt and Jenny were covered by a guard who could instantly spring into action on their behalf.

At first, Burt had been reluctant to agree to this, but when Jenny reminded him that it wouldn't do her a lot of good to have three bodyguards with her, if it meant he got himself captured or worse. These days, he was, by association, in as much peril as Jenny was.

She was startled when she felt two hands placed over her eyes, but calmed immediately when she heard Burt's voice: "Guess who?"

She laughed, turned to the side of the chaise, and stood to give him a welcoming hug. "How'd it go?"

"Well, those scientists at the Switzerland gate are all aflutter. They made some connections that seem to have even escaped Cornelium, Bob, and Merv, not to mention the Alliance headquarters science lab." He grinned in satisfaction, putting his thumbs into make-believe suspenders and putting on a face of pure satisfaction.

They sat down next to each other on the chaise and Burt leaned over with his face beside hers, putting them cheek to cheek.

"Let me put a bug in your ear," he whispered, and tapped her right ear, which began to tingle.

"Meet Nink," he continued as she squirmed, and then a mental voice touched her gently.

"Hello, Jenny, I'm Nink. It is good to make your acquaintance. I understand I will be spending a lot of time with you for the duration, if you will have me."

Jenny drew back to look into Burt's eyes which were crinkled from his mischievous grin. "What is this?" she asked, as he shook in her arms with suppressed mirth.

"Nink, pardon me, but I didn't tell her ahead of time that you would be visiting her," he sent. Then he continued, *"Jenny, Nink is, as you may have already guessed, a Nanoite. He has agreed to stay with you and help you to communicate*

in a new way. In the past you have used your gifts to cross the dimensions, but now we have a new medium, completely unhackable and undetectable, which every agent or Alliance representative can use, if they qualify, even if they don't have your incredible mental gifts.

"Nink doesn't need to be fed, as he feeds off of energy that is inherent in all atmospheres. He is in communication with every Nanoite in every MDP throughout the dimensions. Every agent or gate guardian or gate keeper who agrees to host one of these Nanoites will be able to communicate across the dimensions at will, at a moment's notice, with any other person who hosts a Nanoite.

"This means we now have three levels of communication, two of which are secure and one that is not. Liliath agrees that we will continue to communicate nonessential, non-sensitive, and often deliberately misleading information via the old network. All essential or sensitive information will be communicated via the mental network you have established; and absolutely top-secret information will be instantly communicated across the Nanoite network—but only to those who have a 'need to know.'"

He sat back to look into her eyes, searching her face for any sign of discomfort or dismay. She looked back into his eyes with her heart visible on her face. "It's amazing, Burt! Do Nanoites have the same talent as the linklings, of being able to read my thoughts without me knowing about it?"

"I don't think so. Why don't you ask Nink?"

"Nink, can you enter my thoughts if I don't invite you?"

"Nink can receive only what you send and send only what you are willing to receive in return. Nink cannot even peek into the thoughts of other Nanoites without permission, Jenny. It is considered not only rude but against our strictest laws."

"That is well, Nink. Thank you. I do accept your offer to stay with me. One other thing I need to ask: Are our conversations private? In other words, can another being listen in to what we say to one another or to the sendings you project to your fellow Nanoites, since it is all being transacted in mindspeech?"

"We have a hierarchy within our network, and our agreement with the Alliance is to strictly follow that pattern in our communications. For instance, if you wish to communicate directly with Liliath, I will send the message directly to Liliath's Nanoite, Grif. The message will not flow through multiple channels.

And if you and I are having a private conversation, no one else, not even another Nanoite, can listen in."

"This sounds like it will work well. Are all the Nanoites in agreement about this relationship with the Alliance and its parameters?"

"We are of one mind in this, Jenny. The Alliance rescued us so long ago and allowed us to not only survive but to thrive in a congenial environment. We owe them much and are willing to serve their cause, which appears to us to be a just one. We, of course, will not participate in any activity that is violent or destructive, but we will gladly relay necessary information through our network."

Jenny had to smile at the sincerity of Nink's reply. It was enough. Every new ally in this struggle would play an important role, even if it only meant they were stronger together than they could ever be individually.

"Then, Nink, I am glad to have you as a companion. I do believe you and your kind will prove a significant advantage in the coming days. I'm assuming you won't be lonely, as you have constant access to your fellow beings?"

"That is true, Jenny. Our community network is always in contact with one another. Even from one MDP to the other, we know what is happening at any given time, new things added and different configurations that we had not potentially considered before. Ours is a building-and-creating community.

"For instance, the recent adaptations made to your MDP and Burt's are now being included in all other MDPs. It is an epic project, and we are glad for the opportunity to create a congenial environment for other beings to interact with. Your bodyguards will probably notice continual improvements in their living conditions within the MDP environment."

Jenny was happy to hear that the Nanoites were profiting from their association with the Alliance. She sometimes worried about how they seemed to be taking advantage of the Nanoites, the Mookookie, and yes, even the bots in this struggle. She hoped sincerely that, in the end, every being in the Alliance and beyond would benefit from their moving forward with this struggle.

"Well, Burt? What next? Do I have an agenda, or are we just playing it by ear?"

"Well, my dear wifey-poo, I do believe we are on task to attend Bob, Cornelium, and Merv at a special event, the particulars of which they asked me not to reveal. Are you up for another surprise?" and added his patented evil laugh.

Jenny rolled her eyes and said, "Lead on, my guide. Girls," she called out, and they each stopped what they were doing, all alert and ready to hear anything she had to say, "I hope you're packed."

"Oh," Burt added, almost as an afterthought, "Bob says to be sure to bring Lizziebot."

Chapter 18: Upgrades

They skipped the gateroom this time, Luc taking them directly to Cornelium's lab in the breakroom. Jenny had thought that this would cause the least disruption, as the scientists generally weren't used to people randomly fading into sight within the lab itself.

This occasion also gave Jenny the chance to test her new Nanoite link. Burt had explained as Jenny was loading Lizziebot into her MDP that Bob had already received his Nanoite companion. So she had sent, *"Arriving at the lab in the breakroom in about five minutes."*

She had received back the old ham-radio reply, *"Message received and understood,"* which made her chuckle.

And sure enough, just as the last of their party faded into the huge breakroom, Bob strode in with Merv at his side, both of them with grins that told Jenny that there had been some kind of a new breakthrough.

"Hey, there, chaps! Have a seat, all of you!" The last had obviously been aimed at Jenny's bodyguards, who were immediately in alert status upon being in a new and potentially dangerous environment.

"Yes, you three," Jenny said, gesturing at the recommended chairs. "Do as suggested. We may be here for a while, and there is nothing here for you to guard against. For now, pretend we are in the backyard of my house."

Lyra nodded and they all sat, one at either end of the circle of humanoid sized chairs and one directly in the center, a strategic configuration that Jenny recognized. She could talk about the place being safe until she ran out of breath, but these women would take nothing for granted where Jenny's safety was concerned, which was one reason they had been chosen in the first place.

"Well, then," Merv continued, stroking his chin as if deep in thought. "You're probably wondering what was so important as to interrupt your dimension-wide tour of the gates and your other multiple duties. Jenny, would you please invoke Lizziebot from your MDP?"

Jenny did so without comment. She wasn't about to interrupt Merv's flow, as her curiosity was definitely piqued.

"Lizziebot, what is your task and your purpose?" Merv asked seriously.

"My task is to be an ongoing resource for Jenny and to allow communications and notifications from the Alliance to get to her in a timely manner. My purpose is to serve her in any way necessary to make her job as the Gatekeeper less stressful and to aid her needs, both physical and mental."

Jenny sat there, astounded by this reply. It had never occurred to her that Lizziebot had what her dad would have called a "mission statement."

"Very good. At this time, we wish to give you an additional function that Jenny may consider extraneous, but the Alliance considers necessary. Please report to the lab, where technicians are waiting to apply these new functions to your already considerable abilities."

Lizziebot obediently complied. Evidently, it was within her programming to respond to Merv as one having authority to give her commands.

"So, what are you doing to my bot?" Jenny asked, hoping she kept the plaintive tone out of her voice.

"Nothing and everything. She already has Nanoites installed, which makes her compatible with the new communication system; and from now on, her orders are to send communications only through the Nanoite network. She is also receiving a general upgrade that will be made for only select AI devices that will allow her to access the entire new information network that has been installed on Liliath's MDP. This network is accessible only through the Nanoite network, and it has all the updated information about the gate network, as well as the programming of each level of bots, and the distribution of the space fleet, as well as their access to specific gates that exist in space.

"In addition, she is having some physical alterations that will give her more, er, shall we say, flexibility? Bob has made some incredible discoveries of ways bots can be more than what they appear to be; they will have a certain amount of discretion, the ability to make certain decisions without any input from us."

"Wow!" Jenny couldn't restrain the exclamation. "I knew Bob had expanded his knowledge of robotics and AI and that he had access to a lot of information he didn't have before, but I had no idea—"

"Actually," Merv cut in, as Bob raised a finger as if to add something, "the majority of these advancements happened because of Bob's innate curiosity. He kept asking the other scientists, 'I wonder what would happen if...' and it started a whole avalanche of suggestions of how to use tech we already had available."

"You give me way too much credit," Bob finally cut in. "I just make a few suggestions, and the scientists we've been meeting with already have solutions that they were using for different applications. It was a group project, and it continues to bring together many new ways we can use technology that already exists. That's what happens when thinkers come together." And he tapped his forehead with a meaningful look.

"Way too modest, this chap is," Merv added, with a wink at Jenny. "Our Bob isn't very good at tooting his own horn, as you earthlings like to say."

"It sounds amazing," Jenny agreed. "And Bob has always been that way. When I first met him, he called himself a tinkerer, not adding that he had been hired for several large hush-hush projects from major corporations and governments."

Bob hung his head, obviously not sure how to answer that.

"And Lizziebot isn't the only one getting an upgrade," Burt continued. "As they say in the television commercials, 'But *wait*—there's *more!*'" He waved his arms about like a magician about to unveil an amazing magic trick.

Merv shook his head and laughed in spite of himself. "You're spot on, bloke. Will the three guards and your Daringi escort please stand?"

Bemused, the four of them did as they were told. As they stood there, Merv whistled, as you would when calling a dog. There appeared in the doorway four bots, each about two feet tall and colored in what might have been called "camo" patterns in the Earth military.

"Meet your new assistants! Each of them has a Nanoite in residence, and each of them is attuned to Lizziebot. Each of them will answer to you and is a fount of knowledge. They have already received all the same upgrades that are currently being installed in Lizziebot.

"None of them have a name yet, something you can decide on at your leisure. Their name will be a code that will allow you to install some of your own files and specific commands. Each of you touch the bot in front of you, which will register your DNA with the bot. No one, even with the cleverest disguise, will be able to fool them into thinking they are you."

They each, as instructed, bent and reached out a finger to touch the bot standing before them.

Merv then strode over to touch each of the startled guards and Luc on an ear. "I just gave you another gift. Say hello to your very own Nanoite companion. They will aid you in speaking with your bot in absolute secrecy.

"Do not judge the bots or the Nanoites by their size," Merv continued. "They each have abilities that were inspired by our Mookookie friends. Tell them in mindspeech the command 'taller.'"

All four bots were now the same height as their owners, varying from one bot to another. Jenny imagined that each of them had envisioned being able to "look them in the eye," so to speak. All four faces, seeing this transformation, were wreathed in smiles.

"They have many capacities that you will discover over time, but they also will teach you how to use them to your individual needs. I strongly suggest you spend some time with them. Ask them questions and practice giving them suggestions to see what they respond to. Like any good tool, the more you use them and the variety of tasks you give them will train them to be what you need them to be.

"And you should keep them stored in your MDP at any time you are in the company of someone who does not know about this technology"—and he looked sternly from face to face—"even family and friends. Is this clear?"

They each stood tall and looked him in the eye. "Yes!" they said in chorus.

"Spiffing. Then we can move forward," Merv began, but Jenny interrupted.

"Wait! What about Burt's bot?"

Burt squeezed her hand, their code for "I love you."

"Actually," Burt said soothingly, "DAT was the test subject for all the upgrades Lizziebot is receiving today. I didn't get left out. You could say it was the Guide's duty to test anything before it was handed to the Gatekeeper, to be sure it wasn't going to backfire on us."

"And when did you find time for all this testing?" she retorted. "Haven't you been spending every waking moment with me since you were made my guide?"

"Ah, the key is 'every waking moment.' I know you work in your sleep. I've been getting away in the nighttime on a regular basis while you did your duties, so I could also do mine without disrupting your focus. Am I forgiven?" he asked with mock penitence.

She ruffled his spiky messy hair like he was a little boy caught with his hand in the cookie jar. "Forgiven," she agreed. "Sneaky," she added in a low voice.

"Mea culpa," he replied, and put his arm around her for a one-armed hug.

"Is it getting a little sticky in here?" Bob remarked with a silly grin on his face. "Sciency stuff going on, you know; maybe save the cooing doves and fairy lights for when you're alone?"

"Alone?" Jenny quipped back. "When are we *ever* alone?"

"Ahem," Merv interceded. "Back on topic, wot?"

They all laughed, and Jenny noted that all four bots had resumed their original size and stood next to each of the chairs of their new masters.

"So, now what?" Jenny remarked as the laughter died down to furtive chuckles. "So far, I'm as impressed as I can be, but I get the feeling you aren't done yet."

"Ah, yes, that *more*, that Burt was exclaiming about? Indeed, we do have more. Are you familiar with what Brendan, our dear Aussie, has been busy with? It turns out your old *Star Trek* series has produced yet another scientific brainstorm. Remember replicators?

"It turns out that this is how the Nanoites do what they do. They can take any concept and, when they understand the necessary ingredients, they can recreate just about anything. So, the Nanoites are excited to now also be assigned to the various ships in the interdimensional star fleet.

"Jenny, you had no idea when you did that ride-along with Fidget what you were tapping into. The Nanoites are not only grateful for what the Alliance did for them in the past, but they have caught on to the idea that they aren't limited just to the MDP capsules orbiting a dead planet. Now they can explore the multiverse right alongside the various components of the Alliance.

"Their own recent addition as official members of the Dimensional Alliance has encouraged them to offer their services to our effort to rid the multiverse of the Inseni threat and do it in a way that requires no violent action on their part. Indeed, they may be a large part of the push to end this conflict without large catastrophes of destruction and the loss of life.

"Their credo and discipline are that all intelligence is sacred and should be allowed to bloom into its potential, regardless of its origins, notwithstanding that in that process there are sometimes bad judgments or choices that may affect the other intelligences around them." He paused significantly, gazing into every face to judge their reactions to these revelations.

"I can see that each of you recognizes the potential repercussions of our association with the Nanoites. I urge you to give all of this serious thought.

"We have let them into our strictest confidences, and they are very aware of the contention among our members. They are content that not all of us agree but are also adamant that this never descends into violent conflict. If it does, they will cease to communicate with us or to participate in any of our ventures."

Jenny noticed somberly nodding heads and realized that she too was showing outward agreement with what Merv was explaining to them.

"I, for one," she admitted, "am happy to have them as operatives, and I hope we can live up to the high standards they have set. Hopefully this means we will be successful with our intentions to resolve this conflict in some way that doesn't require us to wipe out a culture, regardless how we differ. But I get the sense that the Nanoites also want to prevent the terrorist incursions the Inseni seem prone to. It gives me something to think about and something to hope for."

About that time, Lizziebot re-entered the room, looking shiny and well-polished. It appeared that the techs not only gave her an upgrade but also detailed her as if she had been a treasured sports car.

"You're looking good, Lizziebot. Tell me, how do you feel?" Jenny asked.

"Feel, Jenny? Hmm. I can't say I have felt in the way you mean the question since I was a corporeal being. However, I can say that I do have many more abilities and ways to communicate to you and the rest of the Alliance.

Not to mention a few new physical adjustments that you may not have expected. For instance..."

Lizziebot protruded from one of her finger joints a small stylus shaped rod and turned it to one of the unoccupied metal chair legs and severed it without a visible beam of light or any appreciable heat.

"I do not intend to ever use it on a living creature," she hastened to explain before their gasps of astonishment had cut off. "It is more like a tool for situations that may require a quick escape."

She then grasped the leg and neatly soldered it back onto the chair with the same tool and set it back upright.

"As you can see, it is also good for mending things," she continued with what seemed to Jenny to be a satisfied tone. Evidently, special tools weren't the only upgrade she had received. Her voice had never sounded robotic to Jenny. Bob claimed the bot sounded almost spookily like her aunt had in real life. But now the voice sounded even more natural, with a spark of what appeared to be underlying emotions.

A thought occurred to Jenny. Mentally, she sent to Lizziebot, including Merv, Bob, and Burt in the conversation. *"Lizziebot, when you aren't interacting with other beings, what do you think about?"*

"Think about?" Lizzie queried. *"Do you refer to contemplation, an internal monologue with myself?"*

"Yes, Lizziebot. When you aren't responding to questions or asked to research something, do you ponder things or imagine things?"

There was an unusual pause. Jenny was used to the bot's responding almost before she could finish her request.

It was as if the entire room were holding its breath, Merv, Bob, and Burt, because the question had caught their attention; and the girls and Luc, who realized that something was going on they weren't privy to and obviously wondering what that was.

Finally, Lizziebot responded, *"My mind is generally blank unless I am processing a request or responding to the things my programming has taught me to pay attention to, such as unexpected loud noises, the voice of a stranger, or voices I recognize speaking on topics that I am constrained to recognize, based on my current programming.*

"This thing humans call contemplation or pondering, isn't in my programming, although I am aware of it, as I refer to Lizzie Japhet's instructions and the records she left behind when she transitioned from a physical being to the next stage of her journey.

"Does that answer your question? I am not prone to self-contemplation or internal dialog unless it is part of one of the aspects of my programming. My assumptions and decisions are completely part of the complex programming necessary to fulfill my function."

Jenny had never heard Lizziebot's mental voice sound more robotic, and yet, she realized that the nature of this question, when posed to a self-aware being, might have been potentially even a little insulting. Lizziebot had responded with complete logic, giving all the information implied in the question, with nothing extraneous or frivolous. Even then, was that a note of longing or hurt in the robotic response?

She sighed mentally and returned to the issue at hand.

"And I assume that it is also a requirement of the Nanoites you are hosting that you only use this as a tool and not as a weapon for either attack or defense?" Jenny asked aloud, ignoring the questioning looks of Luc and her bodyguards.

"The only time I am allowed to use this tool on anything sentient would be for a surgical procedure or to save you from destruction," Lizziebot replied promptly. "The Nanoites recognize the need for your continued existence."

"Nice of them," muttered Burt a bit rebelliously. "Glad they have their priorities straight." And the girls nodded almost in unison with his reply.

"It was a requirement," Bob said simply. "All the bots are allowed to use their various tools to build, to repair, or to defend themselves or other living entities, but never as an attack function. The Nanoites understand self-preservation as a priority. They simply are against deliberate destruction of any self-aware being as an aggressive action."

"That is in complete compliance with Alliance values, although we know that it might come down to violence, which means the bots are more for containing the violence of the opposing forces than wiping out our enemies. I like it much more than what I have seen and experienced with other cultures," Merv agreed, leaning back in his chair, and scanning the circle of faces.

Assured he had their complete attention, he continued, "Which is why we are having this conversation. Just as your bodyguards are not restrained from defending you from whatever comes at you in any way necessary, Lizziebot is not, by agreement with the Nanoites, ever restrained by the Nanoites. By that same agreement, the Nanoites will never be obliged to participate in or contribute to any violent action."

"I think that's clear enough," put in Bob, obviously ready to change the subject. "Now, for the rest of you, your bots are primarily for purposes of communication and ready research resources, but they can also be highly useful in areas such as setting up a tent, or clearing underbrush when going through a jungle, or even doing the dishes." And he winked at Jenny, who couldn't stop the color coming up in her cheeks.

"One of the unique aspects of the bots issued to each of you is that they have immediate access to the high council of the Alliance in any emergency involving Jenny. The head of the military assigned to Jenny's wellbeing is also connected. Luc, you will have coordinates of that being at all times, so you could transport him to where he is needed immediately. He carries with him a complete contingent of Alliance soldiers in his MDP at all times. They take MDP duty in shifts."

Jenny shook her head. She wanted to protest, "All this for me?" but she knew it was a requirement of her job to be defended, as even with a backup Gatekeeper, any changeover would take time they couldn't afford in this crucial endeavor.

Instead, she sighed and then nodded. The others accepted her silent agreement somberly. She knew this was one area in her life over which she had no control, but she looked forward with great anticipation to the time when none of these precautions would prove necessary.

"And that, as they say, is that," Bob pronounced with finality. "We have a lot of other orientations to do before the sun sets, so we will take leave of you all. I highly recommend that you take the tutorials each bot is equipped with, to give you a better idea of what they are capable of. We don't have time to cover the full scope of their abilities or potential applications here and now."

He stood and went to Jenny, raised her up by one hand, and gave her a hearty hug. "We're all so proud of you and what you have done. You may never have a full understanding of how your breakthroughs have affected the evolution of this technology. Don't stop exploring them. I have a feeling that when we get to the most crucial part of this campaign, it will be one of your personal breakthroughs that will turn the tide."

Once again, Jenny colored. She just wasn't used to this kind of praise. She'd never been very good at knowing how to respond to a compliment.

"Thank you, everyone. I'll try not to do anything that will put any of us in more danger than we're already in, but I can't guarantee anything." She paused, realizing what she'd just said. "I honestly don't have any secret plans at the moment," she continued somewhat lamely, looking at Burt, who was giving her a questioning look, and then at the girls, who were now once again standing at attention.

Jenny rolled her eyes. "Honest... Scout's honor... cross my heart and... you get it?" They all nodded, suspicion clear on their faces, and Jenny sighed again.

"Thank you, Bob." Jenny said, "We know you have things to do. See you at the high council chamber this evening? I understand that Liliath also has news to share."

"Yep, we'll be there. See you then." And he and Merv walked out to the lab, leaving Jenny and party to get back to the house on Infinity Loop with Luc's assistance.

Chapter 19: A Dragon's Dilemma

"**W**elcome to our honored guests," Liliath sent, standing before the small gathering that included Jenny and her entourage, along with Bob, Merv, and Cornelium, as well as several troopers and what Jenny recognized as Alliance headquarters security team members.

"We will keep this meeting brief. However, it is necessary to update this particular group in person and without any potential security leaks. Every person in this room is vetted by their history with the Alliance and the courage and honor they have shown in completing their various assignments.

"At this time, I need to inform you of the situation that seems to be enlarging within the ranks of the Alliance membership. There is a movement that began as only a small annoyance, which now appears to be spreading faster than we had expected. It still is far from reaching a majority, however, so although there is no need to panic or worry that this movement may overturn the agreed-upon plans for stopping the Insenium in its tracks, it still is something we need to be keenly aware of and take necessary security precautions.

"Jenny, as you have noticed, we have stepped up security in major ways to prevent your being used as a tool against us. We know you are steadfast, and we have no qualms about your loyalty, but we also cannot allow the entire gate system to be compromised to save one life, however necessary your skills may be to our eventual success.

"We have also removed Anela to a remote dimension that we will not reveal at this time. In addition, we have created a secret group of backup high councilors, who are being prepared in case of another attack on the council itself.

"My personal issue with all this is that my own species is currently highly divided about the existing situation, and this small rebellion is being led by my own brother.

"*Therefore, we very well may not have the support of dragonkind in the future conflict. This has changed many of the strategies and tactics we have used successfully in the past. It is fortunate that Bob and Merv, with the help of many other beings on planets we are also keeping secret, have been creating mechanical servants to allow us to do things that normally in a situation like this would be handled by organic beings.*"

She paused here, noting nodding heads and looks of approval from the gathering.

"*Currently, the most important concern is how to gather intelligence regarding the actual incursions by the Insenium, especially with regard to whether or not any of those planets that have been invaded also have previously unknown gateways that may connect in any way to the Alliance gate network.*"

Merv stood, interrupting Liliath's flow. "*Excuse me, but how exactly do you intend to do that? It's true that we theoretically have access to a few of their portals on Earth, the Mookookie planet, and Engoza's planet...and that we have a bit of their tech to allow us to use them, but without coordinates and some way of disguising our activity, I'm not sure how that will help us.*"

Liliath nodded solemnly, not even shifting color the slightest at what could have been construed as rude, coming from just about anyone else.

"*You are exactly right, Merv. Fortunately, some of those we rescued in our initial confrontation with the Insenium come from these dimensions and were reluctant to return because of the continuing Inseni occupation of their homelands.*

"*When we offered them a chance to create a rebellion similar to what was done to Peril's regime on the Mookookie world, they were more than a little willing to participate. Although we explained carefully to them that we won't be able to guarantee their safety or their success, the majority of them not only were willing but were very forthcoming about information that could prove useful.*

"*Obviously, this isn't something that we can bring up in a general council meeting, but we felt that this private group is representative of the consensus about how we need to proceed with this endeavor.*

"*So, I'm putting it to this small group. What are your thoughts about this? How can we do this with the least amount of risk to the participants? How would you go about making this happen without alerting the Insenium that something is afoot?*"

"We already have the Mookookie engaged in creating a certain amount of havoc within the camps of the Inseni invaders," Burt sent. *"They have been given instructions to eat anything that they wish, especially when it comes to essential materials and tools used by the Inseni, including weapons.*

"Their orders are to do it in small increments in ways that will not incriminate the local population. It is vital that we not create hostility within the occupying forces towards the natives, at least any more than already exists. We understand that the disappearance of these tools and weapons and equipment are a complete mystery to the troops on these planets.

"And we were careful not to let the natives know this was happening or how, as we didn't want to implicate them in any way."

Liliath nodded. *"That will be helpful, I am sure. Do you think, when the time is right, we will be able to get the Mookookie to increase their incursions? When we are ready to trigger the revolution among the locals, assuming they agree to it, will the Mookookie actively create more havoc?"*

"Indeed, the Mookookie are actually looking forward to it, as far as I can tell. They are mischievous by nature and think of it as a fine joke, stopping the 'bad ones,' as they call them, in their tracks by simply doing what they do best, eating anything and everything within reach. We do need to be prepared, however, afterwards, for a radical increase in the Mookookie population."

Merv chimed in with a smug twist to his mouth. *"Having breached this with our native co-conspirators, they seem to be of the opinion that having Mookookie on their planet in large numbers is not a problem and worth the exchange of services, so to speak."*

"When it comes down to it, I think we can see this thing through, especially since we now have instant communication with each of the Mookookie leaders on each planet, thanks to our friends the Nanoites.

"As you probably know, Mookookie ended up hitching a ride with various Inseni troops during our last encounter. Of course, none of the soldiers or officers had any idea they were hosting a stowaway. As a result, Mookookie found themselves on about a dozen different invaded territories.

"When they communicated their predicament to their elders, they were told to stay put and stay out of sight and to continue their covert operations to hinder the Inseni without casting blame on the local inhabitants.

"Recently, our Daringi scouts have been transporting Nanoites to the various Mookookie populations at all locations we have access to for a couple weeks now. It's strictly an in-and-out mission, taking only seconds to accomplish.

"The Mookookie sends the coordinates to the scout via the Mookookie network during a moment when there is no one around. The Daringi goes to the Mookookie, installs the Nanoite, and then goes home.

"Thanks to Jenny opening our eyes to new ways of communicating across the dimensions, we may be able to scrap the old communications network, after this conflict is over. Until then, we will continue to keep up the illusion that we are reliant on that network for all our communications needs."

Bob added, with a wicked grin, *"And we have the bots to supplement. We have been using a number of unusual 'attacks,' if we could even call them that, by the bots that will disable, distract, sabotage, or inhibit the Inseni military. I'm learning to love the concept of nonviolent warfare. It's a lot more like a chess game, or a game of cubes, when your design is only to keep the enemy from harming you without doing them any damage. It requires thought and preparation, and the challenge is satisfying."*

He held up a hand then. *"Not that it doesn't mean we will use lethal force, if absolutely necessary, but those steps will only be taken by the natural beings of the Alliance, not by any of our bot helpers. I got so tired of deliberate harm during my term in the military. This new approach is not only refreshing but also instructive.*

"While it is true that we may face opposition by those whose greed for power and domination lead them to do violence and destruction on others, it encourages me to know that we do not have to respond in kind."

Liliath smiled her draconic smile, both intimidating and encouraging once you got to know her. *"Indeed, Bob. It still amazes me that so much of the advances we have made and the ability to prosecute this conflict is largely due to our earthling comrades, from a dimension that is not even a full member of the Alliance at this time."*

To her surprise, Jenny noticed that the military and security members were nodding appreciatively. Jenny remembered her dad saying that no one welcomed peace more than a soldier. He did admit that there were a few who were never quite satisfied with a peaceful existence, but the majority truly treasured those times when their services were unnecessary for anything more than helping with the results of a natural disaster or a train or plane wreck.

"I wish to be clear," Liliath continued, after a deep breath, *"my compatriots will not be participating in any of the conflicts outside of their own planet. There is too much internal division among them at this time, and they aren't the only ones who are hesitant to offer any support in our current endeavor.*

"The Daringi are limiting their agents to simple transportation, as in the case of the scouts we mentioned earlier, and not on any battlefield. Their only concession to this is the transport of the Gatekeeper; that she is able to call on a single Daringi to transport her away from a dangerous situation at any time. The Daringi council has been very clear about their desire to stay out of the main conflict completely."

Cornelium had been huffing a little louder and louder. Finally, at these last words, he broke in with, *"And our people, the Alani, will stay out of the conflict entirely as well? I have never been so ashamed of my compatriots. I do know that I spend a lot of time in my lab, but I thought I knew our kind better than that. Is that a blanket requirement, or only the 'official' stand of our council?"*

"As I understand it, the statement was that none would be constrained to participate in a 'war' that we neither initiated nor feel personally threatened by. It does not ban anyone who wishes to participate from doing so," Liliath sent carefully back. *"However, the council will offer no support of any kind, including benevolent aid to any victims of the Inseni conflict."*

Cornelium huffed again. *"So, none of us in our lab will be prevented from offering aid, at our own expense, of time and resources?"*

"Indeed, not. That would violate our freedom of choice, a basic tenet of all we stand for. You may, without any restriction from our governing body, continue to aid our efforts."

Cornelium didn't answer, but simply nodded his huge head, once again appearing to be deep in thought.

There was a silent pause, each of them seeming to also be contemplating what had already been said.

"It appears that we have reached a conclusion. Bob, Merv, and Cornelium, continue with the track you are on. The assumption is that the Sanglarka scientists are a part of your team, so I will give approval for you to communicate the body of this conversation directly to them in a secure environment.

"One of the things we need from the entire science team is a functional method of detecting previously undiscovered gateways. This could very well be the key to preventing a recurrence of this issue in the future.

"Jenny, Burt, and company, keep moving forward with your inspection of the gates and working with the new Nanoite communication system. Jenny, please do not include your current communications specialists in this particular system. If one layer of security is violated, for any reason, we don't want to lose the leverage of the other secure methods available to us.

"Security and troopers, you can see what is before you, and we need you to make careful preparations to move quickly. One of these preparations needs to be the development of MDP-based barracks setups that can be imported into an MDP quickly and efficiently, as the need arises, as we anticipate that most of our troop movements in the near future will be via MDP rather than via gateway."

Liliath looked around her, gazing pointedly into each face before moving on to the next one in the circle of chairs, finally resting upon Cornelium. What passed between the two dragons they might never know, but Cornelium nodded in what could only have been called a satisfied way, and Jenny shivered. That was a dismissal to all of them. There was work to be done.

Chapter 20: Wiggle Room

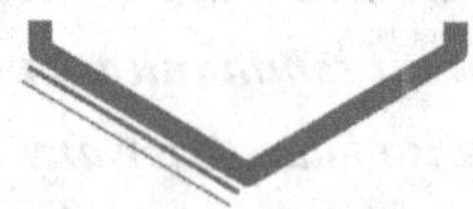

Mi was being very, very still, her face so close to the polished marble floor that she could see the cloud of her breath fogging up her reflected image. She didn't dare move, and only her fear kept her from collapsing in exhaustion.

Vena paced before her, heavy footsteps thudding back and forth and back and forth, a growl deep in her throat, adding to Mi's panic.

"You're saying you can't or you won't?" she sent at Mi like a cannon blast.

And before Mi could answer, Vena continued her rant. *"I thought you said you had her confidence… her trust! I thought you said you now had access to the entire network of the minds of the Alliance! I thought I could trust you!"*

"You can! You can!" Mi interjected quickly, before Vena could build up more steam. *"I have done as I said! I have interjected myself into Jenny's confidence. I have learned the special magic she uses to communicate across the dimensions, but I am currently limited by exactly who I am connected to within that network. It isn't universal. I can't just make up a list of people I want to connect to. I have to be introduced to them and have their permission to communicate.*

"The technique is limited and does not allow me to peer into another's thoughts without their express permission and cooperation. Whoever told you otherwise either doesn't understand how it works or lied to you."

She hesitantly attempted to peek up at Vena, who had stopped her pacing abruptly and now stood staring down at Mi with that one huge eye, the eyebrow furrowing the space between with crinkles and her mouth a stern, thin line—something that did not bode well for anyone unfortunate enough to witness such an expression on her face.

"Then, explain again to me what your restrictions are and what we need to do to widen your influence. Your mission is crucial, and I will not tolerate less than your best effort."

"Simply, it is that this network is reserved for only the most secure messages and to specific groups of people. Part of my training was to be connected to the groups and beings I am personally assigned to. Indeed, one of those personages is Jenny herself—"

Vena snorted at the mention of the dreaded name.

"—and her frequent companions, Mynn, Lyra, and Nona. Their function is as a protection to her against physical attacks.

"I then have connection points with various Gate Guardians within the system, and my function is to relay messages from either side of that network. I report to Jenny twice per lunar cycle; and, as necessary, I also receive her messages at any given time to relay to my specific dimensional contacts."

"Then, perhaps you may prove useful after all," Vena sneered. *"I will consider what you have said. Remove yourself from my presence."*

And with that, Mi carefully stood, without making eye contact, turned gracefully, and, trying not to appear to hurry, left, waiting until well down the mirror-lined corridor before heaving a sigh of blessed relief.

She still couldn't believe she had allowed herself to be trapped into this situation, but for the sake of her mother and her two children whom her mother cared for, she felt she had no choice in the matter. She could not sacrifice them, regardless of the price of conscience she would probably pay for the rest of her life.

She knew that the cause of the Alliance was just and that the Insenium was completely in the wrong under the questionable leadership of Vena. She also knew she did not have the fortitude to see her children, or her mother tortured by that evil being. However, she did long for a way out of this dilemma and couldn't help but wonder what in the world could possibly save her from having to betray what was right into such criminal hands.

She now scurried past other servants, all rushing about their various chores. She didn't have a pass to see her mother and her children. Those were only issued as a sign of approval for something you did right and were few and far between. She seldom got to see them anymore; and when she did, it made her heart hurt.

They were housed in one of the cells deep below the palace and were looking thin and wan, as they hadn't seen the sun in the several months since Vena had captured them. Mi still didn't know how this had happened or why Vena had known to choose her out of the other candidates. But she and her mother and children had been out gathering mung berries together, laughing and enjoying the sunshine.

They had been ushered by force and intimidation through a portal that she had not known existed on her planet, to this horrible place. Vena had instructed Mi that if she didn't cooperate, not only would she and her part of her family be tortured and eventually destroyed, but the rest of her family had been targeted and would also be captured for further destruction.

Vena had made it clear that the potential future of her entire planet was contingent on her cooperation and that it would go ill for them otherwise. Mi's people were peaceful and pastoral, unprepared in any way to defend themselves against an incursion by this dreadful force. Therefore, although it was against everything she believed in, she cooperated, dragging her feet only when she was sure it wouldn't be noticed by the aggressive Inseni ruler.

She arrived at the door she was seeking and entered the laboratory of Rajed, the so-called wizard. She knew better than to buy into the claim that magics were afoot here. Rajed had been a consolation to her. His bouncy, apparently cheerful persona she knew to be his way of fighting back. He was indeed an optimistic person by nature, but the bouncy, enthusiastic front he put on for Vena was a blatant rebellion, which she fortunately was too self-absorbed to recognize.

"Ah... Mi!" Rajed sent, looking up from a diagram he appeared to be studying carefully. *"I was hoping to see you today. I may have news that might cheer you. You see, I have made a connection through the new network that Vena has so conveniently allowed me to establish in her domains. She is convinced that this is all done by unintelligible magics, so she has no interest in the details, as long as it works.*

"I'm assuming she is pressing you harder, as she is me and my associates. Hold fast, Mi. I know you feel your gift has put you in a tenuous position, but there is yet hope. Our strategy will bear fruit.

"I have found an ally in an unlikely place who is, even now, aiding our cause. I won't reveal the details at this time, but just know that I have not for-

gotten *Vena's cavalier destruction of my colleagues and friends, nor her interminable unkindness to my wife and children."*

Mi nodded numbly, restraining herself from breaking into a song of mourning and despair. She straightened her shoulders and looked into the kind eyes of this man who was as troubled as she was and had already endured more than she could imagine, under the thumb of that dreadful being, Vena.

"I feel like I am so weak, compared to others who continue to fight in silent desperation. The song in my heart is of woe and destruction. The song in my heart wells up in the time before sleep and leaves me desolate. My cry goes up to the Creator of All Things to allow me peace and to give us the strength to conquer this threat to all peaceable beings within the multiverse."

Rajed nodded and put a hand on her arm. She was quite a bit taller than he, his head only coming up to her shoulder. He looked up into her eyes and she knew that, regardless of the outcome of the current dilemma, she had a friend here whom she could count on.

An understanding passed between them then. Although he could not afford to tell her the details of his plan at this time, she knew they would both be doing their best to stop the plans of this being of malicious intent. Mi was not alone.

"Have you eaten lately? I smelled some good things from the servant's kitchen earlier. I think they are making soup and I thought I smelled bread baking."

"Then we should go and eat, if you aren't in the middle of something."

"This," he waved dismissively at the diagram he had been studying, *"is only a small project of mine that can wait while we get nourishment. My associates are already down there, so we should probably hurry if we want to get our share."* Taking her hand and once again bouncing on his toes, he led the way to the dining hall.

Chapter 21: Cat in the Yarn Basket

Tarafau stood before the gathered council in the vast council chamber housed several levels up in the Apex pyramid. Before him sat beings from every one of the five native intelligent species on his planet, as well as a delegation of linklings who had been adopted onto his planet years ago. Their small colonies numbered only three on the planet at this time. By agreement, they kept their numbers to a minimum, but they were already well-respected contributors to the communities where they lived.

He found himself musing about how entire civilizations could be affected by a single person; The lone woman, for instance, who had turned the Daringi culture from a greedy and power-centered one into a cooperative that acknowledged the contribution of each member of their society.

There was seldom conflict among them now, and when it did happen, it was usually short-lived. They had learned how to have dialogues from differing viewpoints without having to resort to the disagreeable attitudes Tarafau had experienced in other cultures over his dozens of decades as an agent, ambassador, and guide to several gate guardians and most recently to the Gatekeeper herself.

Now, in his new role as the liaison between the Alliance and his planet, he found himself somewhat torn between two loyalties. On the one hand, he honored and loved his own people, which in his mind included all the different intelligent species represented before him today. On the other hand, he believed strongly in the values and goals of the Dimensional Alliance and the role they played in attempting to keep the multiverse safe from exactly the type of incursions now being imposed on otherwise peaceful beings.

He knew that some of his people were puzzled by his attitude towards the current conflict going on with the Alliance, simply because they didn't feel it affected them in any way.

In the past, their relationship with the Alliance had been congenial, including some trade of goods and ideas. However, many Daringi could not fathom why they should lend any further resources or aid to this conflict, and some parties were becoming unusually vehement about it.

One group of Daringi were employing their shape-changing skills as a type of protest, going about in alternate forms instead of their normal humanoid form. They were seen throughout the Apex at any given time and on the streets and at various gatherings. This was a silent but well-understood statement that they counted themselves among the "antis," or against the current policy of supporting the Alliance with Daringi escorts who could transport Alliance members in and out of touchy situations without the use of gateways.

There were also those who insisted that the Daringi be compensated for this service through an exchange of more advanced technology that the Alliance did not tend to share with cultures who were less advanced than themselves.

The majority of the beings before him were still committed to the cause the Alliance represented, based on the latest polling of the membership, but the last thing Tarafau wanted to see on his planet was division and contention among themselves. They had once lived in that condition, and he had no desire to see it come again.

He realized, of course, that disagreements happen even within family units, but for the last few hundred years, his society had lived in relative peace and had, or so he believed, learned to resolve their differences with open discourse and logical discussions.

Now, as he scanned the beings convened before him, his heart swelled with love and gratitude for his people, his culture, and their general desire for continuing their tradition of mutual respect and consideration of the needs around them.

"My people," he then began, sending in mindspeech to each of the various species. Mindspeech came naturally to them all, although each of them had a spoken language. He was grateful for this. *"My good people, my friends, my*

colleagues. I greet you as the official liaison between the Dimensional Alliance and our people. But more than that, I greet you as someone who loves our cultures and our communities.

"Each of you is poignantly aware of the issue before us now, and I will not bore you with infinite details or tedious reports of the various events that the Alliance is faced with as we speak.

"Instead, I wish to address something much closer to home.

"We have been knit together as a broad community of differing species with differing cultural traditions for a long time, but it was not always so.

"We must ask ourselves if we ever wish to go back to the time of constant conflict between the various species and within each of our own species; a time that history shows us even led to bloodshed and, in some cases, large-scale destruction.

"I see in your faces that none of you wish for this, nor are any of your intentions against the principles we have tried to uphold in our multicultural planetary community. This gives me heart and strength.

"I took on my responsibilities with the Alliance with the firm conviction that this relationship with other like-minded communities would protect our planet—our dimension—from the very threat that threatens the Alliance at this time.

"Two main ideas have occurred to many amongst us. First, the idea that the conflict may spill over into our own domain in some way. Second, that by involving ourselves in the Alliance's plans to eliminate the Inseni threat, we will somehow be taken advantage of and put our own citizens in danger.

"Both of these ideas have merit and, I believe, are based mainly on a true desire to protect our own, a worthy wish. I would suggest, however, that perhaps we aren't looking at the issue from a proper perspective.

"First, is it true that our lack of a known gateway keeps us safe from such a situation as the Alliance finds itself in? I would answer, probably not. Although we have, at least for the present, created a peaceful society, we could still find ourselves in a position of becoming the fodder for entities such as the Inseni.

"The same technology that united the naturally occurring gateways spread throughout the dimensions, is advancing in many ways unforeseen even by the original creators of the gateway network.

"We are also beginning to see that the type of gateways included in the Alliance network are evidently not the only gates that pass between dimensions.

Just because neither of those have been found on our planet or within our orbit doesn't mean they don't exist.

"New gateways are constantly being discovered, even on planets where they thought they had already identified all the existing gateways on that particular world. Most of the time, they are stumbled upon completely by accident.

"Second, what if there truly are no gateways of any kind on our planet? Does that make it any less urgent for us to aid our fellow beings? One of the founding principles of our current planetwide community is the idea that we each contribute to the greater good in different ways, according to our personal abilities and talents.

"We have managed to create a society where the hour of one being's labor is equal to the hour of another being's work, regardless of their skillsets or gifts. Can we not also regard the honest efforts of the Alliance as they seek to extend their aid to dimensions not within their membership as worthy of our respect, and yes, our aid?

"There are those who would say, 'We cannot alleviate the suffering of every being in the multiverse,' and they would be correct in that assumption. But what if it was in your power to help those who, through no fault of their own, are being held hostage by a tyrant, especially if it means preventing any despot from ever using those gateways to encroach upon the rights and freedoms of others?

"I know that our people are, in general, kind and caring, especially towards those who need our help to thrive and then be able to contribute to our society in a positive way.

"I do not enjoin any of you to actively participate in this conflict. It is not, as has rightly been pointed out, of our making. However, can we at the very least offer the small aid the Alliance is asking of us?

"None of those who are serving as escorts are being forced to serve. Each of them has willingly volunteered and will not be constrained to continue any longer than they are willing.

"Can we then lay aside our contention on this matter? I entreat you, by the principles we hold dear, to allow willing volunteers to participate, and I do not propose in any way to ever force a single being to contribute any more than they desire to do.

"We all have our differing views on this matter but let us agree that we can disagree on those views without becoming contentious. Can we do that?"

He stopped, holding out both hands in a pleading manner towards the crowd. At first there was silence. Then, to his delight and gratitude, a swelling tide of applause burst from the crowd.

There were a few, he noticed, who restrained from that enthusiasm, but they were in a tiny minority. He didn't know if that enthusiasm would hold, or even if it would spread; but for now, he had begun as he intended to continue.

The real work still lay before him. He would be actively participating in the Daringi main council, as well as visiting the various communities among the different species of his planet, continuing to encourage and educate them about the importance of their ongoing association with the Alliance.

He felt like there were way too many moving parts as yet and was more than a little overwhelmed by the idea that he could satisfy all the needs of this calling, but he would not, could not, give up. Too much was riding on it, and too many beings he cared about would be affected by the outcome.

Chapter 22: Missing Links

Jenny hated it when she couldn't get a song out of her head, especially when she couldn't remember all the words to it. But for days now, the silly little song about the ant and the rubber tree plant had been going through her brain, specifically the chorus: "He's got high hopes. He's got high hopes. He's got high in the sky, apple pie hopes."

For the life of her, she couldn't remember how the rest of the song went, something about how the ant wanted to bring down a rubber tree plant, for what reason she never could fathom, and how the ant, after multiple tries finally not only took down one plant, but the only other part of one of the verses she could remember was "Whoops! There goes another rubber tree plant."

Why this had come into her head, she couldn't fathom, although she often felt as small as the ant, compared to the giant rubber tree plant. She marveled at how something so big had become such an intrinsic part of her life when she really only had ever wanted to be a writer, even going as far as to work as a writer for other people, never getting credit for what she wrote.

The idea of writing for a living for the rest of her life had been the theme of her entire college career, and she had felt very accomplished, as she set out during her senior year to nail that down by doing freelance jobs for various companies, and doing her job so well that many of them hired her on as a regular contributor.

Now, here she found herself in the center of a multidimensional conflict, doing things and thinking in ways she never would have thought possible. To imagine herself as comfortable with a quarterstaff in her hands, or addressing a large audience in a completely alien dimension so far away from her own that there were no known measurements to describe it, would have never occurred to her as remotely possible, much less a fact of her everyday life.

In one sense, she wouldn't have traded her experiences, so far, for anything that money could buy. After all, it was because of getting mixed up in this unbelievable adventure that she had met her dear husband and had been given the opportunity to experience alien cultures and be friends with more than one dragon. In her wildest imagination, she would have never considered that a remote possibility.

On another note, she felt the weight of the responsibility deeply. Knowing that she was a key player in a situation that stretched her imagination and belief to its ultimate limits did not make her feel elevated or special. Surprisingly, it made her feel so very small, a tiny speck on a somewhat larger speck of a planet, in the grand perspective of the multiverse.

Now, here she was, Jenny Japhet Scout, that little mote of near nothingness, responsible for the welfare of trillions of beings, most of whom would have no idea who she was or where she came from or what she actually did. At the moment, she felt more than a little overwhelmed, and she had no real confidence that she could actually accomplish what she was expected to achieve.

But focusing on her inadequacies wouldn't get anything done. Once again, she heard her dad's voice in her head. *Focus on what you* can *do, and the rest will work out however it will.*

She was excited to have her mom and dad in the loop, as far as her situation was concerned, and she knew that the two of them would team up to do their part. In a way, she almost felt a little selfish about it, since it also meant that more than likely they would receive more protection, doing what they were doing, than she could have offered them herself in her position.

She was aware that special precautions were being taken to prevent the enemy from using her parents as leverage against Jenny. Nevertheless, she still couldn't help but worry that maybe she had gotten them into something that could be potentially harmful.

Then she laughed to herself. She had never known two more courageous and strong people in her life. And she knew the two of them would make one of the strongest teams in the Alliance, once they knew what the Alliance required of them. Of course, not only would they be all right, but they would excel in whatever task was given them.

She shifted her thoughts. Looking out towards the koi pond and Windsong, the yew tree that spread its branches protectively out over the water, she saw Chidwi perched in the branches. She had discovered that Chidwi and Windsong had a close relationship, and it wasn't just the koi undulating below her, sparkling as an occasional ray of sunshine glinted on their golden bodies that fascinated her. She was holding an ongoing conversation with the tree as well.

Chidwi was one of the incredible blessings in her life, a companion who was close to her heart and literally her thoughts, as Chidwi always knew what she was thinking. They were linked, bonded forever. According to Chidwi, this link even extended beyond mortality.

Now, as she contemplated the step she was beginning to think she would soon need to take, she wondered how her choices would affect those closest to her and what she might be able to do or say to prepare them.

She had told her friends that she didn't have anything impulsive planned, and at the time this had been a true statement.

But recently she had been given insights that had begun a process in her mind, a potential solution that seemed far-fetched even to her. But the more she thought about it, the more she realized that she was the only one she knew with all the tools necessary to prevent a dimension-wide disaster.

After going over and over this epiphany in her mind, she knew it would take careful planning, but based on some things she had learned while reading Lizzie's journals, it had occurred to her that the solution was literally within her grasp and that few others could do what she could do.

So, she had prepared a message to be delivered, simultaneous with her planned actions, to all concerned parties through the Nanoites residing in her and in Lizziebot.

Of course, Lizziebot would accompany her, but she doubted she could get away with taking Chidwi with her on her intended journey. Obviously, she couldn't hide her intentions from her linkling companion, but she had time to deal with that before making her move. Chidwi had given no sign that she knew what Jenny was potentially planning, but perhaps she wasn't saying anything since Jenny hadn't made the final decision.

She was unaccustomed to vacillating about crucial decisions. In the past she had almost always done the necessary research to come to a conclusion. It was much like what her dad had taught her: to observe, orient, decide, and then act.

At this point, she felt as sure as she could be that there might be a way to prevent this confrontation from coming to an unnecessarily violent conclusion. Then she really did laugh at herself and asked herself the question that had come to her again and again. Who did she think she was?

Then, shockingly, she heard Chidwi sending: *"Jenny is good and Jenny is wise. Jenny cares about big things, and Jenny isn't a wisher, Jenny is a doer."*

"Then, you know?" and she heard the plaintive note in her mental voice.

"Chidwi always knows. Jenny knows that. Chidwi also understands that there are things Jenny must do. Chidwi will help. Nanoites are building Chidwi a house in Jenny's MDP. Jenny does not have to do this alone."

Jenny almost cried at the tender but firm note in Chidwi's sending.

She would go forward. She had already made some of the preparations that the others would not realize were part of a bigger plan. She had planted certain seeds in places no one realized were at issue.

Certain surprising things had come to her attention from unexpected sources that prompted the plan in the first place.

This time, she needed no prompting in a dream from Miriha, from whom she had not heard since that night in the little cave in an Amazon rainforest in what now seemed like the distant past.

Chidwi's support had been the final piece of her puzzle. And even though the others, including her sweet husband, not only would disapprove but would also be angry with her, she had determined that this was the one thing that might actually make the Alliance's preparations work as they had hoped. She had decided to move forward with it. Now she just had to do it.

Chapter 23: Maybe

"*Crikey, I thought we had it that time!*" Brendan sent to his lieutenant on deck. "*Are you sure?*"

"*We double-checked, Captain. It wasn't what you had hoped. We'll have to get some more parameters. The Alliance gates we have tested all register just fine, but this anomaly isn't what we thought it was. Do you wish for us to check the next one on the list?*"

"*Yes, let's get to those coordinates as soon as possible without straining the engines. Please keep track of the Alliance gate in case we need a quick getaway.*"

"*Aye, Captain. As you say.*" The scrupulously neat lieutenant turned to go relay the orders to the engineers above. Next to Brendan, his bot stood waiting for any orders or questions Brendan might have. The bot had been a godsend, as he didn't have to pay any attention to it and it moved with him around the ship unless ordered to do otherwise.

The bots the Alliance had issued to various components of their military fleet were of three varieties: the personal bot assistants, the server bots who did various chores that didn't require human supervision, and the battle bots.

He had been instructed that the battle bots had very limited use-permissions and were only to be deployed as defensive weapons, except under very special circumstances. Unlike the majority of bots the Alliance was creating these days, these bots had no Nanoites on board. They were simply very clever robots, programmed with very specific uses and stored en masse within the MDPs of the battle coordinators.

His fleet had been given an urgent and very difficult task: to search for alternate dimensional portals in space that might be tied to the portals within the Inseni network, if it could be called that.

The Alliance scientists had come up with a similar device to the ones that had been acquired near the Amazon rainforest portal, attuned to the variances that might indicate a portal, even in the vastness of outer space.

Every moment for the past several weeks, Brendan kept hoping for the equivalent of a shout of "Eureka!" He felt keenly the responsibility to not only continue his search until he had been successful, but to also keep the morale of his crew high, as well as their attentiveness to their duties.

Brendan had been a pilot most of his adult life and had always yearned for travel among the stars as the ultimate piloting experience, but there was one thing he had learned, and it seemed so obvious on the surface.

Space was big... really, really, really *big*. As a matter of fact, there were no words big enough to express the feeling of being so very small, surrounded by such... well... bigness. He knew that many going into space for the first time had expressed not so much awe as intimidation at the sheer vastness of the emptiness that surrounded them.

He often wished he had the slightest inclination to write poetry, as a poet would surely have words that could invoke the feelings that overwhelmed him every time he considered where he was and what he was doing. That the idea of space could actually be expanded by the concept of multiple dimensions, potentially an infinite number, was beyond his ability to comprehend, much less express.

But, then again, perhaps not. His gut tightened as the ship took another tack, although there was no actual sense of movement... not at all like what he would feel in a jet or a plane, but a slight vibration in the deck under his feet told him that they were changing direction. On the controls before him, he could see the little dot that represented his ship and the destination dot before them.

"Maybe this one," he thought again trying to loosen his stomach muscles, grateful that none on the ship had the ability to read his doubts or concerns as they continued their tasks. "Maybe..." he repeated to himself, not liking the potential defeatism in this word.

"Hopefully..." he edited the previous word, changing its tone and the tone in his mind.

They had been searching for weeks now and, although he knew this was definitely the proverbial needle in the haystack, this might prove vital to success in this conflict.

He had been excited to find himself the captain of an actual starship that went beyond any of the limits Earth scientists had ever envisioned of the cosmos. Now, the absolute reality of it all was only beginning to sink in. And captaining a ship in space was so very different than flying a jet or other aircraft.

Even though they were traveling at unimaginable speed through the depths of space, it often felt as if they were only drifting, especially in the area of space they were currently traversing, between one galaxy and another, chasing what sometimes felt like phantoms, tiny irregularities in space that seemed to have similar properties to the dimensional portals they were searching for.

So, now, looking at the viewscreen before him, there were almost no visual reference points to give him a feeling of progress or movement. The only clue was the ever so slight vibration of the deck below his feet, something that many might not have noticed, but to which he had become sensitive while training for his position.

He found it curious that an earthling, a species on a planet not officially on the membership rolls of the Alliance, would find himself in such a role, but he was grateful for it, nevertheless.

"Captain, the target anomaly is directly ahead. Slow trajectory?" sent the navigator from the helm.

"Indeed, lieutenant. Slow by three quarters speed. Scanners forward in a hundred-and-eighty-degree arc. Record all data from here to the destination. This may be what we're looking for." And in his heart he said, "Hopefully...."

Chapter 24: Snits and Do-Nothings

"*Limiting! What do you mean,* limiting?"

Vena's mental shout might possibly have been heard in a distant galaxy, Mi thought, wincing at the forcefulness of it.

It was a private conversation, in Vena's sitting room, as Mi was sure that Vena didn't want this part of her plan known to anyone. As it was, it was all they could do to hide Mi's function from the nits on the planet where she had been assigned by the Alliance. Through some delicate maneuvering by Inseni infiltrators, Mi had ended up doing her duties as a communications specialist on a planet with both the Alliance network gates and a portal that, as far as they could tell, was known only by the Insenium.

One of Vena's few reliable infiltrators of the Alliance headquarters had to be very careful to escape notice, but she was extremely good at making herself unnoticeable, hiding in plain sight and making herself tremendously useful at every opportunity.

Mi could see the intent in Vena's angry eye and realized with trepidation that Vena was using every bit of constraint she could muster not to throttle Mi, her hands twitching and clenching and unclenching nearly uncontrollably.

"*It's not just me,*" she hurried to add. "*All the mental communicators are getting a limited number of contacts, and the messages are very specific to the dimension in question. They have cut in half the number of dimensions I am responsible for, and the messages are fewer than before.*"

"*This was supposed to be the key!*" stormed Vena. "*My way into the secrets of the Alliance. You have failed me. Could you not have persuaded them to give you more responsibility? Told them you were up to a much heavier load? What use are you to me now?*"

"Much use, Great and Exalted One! I still get all the messages related to the conflict that are being privately told to the dimensions I have been assigned—"

"But you don't get all the messages sent back by the dimensions you don't have access to, do you? What the Alliance has to say to their members may not be nearly as important as what their members are saying to the Alliance. Think girl! Think! I thought you were supposed to be this great talent! This amazing gifted one! Did no one gift you with a brain?"

Mi could think of nothing to reply to these inane questions. The answers were too obvious, and she was afraid that any answer would simply increase the intense rage that was sweeping over Vena in waves, the mental communication sending dire signals that she might be seconds from annihilation. Worse yet, she feared that Vena's anger would spill over to harm her mother and children.

So, she didn't say what was in her heart to say. She simply stood there, looking down at the ground, hoping that, if Vena couldn't read the emotion in her face, that she wouldn't follow through with her usual violent reaction.

Vena's tantrums were legendary among the servants and members of Vena's court. Every one of them lived in fear that they or their loved ones might be the target of her next disappointment.

Miraculously, Vena's breathing slowed, and Mi attempted a brief glimpse up. To her amazement, Vena's face had nearly cleared, and she was looking up at the ceiling and saying, *"Yes, yes, that might just work. Do you know, Mi, I think this may actually work out just right. You are dismissed. We will talk again later. Wait for my summons."*

Mi bowed herself out without another word and nearly ran back down the hall to her tiny room in the servant's quarters. She threw herself down on the bed, and only then did she sob until her stomach hurt and there were no more tears left in her to shed.

In the meantime, Vena paced her sitting room, the agitation having left her and an idea swelling in her mind.

Her wizards and their magical contraption! Could it do more than just send her voice to her commanders and their voice to her? Could it trap a portal? Perhaps it could trigger a spell that when organic beings came near, it would suck them through and capture them?

The trap would have to take the captive to one of the smallest of her dominions, of course, since she didn't want the detritus of the multiverse landing on her doorstep. But there was a very specific captive she was looking for. And she had the perfect tool to use as bait. Now... how to bring that being within her clutches....

Chapter 25: You Ain't Seen Nothin'

Bob straightened up from his minute examination of the diagram before him.

Well, he thought, looking around the silent, empty lab, *That's done. Cornelium and Merv should be here any minute.* And he vigorously rubbed his hands together in anticipation.

He carefully stowed the diagram into its folder, musing that no matter how advanced people got with so-called paperless technology, there was something satisfying about putting things on paper. This, of course, had been printed out from its digital version, but now it had pencil marks of various colors all over it. And it would be used to brief the rest of the team in their meeting later that day.

The corrections would be argued about and then agreed upon, and those corrections would be applied to the digital document.

He had no sooner put the folder away than Merv opened the lab door, followed by Cornelium. Once again, Bob found himself so grateful that he had been given this opportunity to do serious science and work with technology so far beyond what had been available to him on Earth.

Even more than that, the two beings before him, both completely alien, had become fast friends: Merv, with his nonchalant attitude and practical approach to every situation, and Cornelium, the logical curmudgeon, who Bob also knew had a heart of gold.

In any of his wildest imaginings, he would never have expected to be mentored by a wizard, by reputation, and a dragon. Yet here he was, hanging out with the infamous "Merlin" of Earth legends and a full-blown dragon, wings and all. It saddened him that for now they had to focus on righting a serious wrong in the multiverse when they could be putting their talents to things more productive and positive, but he still wouldn't have changed his situation for any amount of money or fame on Earth.

He did miss his old neighborhood sometimes and would have liked to have spent more time with his son, but in every great work, sacrifices had to be made.

"Hey, mate," Merv sent as they approached Bob's workstation. *"I hear you have something for us?"*

"Yes, I do, and I think it would be good to head into the breakroom. Cornelium, I'm going to need your opinion on something."

Cornelium huffed, his huge reptilian eyes slitting for a moment. *"I thought we got all the wrinkles out of that last project,"* he sent gruffly. *"Aren't we moving on to the Mookookie issue today?"*

"Actually, this is something new, but I do think it is a priority, or at least I think that you will agree, when you see it, that it is. And the Mookookie issue is resolved. They have agreed not to eat any of the tech they find in the Insenium military camps. They will only consume weaponry and other supplies."

"Hmmph. Well, then, let's get to it. I have several loose ends I need to tie up on the issue of nonlethal weaponry, and we still need to test the gases the Sanglarka lab sent us on some of our captured Inseni."

"Got it. I promise this won't take a long time, and you may be glad that we put this first on the agenda."

The three of them settled into their usual seats in the large circle where the various techs and scientists held their conferences or sometimes just hung out to eat and chat about what was going on in their various projects.

Bob loved that those arrangements had been made for intense and personal interaction among the scientists and techs, each working on a different aspect of their preparations for the upcoming conflict. It meant they got to pick each other's brains and get a different viewpoint on a project that seemed to be stuck at any given time.

Bob had long since learned to interpret the expressions on Cornelium's draconic face, and he could see some impatience there, so he launched right into it. He would have loved to draw out the suspense a little longer, but he didn't want his surprise ruined by an unhappy dragon.

"So, I know you have a pretty heavy load of things that need doing and not nearly as much help as you would like. You made a suggestion to me awhile

back, and I have been incorporating creating a solution into my evening work. At night, the lab is quiet, not nearly as many distractions as during the day.

"At any rate, I came up with this, and I want your opinion." And looking directly into Cornelium's face, he invoked from his MDP a robotic dragon in the same coloring and configuration as Cornelium, but smaller—at least, smaller compared to the original. The new dragon stood a good three feet taller than Bob or Merv.

The bot swiveled his large head towards Cornelium on his long neck and intoned in mindspeech, *"Good day to you, master. How may I help you today?"*

The tone of the mental voice was nearly identical to Cornelium's, and Bob was satisfied to see Cornelium's eyes widen in surprise and disbelief.

"Incredible," he intoned. *"When in all creation did you find time to do this?"*

"I didn't do it by myself. I had help from some of the other techs and the factory where we have been creating the other bots. They want to know if we want more of them."

"More? Really?" Cornelium's huge head swung back and forth, and for a moment Bob thought this must be a negative response.

"Well, I mean, if you don't think it would be worthwhile," Bob began, but Cornelium quickly cut him off.

"Not worthwhile? Worthwhile? Wait until Liliath sees this! But wait... does he fly?"

"Would you like to try it?" Bob returned, now feeling elated to see this kind of enthusiasm.

"Yes, but put it back in your MDP for now while we head to the launch door."

Bob complied, trying not to feel too smug about this reaction.

On the far end of the lab was what you might call a very large balcony that the few dragon scientists used to travel directly from the lab to other areas of the planet, eliminating the need for them to go into the lower floors of the palace. It was attached to the dragon-sized lab for their convenience.

A few techs were already at their stations on the humanoid side, working away, and another draconic scientist deep in thought at her station, who didn't even look up as the three of them strode to the balcony.

The view from there was breathtaking, nearly literally, since the air at this altitude was a bit thin. The balcony looked out over the big gap between two mountain ranges. Peering down from this height, you could only see the narrow floor of the canyon below. Completely surrounding the vista were multiple rocky peaks. As they were far above the timber line, there was nothing to block their view.

"*Now,*" Cornelium instructed, "*let's see him fly.*"

Bob obediently removed the dragon bot from his MDP.

"*He will take your command,*" he sent to Cornelium.

"*Fly to the peak straight on from here and return,*" Cornelium sent.

The bot nodded and from the standing position leapt high into the air and soared, first in a downward glide and then, picking up speed, leveled out and headed straight as an arrow to the peak just beyond them.

Just as he approached the peak, he did a mid-air pivot and returned. The flight took only a few minutes to traverse what Bob judged to be about forty Earth miles.

It landed with surprising grace and only a slight thump on the stone floor of the balcony.

"*Be at ease,*" Cornelium commanded the bot. "*Bob, did you say something about creating more of these? What other things can it do?*"

"*Yes, Cornelium, but only if you desire it. I didn't know if you would want to keep this to yourself or not. Your bot can do nearly anything you can do, as well as recording discussion, as you choose, storing computer data, and even common chores, such as straightening and cleaning areas in the lab. It has Nanoites installed in it, meaning you can instantly communicate with anyone else in the dimensions who has a bot with similar abilities. It also has some defensive capabilities, and you can add other things to its programming as needed.*"

"*I will consider it,*" Cornelium replied, tapping his chin with one clawed finger. "*And no one knows about this but us?*"

"*No one. Of course, the other associates in the lab will know, but I haven't even told Liliath yet.*"

Merv nodded, when Cornelium looked his way. "*It's a surprise to me as well, mate. Bob never even gave a hint of what he was up to.*" And he looked accusingly at Bob.

Bob shrugged. *"A secret is more likely to stay a secret, the fewer people who know about it."*

Merv nodded and slapped him on the back. *"Well, you nailed this one, you barmy bloke. Don't get me wrong, I love my own little guy. He comes in handy, but I think you've outdone yourself on this one. Hey Cornelium, this little work of art needs a name. Got any ideas?"*

"You are right, of course, if nothing else to set him off from the other bots. Let me see...." He cocked his huge head, examining the dragon bot from his huge head to his clawed feet. *"I think I will christen him Nimble, as it is my hope that he will be nimble and able to take my commands and make my work a lot easier. Thank you, Bob, for taking time out to create this for me. Do you ever sleep?"* he added shaking his head.

"Oh, I get enough. You must remember that the days on my planet are only twenty-four Earth hours long and I'm not used to sleeping as long as the regular sleep cycle for the inhabitants of this planet. So, I use the extra time for things outside of my regular schedule of work."

Cornelium chuckled. Bob was always amazed at how intimidating that sound was, coming from a dragon.

"Well, then, speaking of work, we have a trap to lay in the Alliance communications network, as Liliath tells me there may have been other ears listening in on our conversations, and she would like to figure out just who that might be."

Chapter 26: Tracking the Beast

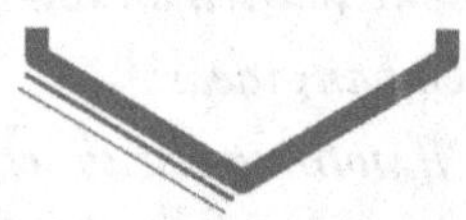

It didn't seem fair, somehow, Arvid reflected, watching his students spar with one another, especially noting the natural style of Donna, Jenny's mother, as she sparred with one of the agent recruits.

Donna not only had an inherent grace and style in her movements, but she had already beaten him twice in the several matches they had sparred in. This puzzled him to no end, as he had a reputation for being unbeatable.

He didn't consider himself prideful or full of himself, but he had become very accustomed to his status as the undefeated champion at Sanglarka, even against the daunting Tarafau.

And, to add to his dilemma, she was an even better cook than he was, or at least as good. These days, they prepared meals side by side, and he couldn't even complain about her messing up his kitchen. She was an orderly and efficient cook, cleaning as she went, so there was almost never a mess to clean up when she was finished.

She taught him some of her favorite recipes, including her famous (so she called it) tuna casserole and her meatloaf that everyone had raved about at their last supper together.

And to add to his frustration, he actually liked her. He could see where Jenny got her temperament.

Currently, he wasn't sparring with anyone, evaluating each of the sparring partners carefully, as this class would soon be graduating to the actual Alliance agent training facility, and they probably wouldn't see this group together at any point in the future. Their individual assignments, especially during their internship, would take them to very distant places within the Alliance member network.

He remembered his own early agent days with a bit of wistfulness, but he liked doing what he did these days... at least most of the time.

Donna finished off her opponent with a swirling whack to the back thighs at just about the same time as her husband, Ed, tapped his opponent on one shoulder, just hard enough to elicit an "Ow!" but not hard enough to cause any real damage.

Arvid clapped his hands, and everyone turned from their partners to listen. *"I can see that you are nearly ready to go to your next level. And in some cases,"* and he looked pointedly at Donna, *"some of you may teach them a thing or two. Let's break for lunch, and then we will be working on our tracking skills. Assemble after lunch in your hiking attire. You may, if you wish, bring one of your quarterstaffs with you as a hiking stick.*

Dismissed."

They all obediently stowed their staffs and headed out into the dining room. Donna joined Arvid in the direction of the kitchen. The lodge staff would be in there completing the more boring tasks of setting up the smorgasbord with the food that had been prepared ahead of time and setting the long dining table, but Arvid always liked to oversee that all was in order. He had timed it so that the bread would have already come out of the oven a few minutes before, and he would butter the tops of the rolls himself to ensure that beautiful silky sheen.

Donna also had something to take care of, as the brownies she had made had cooled and were ready to cut into serving sizes. Brownies hadn't been an offering in the usual Sanglarka fare before, but they would definitely continue, as the staff seemed to really like them, almost as much as Arvid's classic spicy sugar cookies.

The meal was congenial and, as usual, the Sanglarka team ate with gusto, many mental conversations ranging around the table, based on the facial expressions and body language of the various earthlings.

These days, with Meta back to working with the new agents at the training center, Arvid was the only non-earthling at the lodge. He didn't mind it at all, as there was plenty for him to do and he really liked all his earthling friends.

He had been at Sanglarka for so long that he might have forgotten his origins if it wasn't for the convenience of the gateway that led back to his own dimension. He took some time off between new groups of agent recruits to visit his home, but more and more he felt at home in Sanglarka and its environment.

One of the things he loved was to go out with the groups of agents on their hiking workout. They ran a course that led through wooded areas, across streams, and up and down hills, with stops at different stations where they did specific calisthenics before continuing through the entire sequence.

This group was in pretty good shape and fairly well matched in stamina and resilience. Today, however, their task would be slightly different. One of the skills every agent learned was the ability to navigate in unknown territory and how to recognize the signs that allowed you to track something in a natural setting.

Arvid considered himself accomplished in this area and was hopeful that this was finally something in which he could outdo and outpace Donna, who, in spite of the fact that he actually liked her, was becoming a bit of an irritant, at least where his ego was concerned.

They met in the lobby, all appropriately dressed, and most of them had opted not to carry a staff, at least for now. They all knew that at any point, in an instant they could pull a staff from their MDPs, something they had practiced over and over again as part of their training.

"Today we will be tracking a bear I know to be wandering the woods lately. She recently lost her two cubs to predators and is not very happy. We won't be confronting her, but she has left some pretty obvious tracks, and we will be examining them to see how your lessons have sunk in. I will be asking each of you to tell me her story based on her tracks."

Every head nodded, most of them solemn, and some looking a bit alarmed. "No student loves a pop quiz," he thought to himself with a grin.

"So let us begin. Ed, when we find the tracks just inside the forest, I want you to take the lead. When you see the first difference, stop and tell us what you found. The rest of us will remain a few paces back to keep from tracking over the spoor."

Ed, in his usual businesslike manner, nodded and they began.

Arvid remembered one smart aleck recruit who had questioned the need for this kind of training. Arvid had told him that there were a lot of different kinds of tracks they would be watching for over the course of their time as an agent, most of which would not be animal tracks.

The point of the exercise was to learn to draw larger conclusions from small observations. However, he also told the young know-it-all about the time he had participated in a search for a lost agent in a swamp in the Amazon jungle, the time they had found the Groga encampment and nearly lost Jenny.

The young man had not complained about it after that and afterward actually became a terrific tracker. Arvid still got good reports about him and his attention to detail.

So, now he paid attention as each of the agents in training stopped at various points to explain the deductions they had made, regarding various aspects of the tracks they were examining. He was pleased to see that most of them were able to discern small variations that allowed them to make conclusions about where the bear might go next and what she was engaged in at the time.

He was just about to tell them to head back to the lodge when all of a sudden, the young man in the lead at the time let out a mental shout, *"Bear!"*

They all froze at that call. Donna had been right beside the young man, peering down at the track, watching what he had been pointing at. She looked up and saw the bear who was on all fours, looking at the group.

"Look her in the eyes!" she sent urgently. *"Make yourself as large as you can. Don't show fear, but don't move towards her. If she starts towards any of us, then everyone should shout, wave your arms, and get as loud as you can! But do* not *run away from her. That's a race you cannot win!"*

The bear rumbled more of a pleading sort of sound than an angry growl.

Everyone followed Donna's instructions to the letter, each standing tall, with arms outstretched, looking the bear right in the eyes.

The moments ticked by with no sound except the normal rustling of the leaves in the light breeze that seemed to always blow in the valley where Sanglarka was situated.

Suddenly, with a mewling cry, the bear turned and trotted away in the direction she had come from.

"And that concludes our lesson for today," Arvid sent to the group. *"Let's go home. I don't know about the rest of you, but I could use a break."*

She had done it again! Once more Donna had shown herself courageous, and she had taken charge before her military husband had noticed there was a threat. Now Arvid understood why Lizzie had chosen Jenny. He would bet anything that she had known Jenny's mom well.

"My dad used to take me hunting as a kid," she explained to him as they hiked back. It was almost an apology. *"I didn't think, just reacted the way I was taught."*

"Well, we appreciate it," Arvid admitted. *"I think the bear was more sad than in defensive mode, after the loss of her cubs, but there is no predicting what a distraught mother bear will do if provoked. You were exactly right and may have saved a life or prevented a serious injury today. Thank you."*

Arvid resigned himself, then and there, that he wouldn't even worry about keeping up with Jenny's mom. He admitted to himself that he admired her husband. Ed must have realized early on that he had taken on more than he expected when he married that one, and he didn't even seem surprised when she outperformed most of the others in the company.

He watched as Ed caught up with his wife and put an arm around her waist, and she looked up into his face with a grin.

He sighed and trudged forward with the rest. "Just goes to show," he thought, "that the teacher can learn as much from his students as the other way around."

Chapter 27: Rubber Tree Plants

Jenny grunted as she tripped on her own quarterstaff while trying to counter Mynn's attack during their sparring match.

"Something on your mind?" Mynn asked observantly. "It's usually your opponent who is supposed to execute that particular move. It isn't like you to inflict it on yourself." Her mouth was trembling, trying to keep from grinning at her own wit.

"Yeah, well, you know, Gatekeeper stuff and sciency stuff and family stuff…. It's amazing to me how it all adds up, each thing affecting another thing," Jenny retorted, resting on her staff and breathing harder than she usually did during one of their matches.

"Something just occurred to me that surprised me," Jenny confessed. "I realized there is a chance that, although we all agree that a frontal attack on the Insenium would be a big mistake, what if trying to be too subtle doesn't work either?"

"Man, I wish I could think like you do. Most of the time I'm just focusing on where the next attack might come from and how fast I can react to protect you. Mental wanderings aren't really in my character, I suppose."

"You weren't raised by my parents. They're both heavy thinkers: Dad, because of his military service and having to strategize and second-guess the enemy in order to give his soldiers the best possible chance to survive and to complete their objective; my mom, because she has been so actively engaged in the community in every new place we lived. She helped plan huge events and organized folks in the community for big projects, all while raising and taking care of a family.

"Both of them taught me a different kind of thinking and encouraged me by discussing deep-thought topics almost every night at the supper table.

"But here's the thing. One thing I've learned so far in my life is that different minds in different situations may not see the situation the same way. Motivations are different from one person to the next, and sometimes the 'why' someone does something is more important than the thing itself.

"We really don't know why the Insenium is doing what they are doing. That could change everything.

"We don't know if it is the Inseni people, or just their leaders. And, if it is their leaders, what makes them want to do what they are doing?"

"Really? Isn't it just because they are just plain evil and only want bad things?" Mynn often seemed mystified by Jenny's ideas. Of the three of her bodyguards, Mynn was the most interested in the sciences and logic, but nuances and subtleties often escaped her.

"I know it may sound silly, but I honestly don't think there is such a thing as pure evil. Not to excuse people who do bad things to others, but when it comes down to it, I think there is nearly always a spark of good in a person. I could be wrong about that, of course, but I would like to think that there is some good in pretty much every being ever created."

Mynn didn't look convinced, but Jenny knew it wasn't her job to persuade her. Nevertheless, she appreciated that Mynn listened and let her get these thoughts out into the open air.

"So, what's on the agenda today?" Mynn said, not so deftly changing the subject.

"We're all going to the Amazon portal to check for new incursions. No need to keep you all in the MDPs, as you will be our lookouts. Luc will be transporting us there. We'll leave after lunch."

"Got it. Well, I think Nona and Lyra are probably finished with cleaning the apartment, and I saw Luc out on the patio earlier. I think he is as fascinated by the koi as Tidbit and Chidwi." And she chuckled at that.

Jenny had noticed that Mynn seemed to be fascinated by Luc, who alternated between being a tortoise-shell cat and his usual self, similar to Tarafau's pattern. But they called him Luc in either form. Jenny no longer found herself in the situation where she needed to hide her activities from the neighbors, as the houses on either side were inhabited by Alliance agents.

She hadn't had a lot of time recently to visit them or to have them over for backyard barbeques, but she was in mental contact with them frequently, and they continued to keep an eye out for any suspicious activity in the neighborhood.

Once again, she felt a pang about what she was about to do. It couldn't be helped. The others needed to be completely clueless, or her ruse would be in vain and she wouldn't accomplish the task she knew that only she could do. It might not even work. She knew that and was willing to take responsibility for the fallout from her friends, associates, and even her sweet husband.

Burt was going to be beside himself, she knew, and more than likely would feel betrayed, but it couldn't be helped. She needed them to express genuine reactions from her escapade, in case others were watching for discrepancies in their behavior.

Her most recent nighttime mental work had turned up an interesting bit of information from an even more interesting source. She couldn't ignore it, and she also knew she wouldn't be able to take advantage of it unless she acted carefully and kept it to herself.

She had also concluded that she couldn't risk Chidwi in this venture. Chidwi was aware and not at all happy about it, but was willing to stay behind, having been forcefully convinced by Jenny that she had taken every other option into account before making such a seemingly radical choice.

"Well, let's get out there and get it all together," was all she said to Mynn.

Chapter 28: They're Playin' Our Song

Jenny made sure to pack some very specific things, including Lizziebot, her tablet, and necessary hygiene supplies, although since she had a full-fledged apartment in her MDP it probably had more than enough to go on with. Of course, she couldn't live in her own MDP, since she carried it on her wrist, but she had full access to everything in it, and she planned to use it to her full advantage.

She tried to appear casual about the whole thing, as she wasn't exactly alone while she was making all her preparations. Burt was staying close; and when he wasn't by her side, one or more of her bodyguards were.

Jenny didn't necessarily consider herself a very sneaky person, but she had loved the theater classes she had taken in high school and felt like she was a fairly good actress when she set her mind to it.

Chidwi was doing a good job of just behaving as if everything was normal. She also had a part to play in the coming charade and had promised faithfully to do what she had been asked to do, as she understood perfectly the mental process Jenny had gone through in order to make these decisions. That was the advantage of a linkling. Since they could read your mind, you didn't have to do a lot of explaining.

In Jenny and Chidwi's case, Chidwi pointed out a few concerns that Jenny hadn't considered; and when Jenny could answer those concerns satisfactorily, Chidwi agreed with Jenny's reasoning.

Now she just had to follow through. Her dad had always told her that success was often more about the follow-through than the initial work, and so Jenny continued to plan and prepare in the short time she had to get ready.

She knew that more ideas would come to her as she continued to work through her plan. She also knew that everything could easily go horribly wrong.

She smiled her best smile as Burt put his arm around her when she straightened from grabbing some notebooks and pens.

"Planning on doing some sketching? You know, Lizziebot can take notes for you, as you need. You don't even have to speak out loud. You can think them to her."

"Not sure, but I'd feel pretty foolish if I needed pen and paper for something and I remembered that I could have taken it and didn't, now, wouldn't I?"

"Can't escape that kind of logic, I suppose, especially when anything you decide to pack doesn't add a single ounce to your burden. I notice you got out your old hiking boots. You know we won't be doing all that much walking, since Luc can take us directly to the clearing, right?"

"Yeah, but these are broken in and as comfortable as my bedroom slippers. They support my ankles and may save me some pain if I accidentally step into a hole or something."

"I suppose. Are you going to take a sun hat too?"

She laughed. "Actually, I have that packed, and a parasol as well. I like my comforts, you know."

She was enjoying their usual bantering so much. Once again, she felt a stab of regret for what she was about to do to them all, especially Burt. But she hardened her inner resolve and Burt looked at her curiously, as if he sensed a bit of stiffness in her.

"Well, let's go grab the girls and Luc," she said, as she added the bundle of pens resolutely into her MDP.

"Just one minute," he said; and whirling her into both arms, he kissed her fervently, to the point that she thought her toes rose off the floor, hiking boots and all.

"Okay," he said, as he withdrew, looking deep into her eyes. "Now we can go. Just thought one more kiss for luck without prying eyes...."

"Oh, yes," she agreed breathlessly, "maybe two..." and she gave back as good as she had gotten until they both were swaying together as if in a dance.

"Do you really want to go... now?" he said as they drew apart once again. "Now?"

"I think we'd better, but I'll be up for an encore later."

"That's a deal. Okay. Got your bug repellent?"

"Yep, and enough for you as well. Let's go."

They took their time wandering out to the patio where the rest were gathered, Jenny saying goodbye to Windsong, the girls all set and ready for a jungle journey and Luc in his cat form.

"Okay, everyone got on clean underwear?" Burt asked as they walked into the California sunlight.

The girls rolled their eyes, and Chidwi sent Jenny a puzzled thought.

"Ready, big brother," Nona replied, with more than a little sauce in her voice; and suiting words to action, she led the way back into the house to the gate office door.

On the desk was a letter she had received from her mother with little stickers all over it. It just told her that she and Jenny's dad were doing well; and as a side note, as if it didn't really matter, told Jenny she had beaten Arvid in another sparring match and that she had stared down a bear!

Jenny shook her head. Leave it to her mom to make her laugh, even when things were stressful. Of course, Jenny was sure that she couldn't have beaten Arvid again. She wasn't quite so sure about the bear, however.

As soon as the door closed behind the tortoise-shell cat, he faded into his usual form.

"Take us here," Burt sent to Luc, pointing to his own head, and Luc nodded.

With a hand on each shoulder, the gate office faded away. Suddenly, Jenny, Burt and Luc were standing at the edge of a familiar clearing bordered on all sides by the overgrowth of the Amazon rainforest.

They stood there for a moment, Luc taking it in. Then, with a salute to Burt, he faded back out and in again twice more, once with Nona and Mynn and the third time with Lyra.

The girls were familiar with this place. Besides their initial adventure in the Amazon, they had come here several times with Jenny and Burt to check for any signs of recent gate activity.

"Okay," Burt said, scanning the group. "Luc and Mynn, you check the perimeter on that side. Nona and Lyra, you check the perimeter on the other side. Jenny and I will stay here until we get the 'all clear' from both parties."

There was no argument. Burt and Jenny waited while the other four split and headed off in either direction.

"Do you really think we need to go to all this trouble? After all, we haven't seen a single soul any of the other times we've done this," Jenny asked Burt, cherishing this moment of quiet with him, but anxious for the others on her team.

"Just not gonna take any chances, that's all. Remember what Liliath said in our mental conference last night. She thinks there have been some shifts in Inseni movements and that, even though they look like they're settling in and don't seem to be interested in acquiring more territory at the moment, she thinks something is fishy and that we should be even more on our guard than before."

"Yes, of course. But here? This place has practically gotten boring lately. Not much new since I picked up that coin; and even then it turned out to not be the big deal it seemed to be."

"You don't know that for certain, Jenny. The fact that we still don't know what that coin does, feels a little creepy to me."

"Well, I'll let you worry about it, I guess. It's far away in the Switzerland observatory, so not an issue for us right now."

"Yes, dear," he said in a falsely submissive tone. "Anything you say, dear."

"Grrr..." she growled back at him.

And he snugged his arm a little tighter around her shoulders. "I love your growl." He said, his cocky grin warming her heart. She remembered clearly the first time she met him and thought him to be a brash kid who was a bit full of himself. She had since learned of his caring heart and determination to do good things, and she loved him for it.

Their scouts returned maybe sooner than Jenny would have liked, enjoying this brief respite from what she knew lay ahead.

"Nothing unusual," reported Lyra.

"All appears to be well," agreed Luc.

"So," Burt instructed them. "What we need is for two of you to stay at this vantage point while two of you come with us. We are going to go very slowly, examining the ground carefully for any new signs that anyone has been here. We will attempt to determine if there has been any recent portal activity and whether the signs we see were made by our enemy or are simply the wanderings of the natives."

Mynn and Lyra stepped forward, and Luc and Nona hung back.

The four of them inched along carefully, scanning the ground ahead of them, looking for any unusual indentations in the patchy grass and dirt. Jenny didn't expect to see anything right away, but she knew it would be easy to miss an important clue; and regardless of the outcome of their adventure today, she at least wanted Burt to go back to the Alliance with any useful information that might help them moving forward.

As they moved, she could tell her bodyguards were using every one of their senses, including smelling the air and listening for any unusual sounds. By this time, they had been there often enough to be able to identify the difference between a bird call and a human whistle or the slither of a snake compared to the quiet tread of human feet.

She was proud of them, as they weren't jumpy, startling at every little noise or shadow; but they were alert and ready to defend Jenny and Burt at the cost of their own lives if necessary. She hoped it would never come to that.

"Look here," Burt said, reverting to mindspeech to prevent anyone from overhearing their comments. *"See how the grass is bent about four feet out? Can you make out footprints?"*

"Actually," put in Lyra, squinting ahead of her own position, *"I think they were dragging something. Do you see that trough-like pattern just to my side of your footprints?"*

"I think you're right," Mynn agreed, also looking just to the side of Lyra's trough pattern. *"See, the footprints continue to the side. Like people dragging another person between them. Or maybe something heavy that isn't a person. It's hard to tell until we get closer."*

Burt removed a credit-card-sized device from his shirt pocket. Jenny knew he was going to photograph the footsteps and the trough for closer examination in the lab.

"That's what I forgot!" he said, miming hitting himself in the forehead. *"Bob gave me a new mini drone. It's soundless, and we could have had it photo-*

graph the ground before we came out here. Darn it all! And here I was, fussing at you for packing things that weren't necessary. 'Stay in your own runway,' Bob would have said to me. Sorry, Jenny."

"Not to worry, Burt. I don't see pens and notebooks helping us much at the moment, either."

"What about this?" Lyra asked. *"Do we keep moving forward?"*

"Go ahead. I got photos of the next dozen feet. We'll pause again if we find anything new or interesting."

So they continued to move a half a step at a time, being careful to note every bent piece of grass or indentation. So far, there were just more footprints and the long, continued trough of something being dragged straight ahead. Jenny realized, because of its abrupt beginning, that it was almost like something had been dropped from an airplane or helicopter at this point and then was being taken towards the portal.

She knew there was nothing to clearly mark the portal entrance except the footprints that disappeared as if cut off by a knife, half a boot print either coming or going. That was the only indication of anything strange.

The sudden appearance of these footprints and their apparent load of something that had to be dragged along was just not right. Jenny was about to say something when Burt popped up with, *"Am I the only one who noticed how suddenly those footprints appeared?"*

She wanted to laugh. Evidently, she and Burt were already beginning to think alike, something she knew eventually happened with married couples.

"Actually, I was just thinking that these people, whoever they are, appear to have dropped from the sky."

"Do you see how amazing my wife is? How brilliant?" he sent to the others. *"She catches on so quickly."*

Jenny didn't retort, just shook her head.

"Wait! Look at that!" this from Mynn, who was kneeling and pointing at something half buried in the ground just in front of her.

"Don't touch it!" Jenny warned. *"If we don't know what it is, what is the chance it's something like that dratted coin?"*

Mynn pulled her outstretched finger back as if burned. *"So how can we tell what it is?"*

"Stand up and move back about a foot," instructed Burt. Let me get close enough to take a photo. She did as told, and Burt once again scanned the object with his device. Jenny knew that he wasn't just taking a casual photograph but was scanning for things like radiation and other resonances that would allow them to potentially identify the strange thing.

From where Jenny was standing, on the other side of Burt, she could only see that the part sticking out of the ground was disc-shaped, about a half inch thick and about nine inches across at the widest part they could see. It was about the color of a terra cotta tile and didn't look like any piece of tech she had ever seen.

"I interned with an archeologist once. This almost looks like the kind of thing he would have gotten excited about." Burt said as he continued his careful scan. *"It doesn't appear to have any unusual radiation, nor is it emitting any chemical signals. But there is something not quite right. Do you feel the vibrations? Everybody back!"* And he pointed behind them. *"Run!"*

They all responded immediately, running flat out until they arrived under the trees that hid Luc and Nona from sight.

"What was that thing, and why were we running?" Lyra asked. *"Was Mynn exposed to something dangerous?"*

"'I don't know' is the answer to both questions. Let me look more carefully at the results," And he invoked his bot out of his MDP.

"DAT, I want you to take a look at this," he said, immediately pushing his device into a slot in DAT's chest, apparently created for just that purpose.

"Got it, boss," and there was silence for a long moment. *"Sensors tell me it is alien, not made of any local metals, and not as simple as it seems. It..."* But whatever he was about to say was interrupted by an explosion from where they had found the disk.

"... is a land mine," DAT finished, once the dust had settled.

"Come on, kiddos." Burt said as he reinstalled DAT into his MDP. *"We're going home. This needs reporting. And next time we're sending in the troopers and their gizmos before we try this again. Something needs rethinking, and this isn't the time or place."*

No one argued. Jenny felt Luc's hand on her shoulder. The gate office faded into view and before she could fully adjust, the others were there around her.

"Well, that was fun," was all Burt said. The rest shook their heads.

All Jenny could think, however, was how in the world she was going to get back there. She had something that needed doing, and this event made it feel more urgent than ever.

Chapter 29: A Will and a Way

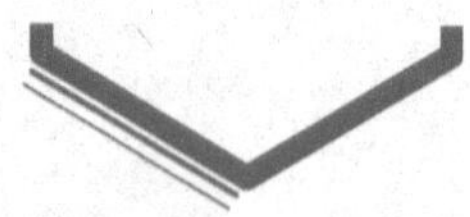

Jenny couldn't believe how close she had come and was struggling to figure out how to get back there at this point. She knew, if she let any of her constant companions know what she was about to do, that they would likely do everything in their power to prevent her from accomplishing her goal.

She also knew that most people would consider it a foolish risk and would perhaps chide her for her audacity to think that she was the only one who could do it. From a purely logical point of view, and without the intense urgings within her that it had to be her and it had to be exactly as she had envisioned it, she would have been skeptical herself.

However, her time and experiences with the Alliance had taught her that not everything always made sense, and that not everything was as it seemed, nor did it always make sense until after the fact.

Burt had sent a troop of drones to the Amazon clearing immediately following their return. One of them was instructed to film the entire venture, and the others were to scan the area for any other mines and detonate them after they had thoroughly photographed every square inch of the clearing so that the scientists at all three labs could examine them.

Jenny knew that with all the protections she had been given and the instructions that had been given to her protectors, it was unlikely that she would manage even one moment alone any time soon.

Lately, she had taken to sparring in the workout room with just Mynn, explaining that she was using the time these days for focus as well as the workout and that the constant sound of the clacking of the other staves in the room was distracting.

Mynn was happy to be her partner and delighted in the pre-sparring time of breathing and meditating together. Of the three of her bodyguards, Mynn had the greatest interest in what Burt termed "sciency stuff," and Jenny and she would often spend time together out on the patio, discussing the various projects going on in the Alliance science labs while the other two played almost vicious games of cubes.

The cubes thing had become a passion for Lyra and Nona, each wanting to be the absolute conqueror. But they were pretty evenly matched, so it wasn't unusual for one or the other to come out hooting in triumph, with the other one grumpy and exuding defeat. It was actually pretty funny, and Jenny and Mynn often speculated as to which one would triumph this time.

So, she found herself contemplating all this as she and Mynn went through the quarterstaff forms together like a well-choreographed dance. Jenny remembered with fondness her opportunity to see her mother defeat Arvid and found herself wondering what her parents would think about the task she was contemplating.

"Earth to Jenny!" Mynn exclaimed, as she tapped Jenny lightly on her behind with her quarterstaff. "Forms are complete, and you're still moving!"

Jenny stopped with a grimace. "Yeah, sorry about that. I've got a few things on my mind."

"So I've noticed," Mynn shot back. "Look... do you need to talk about it? I don't know if anyone else has noticed, but you've been unusually quiet lately, more than just all the mental communications. Even at mealtimes, you haven't been saying much. I know you have Burt, but I think there are some things that maybe you might not necessarily want to share with him."

"Thanks, Mynn. I think that...," and she paused as a sudden thought struck her, "that you are trustworthy. But you should know I have put my trust in the wrong place before now, and it didn't work out very well."

"Ah, yes," Mynn said, leaning on her staff. "I heard about that. A buddy of yours, Sam, I think that's what they called her, turned out to be a leader of the Groga and fast in the grasp of the Insenium. A rude awakening, I'm sure. But didn't she actually do some serious damage to one of the Inseni outposts in the end? I'm pretty sure everyone thought that would be the end of it."

"Yes," Jenny admitted, her heart still not completely comforted by the fact that Sam had, in the end, given her life to destroy Gall. Miriha had shown her Sam's last mortal moments, and she knew there had been genuine remorse there. But the betrayal still made her hesitant to trust too much in an evident friendship.

"Well, then, it makes sense that you hesitate to trust much. However, I think that perhaps it also puts more of a burden on you than is necessary.

"Look, I know we haven't known each other for very long, but you must know that any of the three of us would give our lives in your defense. I think by now we've proven that. What if I promised on my vows as an Alliance agent that I wouldn't reveal anything you said to the others or anyone else you didn't want to hear about it?"

At that point, Chidwi sent from the bench at the side of the workout room where she always watched the workouts and sparring matches, *"She means every word of it, Jenny. She is sincere."*

Jenny was startled by this. She knew that Chidwi could read the minds of those around her, but she also knew that she generally didn't listen in on a person's thoughts without a reason. She had obviously been paying attention to the exchange between Jenny and Mynn.

"So, what if it's about something that you might not like or agree with?" Jenny countered, not believing what she was considering at that moment.

"The promise holds. You will find that I am very good at keeping confidences." And Mynn looked straight into Jenny's eyes. Jenny could feel the promise there.

Chidwi nodded.

Jenny hesitated one more moment. She couldn't believe she was about to confide in this person, even though they had spent so much time together and Mynn had put herself out there in Jenny's defense. She was, after all, her bodyguard. Even if she did keep the confidence, would she try to prevent Jenny from what she was about to do?

"Okay, I'm about to tell you something that you shouldn't reveal until after the fact. And you may not decide to do that even then, since after I do this, all those who need to know about it will be notified anyhow. Not even Burt knows about this.

"I will not give you all the details. But you should know that I have discovered things that could make a huge difference in our likelihood of success in our mission to defeat the Inseni. For most people, this won't make any sense and will seem like a foolish and overhasty decision, but I have considered it from every angle and I can't see any alternative that won't require the loss of many lives and the potential destruction of entire societies.

"The Alliance believes they know what they're up against, but the fact is, we may be going about this the wrong way. It's one of the reasons there is so much contention among the Alliance members. It's why we've had to make so many adjustments to our plans, based on the restrictions the Nanoites and Mookookie have placed on their participation.

"I know that the natural reaction to the attack of an inimical force is usually to meet force with force, but I'm becoming more and more convinced that this might not be the answer.

"I've been exposed to many alien cultures, even in my short term as the Gatekeeper, and I have learned so much from them. My Earth heritage has taught me a lot about armed conflict and its consequences; and when I apply those lessons, along with the lessons I am learning from the many cultures throughout the multiverse, I realized that maybe it's time to take a different view."

Mynn didn't speak but was nodding seriously as Jenny continued.

"I have come to the conclusion that perhaps I might be the only person who might be able to carry this off."

"And 'this' might be what?" Mynn finally broke in.

"I won't reveal that much even to you, any more than I could confide it to Burt. All I can tell you is that I have a plan and I think it will work, but I need to get to a certain place without anyone being the wiser, in order to make it happen, and I need to go alone."

"Hmm." Mynn shook her head, obviously taking it in.

"So, you mean to pull another stunt like the one you did on Peril's planet?" was all she said.

"Kind of, but definitely different. This time I hope not to have to get hit on the head to accomplish my goals." Jenny quipped. "I intend to walk into a trap with my eyes wide open and my skull undamaged."

Mynn whistled through her teeth, shaking her head.

"You promised..." Jenny began.

Mynn nodded, holding up a hand to stop the rest of her sentence. "I promised. I will keep that promise. So the next logical question is, how can I help?"

Chapter 30: Rocks and Hard Places

Burt couldn't sleep. His beautiful wife lay beside him in their comfy bed in their safe little house, but he had been feeling antsy all week, since the adventure in the Amazon. Something about Jenny and the way she looked even more pensive than ever....

Sure, she still joked with the girls and did her nightly rounds in her mental communications network, while she intently studied the course the Alliance scientists had given her regarding the gate network and her responsibilities as the Gatekeeper.

Having never been given the chance to go through the formal training that Anela and former Gatekeepers had been put through, she was playing catch-up as fast as she could, lamenting the fact that she was having to learn her responsibilities in what she called "on-the-job-training," what Burt would have called an internship.

He worried that she still had far too much on her plate, even though the majority of the mental communications network had been taken off of her plate due to the training of other specialists after they had discovered that this was a skill that could be learned by those with the coinciding talents.

This had not quite been what he had expected out of married life. In the world he had grown up in, even though both of his parents had worked outside the home, his dad had always been the primary breadwinner. As an only child, he had spent a great deal of time in daycare, but when he was home, he had been given the full attention of his parents.

Somehow, he had thought that, though he and Jenny both had some heavy responsibilities, he would somehow be able to ease her burden and spend more time with his beautiful wife. Becoming her guide had given him hope for that goal.

He admired her persistent and generally optimistic attitude and her strength and competence. But mostly, he would have been completely content, at this point in their lives, to have lived in that little cabin by the Merced River and left the Alliance to its own troubles.

And he immediately corrected himself. No, he couldn't have lived with himself, knowing what he knew, if he had simply tried to ignore the threat to Earth, but he also had to admit to himself that there was something to be said for ignorant bliss.

Now, leaning up on one elbow and watching her sleep, he resisted the impulse to kiss her awake and just spend some time holding her in his arms. He was never happier than when he could have an armful of Jenny, and he realized that he had never felt complete until he and Jenny had said their vows and were officially man and wife.

Lately, he had experienced an uneasy feeling that an even greater disaster was pending and that it would involve Jenny. He knew that the one thing he would never be able to accept was that she might be in danger; and yet, he knew that because of her position in the Alliance, this was illogical.

So, he sighed and quietly crept out of bed and out the door, down the hall and into the kitchen to grab a cup of hot cocoa, something that would potentially soothe him and allow him to go back to bed and get some sleep. Lizziebot was there.

"Hey, Lizziebot, are you awake?" he asked wryly, knowing, of course, that the robot never actually slept.

"Good evening, Burt, you know better. What is troubling you this night? You don't tend to miss sleep whenever you can get it, like any good soldier."

Burt could never shake off the fact that Lizziebot's voice was nearly identical to Lizzie's. He had known her before she had passed away and had liked her straightforward manner and the way she would cut to the chase, without apology. This bot had been programmed by her and Bob, who also knew her well, so the similarity was almost eerie.

"You know me too well, Lizziebot. Couldn't sleep. A lot on my mind. Tell me... why did you choose Jenny for her position as a gate guardian?"

"Actually, there were several reasons. You may not know that Jenny was host to one of those clever little nanobots created by the Alliance to track their agents.

It was just before she went to college. I had been considering a few different prospects, as I was told to do as part of my gate guardian responsibilities.

"I was able to listen in as she went about her life as a college student, including going on hikes in the mountains and the few dates she had. She showed herself as a responsible, honest, and dependable person, but besides all that, she had a firm desire to do good things and an insatiable curiosity about the cosmos.

"One of her other qualities was that she was a self-starter. She didn't need a lot of supervision to start and finish a task. Her one flaw was that she was a bit over-critical of herself, always holding herself to a higher standard than anyone else would have done.

"Of the other two I had been considering, she was the one who kept my attention, and I felt strongly that she would be the most appropriate choice. I knew that when she decided to do something, she would follow through one hundred percent."

"Yep," Burt agreed. "That's our Jenny all right. Do you ever regret your choice?"

"Ah, Burt, you know, of course, that I am just a mechanical construct, very cleverly programmed. I don't feel in the way a human does. I do know that Lizzie felt confident in her choice. And the evidence shows that she was correct in that assumption."

Burt could only nod in agreement. And here he was, so worried about Jenny and whether she was going to be safe. He knew she hated it when he did that. She had expressed that before they were finally married. She considered it a lack of his trust in her decisions and her abilities.

He knew it wasn't any of those things. It was just that she was precious to him, and he could no longer imagine his life without her. All the more reason for them to get this issue with the Insenium resolved as quickly and permanently as possible.

He couldn't change his and Jenny's situation by going without sleep, and he knew there was nothing he could do about her determination to be actively involved.

He sighed. That didn't mean he had to like it.

Chapter 31: When a Plan Comes Together

Mynn couldn't believe she was doing this. In all her time as an Alliance agent, she had never felt so torn between two differing duties. On the one hand, she had given Jenny her word, and nothing within her would allow her to forswear herself.

On the other hand, her assignment, given by the Alliance high council itself, was to protect Jenny with her life, if necessary. How could she ever reconcile the two contrary commitments?

Jenny hadn't given her a lot of detail, only allowing her to know the part that she would play in aiding Jenny in her task. She knew, if the others ever found out about it, she would never be trusted again. Jenny had outlined a plan to allow her to feign ignorance, but she wasn't sure if she could carry it off.

She had always prided herself on her honest and forthright nature and the fact that she was true to her word. Now she found herself wishing she hadn't reached out to Jenny, even though she had noticed her weary and resigned attitude. She wished she had phrased her promise differently, to give herself at least a little wiggle room, but that just wasn't who she was.

She tried to be as honest with herself as she was with others, but now she was in a terrible position and would have to figure out how to deal with it. She puttered around for a bit longer in the apartment over the garage, pretending to straighten and clean, but her mind wasn't at all engaged. She wasn't used to pretense, and she realized she didn't like it much.

She found herself wondering how Jenny's friend Sam had managed to succeed in her charade for so long, especially when she had been told by Jenny that Sam had struggled with her growing attachment to Jenny, a foreign concept for her. According to Jenny, Sam had felt deep regret in the end for her deception, having gotten used to having a real friend for the first time in her life.

Of course, this was different, as Mynn was trying to do what was right, but she also had her doubts as to whether Jenny had thought this through completely enough, especially since she had not been made privy to the details of the plan.

She had only been told where Jenny needed to go and that it had to be kept secret from the rest of the group until the final moment.

She had been reassured by Jenny that there would be constant communication via the bots her companions had been issued by the Alliance, thanks to the Nanoites who now lived in selected bots issued to a very select group of people. And Jenny had guaranteed Mynn that she would never reveal to the rest the part Mynn had played in her plan.

She could delay no longer. The others would be assembling on the patio any minute now.

She emerged out into the sunlight to see them, as she had expected, hanging out around the patio table, a snack set out with the usual frosty root beers. They had already started in on the veggies and dips, not to mention a plate of Arvid's spicy sugar cookies.

"It's about time!" Nona chided her amiably. "We were about to eat your share of the cookies!"

"Well, we can't have that!" Mynn quipped back. "That's Arvid's cookie recipe, after all. Lizzie does a great job replicating it, to be sure."

They all laughed as Mynn snatched a cookie off the plate and grabbed the only root beer that wasn't already in someone's hand. Mentally she shook her head, realizing that they wouldn't be so nice to her if they understood what she was about to do. This might be the last lighthearted moment for a long time, if she and Jenny succeeded.

Luc had often gotten paired with Mynn in the last little bit for Jenny watch, so it wasn't surprising to anyone, once they had imbibed the last of their root beer and finished up the last cookie crumb, that Jenny told them she had something she had to do in the gate office, and could Mynn and Luc accompany her while the rest cleaned up the mess of their snack?

The rest agreed good-naturedly and returned to their discussion about whether Chidwi was having a conversation with the koi or not.

Jenny walked at a normal pace to the hallway door and opened it, allowing Mynn and Luc to precede her into the office.

As usual, Luc immediately faded into his natural form as soon as the door closed behind them.

"Okay, Jenny, what do you really want?" Luc sent as soon as she turned to them. *"I don't think anyone else noticed anything, but you've been acting strangely for the past week. Mynn, are you in on this?"*

Mynn didn't answer, waiting for Jenny as she had been instructed.

"This isn't about Mynn, Luc. It's about something I need to do, and I am trying to obey protocol. I left something at the Amazon portal site that I need to recover, and I didn't want to make it a big deal. I just need you to take us to the apex of the portal area. As you noticed, I have a bodyguard with us, and the two of you should be sufficient. I promise you, we won't be gone long."

"Do the rest know about this?" he queried suspiciously.

"They will," she promised, and Mynn knew that she would keep that promise, as all the rest would be informed by the time Mynn and Luc returned. Chidwi was deliberately being left behind, and Lizziebot had already been programmed with instructions to pass the information out from the MDP via the Nanoite network to those who needed to know.

Once again, Mynn felt a twinge of guilt. She didn't look at Luc but looked directly at Jenny, as if waiting for instructions. She knew if he looked into her eyes, he would realize that something wasn't quite right.

"Okay, just there and back again?" he confirmed.

"You'll be back before anyone knows we've left." Jenny promised, and Mynn realized that Luc probably didn't notice that she had said *"You'll be back,"* and not *"We'll be back."*

"Then let's do this. I understand that Nona and Lyra are about to start another cubes match, and I want to be there to plague the loser." And he chuckled at that, his cat fangs showing slightly through his lips as he laughed.

He placed a hand on Jenny's and Mynn's shoulders; and in no time, they were fading into the familiar clearing.

Jenny immediately set off around the perimeter, and Mynn noted several small craters where it was obvious that mines had been located and detonated. Jenny didn't speak to either of them, but just led them forward at a determined, fast-paced walk.

Mynn knew that Jenny was anxious to get this over with, and she couldn't blame her. She knew her part in this was just beginning, and she wasn't looking forward to continuing the deception. She knew that if anything happened to Jenny as a result of her compliance in this scheme of hers, she would never be able to forgive herself.

The space was quiet, nothing but the rustling of the foliage in the mild breeze. Mynn had to keep reminding herself to breathe. She really didn't know what was about to happen, but she also knew if it was something Jenny needed to hide from everyone else, it couldn't be good.

Jenny was about two paces ahead of Mynn and Luc, who followed her side by side, looking around them, attentive to anything at all suspicious, but the area remained quiet and there was nothing, not even a bird on the wing to disturb the calm.

Jenny gave the hiking sign for them to stop. She had been scanning the ground the entire time they walked and seemed to have found what she was looking for.

"I want you both to know how much I appreciate your help. I am aware that what happens next may not make you happy, but it must be done. Please stand very still."

She briefly peered into their troubled and confused faces and then suddenly whirled around, took three running steps, and disappeared into what looked like a sudden heat haze, which then vanished into nothingness.

They both started forward, ready to follow her; but although they ran directly through the area where she had disappeared, there was nothing there, and no sign she had ever been there except her cell phone, which she had dropped as she had stepped through what was obvious to them now, the Inseni portal.

Chapter 32: The Den of the Beast

Jenny nearly tripped over the rock just on the other side of the portal. Two startled, one-eyed beings that she thought must be male, immediately reached for her, one taking each arm. She didn't resist and couldn't help but send to them, *"Take me to your leader."*

"Just who do you think you are?" one of them sent gruffly. *"Our leader is pretty choosy about who may bask in her glorious presence."*

"Tell her the Gatekeeper has come calling. She'll be very happy to hear it," Jenny retorted with a show of confidence she didn't really feel. These men reminded her of Gall, the fearsome creature she, as a helpless bystander, had watched apparently disintegrate Burt before her eyes, what seemed like ages ago.

"And while you're at it," she continued in what was hopefully a haughty voice, *"You can take your hands off me. I don't think she will be well pleased if you give her damaged goods."*

One of them was apparently amused at this, but the other one loosened his grip with a shudder. The other followed suit after the more serious one gave him a pointed look, the one eye speaking as many volumes as two would have done.

"Listen, earthling, you will soon find yourself in the presence of The Great One. I would hope you will show more respect to her than to us, as she is not nearly as tolerant as we are." And he shook her arm to emphasize his point.

Jenny didn't respond with either facial expression or words. She was bound and determined not to show the mixed emotions roiling in her gut at the moment. Let them think whatever they wanted. She had accomplished step one of her plan. She had walked—no, she had run, right into the trap the enemy had thought she had laid for her. Little did she know that Jenny had laid traps of her own, and only time would tell who had been the more successful.

The two men marched her to a nearby building that had obviously been quickly thrown together. Jenny had to assume that the invading army had either erected it or had some of the locals do it for them. Either way, it was so poorly done that even a bunch of kids at summer camp wouldn't have claimed that level of workmanship.

They shoved her in through the door and then slammed it shut, and Jenny assumed it to either be locked or guarded. Either way, she had them right where they wanted her, as her mom would have said.

Jenny didn't have much time to contemplate her mom's funny sayings, since before Jenny could even register the scant furnishings of the room, the door opened again and the two guards reappeared with a taller female of the same species, which Jenny assumed to be Inseni.

"You will come with me now," an obviously female voice sent, although it was gruff and harsh. *"The Great One will see you now."*

Jenny noted, without surprise, that she was being ushered back through the portal, one of the guards manipulating one of the contraptions they had found back in the initial assault of the Amazon clearing in the beginnings of her adventures.

They stepped through an arch into a garden-like terrace, although the plants, while healthy, were sparse. Before them stood a very tall, square-built woman with one eye in the middle of her forehead, the brow furrowed threateningly and both hands on her hips in a challenging gesture.

"Our little Jenny fell into our clever trap. Now, you are mine and will tell me all the secrets of the Alliance; and together we will stop them from ever interfering with our plans again."

"Not so fast, missy," and Jenny couldn't help but grin, since she heard her mother's words come out of her own mouth and the others on the terrace gasped at her impertinence. *"You have some explaining to do."* And she imitated the hands-on-hips gesture. *"After all, you started this whole mess. And I have every intention of seeing you finish it."*

"With your ugly two-eyed head on a spike in my throne room, you will see nothing," Vena retorted. *"And the proper address from a worm like yourself is 'Great One' or 'Your Excellency.'"*

"And the proper address from a one-eyed non-entity like yourself would be 'Gatekeeper,' thank you very much," Jenny retorted, knowing that she would probably get nowhere with someone like this by kowtowing before her. It was important to establish right from the beginning the rules of this game.

She had dealt with bullies in her junior high school days and had discovered that the only way to keep from bowing and scraping every minute she was in school was to stand up to them with at least a show of confidence. Her dad had taught her that, and it had always seemed to work. She discovered that if you gave in to the major bullies, the minor ones would line up right behind them and make your life miserable.

She already knew her life would be miserable here, but, if her source of information was accurate, she was not being brought here to be killed, but as a trophy, a hostage, and a potential source of information.

Of course, in the end, her enemy would be terribly disappointed, because Jenny had a plan that not even Merv probably would have thought of.

But before she could put her plan into action, she needed to establish the ground rules. She knew a lot of things Vena (for her information source had told her that this was the name of the being before her) did not know.

"Well, Gatekeeper," and Vena sneered the name in her mental voice, *"we will see what we will see."*

She turned to two uniformed, one-eyed beings behind her. *"Take this slime-infested Gatekeeper, and escort her to her chambers. I am sure they will be to her liking. Do not speak with her or explain anything. Let her wonder if maybe she might have been a little more respectful to her betters."*

The two guards nodded without expression, the one eye in each head looking directly at Jenny. Jenny showed no fear. She also did not retort to Vena's remarks. *Let her wonder,* Jenny thought to herself; and with that, she couldn't suppress a smug little smile.

The guards led her down a long corridor to a gaping tunnel that wound down and down, past doors to what were obviously other levels of the palace she had briefly glimpsed before entering the tunnel.

Finally, they arrived at an iron gateway, behind which stood another one-eyed guard in uniform.

"Last cell, by the parents," was all he sent, unlocking the gate and passing them through.

Which parents, of whom? Jenny thought as she walked silently along, making a point not to look right or left, although she could hear occasional movement from one side or another, like someone moving towards one of the barred cell doors they were passing. From time to time, she heard a murmur in a foreign language or a sigh or even a sob, but no loud noises or cat-calls like one might expect in a prison movie scene.

It seemed like they walked forever in that stifling, uncommunicative silence until after a turn at a t-shaped corridor, they slowed and stopped. One of them opened the door located one door to the right of the center door of the 't' and jerked his head towards the interior, true to the command that they should not speak to her.

She didn't flinch or cringe when he slammed the metal barred door behind her. She didn't even turn towards the door, seeing, by what appeared to be a single glow-stick, the pallet on the floor with one thin blanket and no pillow and in one corner a pot that she assumed was to pee in.

There wasn't a chair or even a stool to sit on, or anything remotely resembling a table or shelf.

But Jenny hummed to herself as she stooped and sat cross-legged on the pallet.

She took her tablet out of her MDP, fully charged whenever it was re-installed there, so there was no danger of her running out of battery. She was happy that one of Lizziebot's Nanoites had agreed to live there for the duration of Jenny's situation.

"I'm where none of you will be able to find me for now, but don't worry. I have a plan, and it was important that our enemies not know that I actually allowed myself to be captured. Please put on a convincing show for anyone who might be listening in or watching you. I'm actually quite safe, which is all I can tell you for now, but I will have a lot more to give you in the coming days or weeks. Please don't be too angry with me. It had to be this way." And she pushed the send button to signal the Nanoite that the message was complete. It would immediately be sent to all the key people, especially Burt and Liliath.

Then, she went into her deep breathing exercises and found herself in the studio of the communications room. As she expected, Mi was there.

"I'm in, Mi," she said, walking to the woebegone-looking young woman. "You did the right thing. We have work to do."

The End

Also by Bonnie K.T. Dillabough

The Dimensional Alliance
Links to Infinity
Threads of Infinity
Tangles of Infinity

The Dimensional Alliance 2nd edition
The House on Infinity Loop
Infinity on Fire
Mirrors of Infinity
Ripples of Infinity
Chords of Infinity

Watch for more at https://dimensionalallianceheadquarters.com.

About the Author

To write or not to write has never been the question... She wrote her first 26 line poem at age 8, entitled "My Christmas ABCs". She then memorized it and performed it for the church Christmas party. This wasn't terribly surprising. She started reading before Kindergarten and Dr. Seuss was one of her favorite authors, so rhyme came very naturally to her. She has been writing all of her life, as long as she can remember. A lot of poetry, short stories and, of course, the usual school reports. she always got high grades on her writing assignments, even when she didn't in other classes, simply because she loved to write. Then, adulthood set in. Always a voracious reader, she dreamt of writing a novel, but got gloriously side-tracked with a wonderful husband and six amazing children. During that time, she still wrote: Musical plays for her kids at church and school, songs, poetry and even an occasional newspaper article streamed from her pen. Then, she got involved in jobs that required clear concise writing and a lot of marketing copy. She put up her first website in 1996 and made her living on the internet for over 20 years, writing everything from blog posts to sales copy to scripts for online videos, not to mention copy for the websites she built for her clients. Now, at age 65 she has finally published the first novel in an ongoing series. "The House on Infinity Loop" is the first book in a trilogy that will become just the first part of the Dimensional Alliance series. When she is not writing, she likes to read, crochet hats for the homeless and gifts for friends and family, is active in her church and looks forward to being very involved with the fans of her books from her website: DimensionalAllianceHeadquarters.com

Read more at https://dimensionalallianceheadquarters.com.